EVERYTHING
HAPPENS
FOR A
REASON...

EVERYTHING HAPPENS FOR A REASON...

Daisy Jordan

iUniverse, Inc.

New York Lincoln Shanghai

Everything Happens for a Reason...

Copyright © 2005 by Daisy Jordan

iUniverse books may be ordered through booksellers or by contacting:

iUniverse
2021 Pine Lake Road, Suite 100
Lincoln, NE 68512
www.iuniverse.com
1-800-Authors (1-800-288-4677)

This book is a work of fiction. Names, characters, places and incidents are products of the author's imagination or are used fictitiously. Any resemblance to actual events or locales or persons, living or dead, is entirely coincidental.

ISBN-13: 978-0-595-36273-8 (pbk)
ISBN-13: 978-0-595-80718-5 (ebk)
ISBN-10: 0-595-36273-7 (pbk)
ISBN-10: 0-595-80718-6 (ebk)

Printed in the United States of America

To Calli, Shadow, Tigger, Malibu, and Wrigley

and in remembrance of Domino and Abby

Acknowledgements

I want to offer a special thanks to:

All my college friends and roommates who have made life interesting and helped inspire my characters, scenes, and dialogue...you can probably all see aspects of yourselves in this book...this also goes for friends from high school who have been part of my life during college even though we go to different schools...you all know who you are...

Derick because our relationship over the last eight years has strengthened my belief that everything happens for a reason...

Mom and Lyns for reading this before I ever got to the publishing stage and offering me lots of great feedback and encouragement...

Summer for supporting me through Summer's Stories...

And of course my wonderful family: Dad, Mom, and Josh...with an extra-special thanks to Josh who will be playing almost every role when this is made into a movie..."HAEIOUNMGH!!!"

Read between the lines
What's fucked up and everything's all right….

~Green Day, "Boulevard of Broken Dreams"

Late February 2004

The apartment was dark except for the three blacklight bulbs hanging from the light fixture on the ceiling fan in the living room and the sliver of light coming from behind the partially closed door to Laney's bathroom. Jill figured someone was probably in there puking up the Jungle Juice Justin and Adam had made. It was in a big cooler Adam had brought over for the party and after mixing it, he and Justin had asked Laney and Jill to try it. When the girls had proclaimed that it tasted good, the boys had decided it wasn't strong enough and added another whole bottle of some cheap-ass brand of vodka.

Now Jill had consumed at least five Turtle cups full of it, along with a few Jell-O shots. Even though she knew the light fixture in the fan was stationary, the lights seemed to be swirling around as Jill and Laney sandwiched Justin and grinded to the music that blared from their roommate Hilton's computer speakers, which were hooked up in the living room for the party.

As Jill gazed at the swirling lights above, someone grabbed her left arm.

"Hey!" she cried as her Turtle cup tilted and her drink sloshed dangerously near the edge. She turned and saw Hilton standing on the coffee table.

"Sorry, babe! I almost fell!" Hilton exclaimed, jerking her hand back to cover her O-shaped mouth, then letting out a whoosh of breath as if she and Jill had just nearly avoided some huge disaster. Then she burst out laughing. Jill flashed Hilton a huge drunken smile to indicate she was not mad at Hilton for nearly spilling her drink and then climbed up on the coffee table to join her.

As they danced on the coffee table Jill surveyed the room and noticed Adam making out with the brunette in the white, off-the-shoulder top and low-cut jeans she'd seen him talking to earlier. She felt her stomach clench and turned away, pretending not to see. As she turned, she saw Laney still dancing with Justin, people smoking out on the balcony, her other roommate Natalie doing a kegstand as Jill's best friend Todd and Justin's sister Kylie held her feet up….Then the whole room was spinning and all she could see was the blur of the blacklights as the music seemed to get faster and faster….

The next thing Jill knew she was in bed and there was a pounding on her door.

"Jill!" Laney was calling her.

Jill started to get up as she called for Laney to come in and then realized in a panic she was naked. She flung herself back down on the bed in an attempt to get the covers up before Laney opened the door, but for some reason the door didn't open and Laney continued to knock and yell her name.

"Jill! Wake up, girl! It's 9:00. We're leaving in an hour!"

Jill suddenly jolted awake and her head jerked off the pillow. She was relieved to find the party and her nakedness had been a dream and she was wearing the same jeans and Dale University sweatshirt she'd had on all day. It wasn't the morning after the party, as she'd thought in her dream, but a Thursday night.

"I'm awake!" she snapped irritably at the closed door.

"How the hell can you be sleeping that hard?" Laney asked through the door. "You've only been asleep for half an hour!"

Jill glanced at the clock and realized Laney was right; she had only been asleep since 8:30, when she had come in her room after *Friends* to take a brief nap before heading to the Turtle.

"Well, I'm awake now!" she snapped.

"Okay, well I just wanted to make sure you'd be ready by ten."

"I'm not in the mood to go anymore," Jill groaned. "I'm too tired."

"Whatever, you just don't wanna go 'cause it's your turn to be sober bitch," Laney teased.

Jill rolled her eyes at the door and a small, almost bitter smile curled the edges of her lips.

"Yeah," she said sarcastically to the door, "I'm pissed 'cause now I have no excuse to get wasted and try to get on Adam."

Laney laughed and Jill heard her footsteps retreating across the living room to her own bedroom.

Still sitting in bed, Jill glared at the closed door and rolled her eyes again, then slowly climbed out of bed and headed toward her bathroom. As she turned the shower on and undressed, she replayed her dream in her head but as soon as she stepped into the hot, steamy water and it began to rain down on her head and back, the image of blurring lights and swaying people in her mind dulled and grew dimmer until it finally disappeared, and Jill grabbed her shampoo and began to wash her hair.

"Vodka and cranberry," Jill's roommate Natalie said as she squeezed into an open space in front of the bar and slid her empty Turtle cup across the counter for the bartender to refill.

As Jill waited off to the side she scanned the dance floor below them in the center of the room, searching for Adam but half afraid to see him because she was sure he'd be making out with some cute girl.

"It's fucking packed in here!" Natalie yelled over the music as she wound her way back to Jill through the throng of people pushing up to the bar.

"It's Thursday, what do you expect?" Jill responded absent-mindedly as she continued her search for Adam. Thursday was the beginning of the weekend in the minds of many Dale students, and just as big of a party night as Friday. The Purple Turtle was the hot spot on Thursdays because it was Thirsty Turtle night. The special was thirty-ounce mugs which could be purchased for one dollar and filled and refilled all night with either twenty-five cent beers or one dollar mixed drinks. The mugs could then be taken home and reused the next week. Thursdays also always drew a large crowd at Mike's, the karaoke bar adjacent to the Turtle. Sometimes the girls went to Mike's, but the line to get in was way too long tonight and they hadn't felt like waiting.

"Hey, there's Hilton and Luke and Laney. Let's go!" Natalie shouted, grabbing Jill's arm and pulling her along. Natalie's long, wavy blonde hair swung loosely behind her, almost reaching her waist.

"I don't feel like dancing!" Jill shouted back, trying to make herself heard over the earsplitting dance mix of a popular rap song. Why did they have to ruin songs that were already perfectly good dance songs by making a so-called dance remix? It was completely beyond Jill.

Natalie either ignored her or didn't hear her. "Hey look, there's Adam too!" She turned and winked at Jill and continued to pull her down onto the dance floor.

"Well all right, maybe I'll dance for a little while then," Jill muttered as she followed Natalie down the six steps onto the floor.

"Hey guys!" Natalie cried as she glided up to Hilton, Luke, and Laney.

Hilton momentarily stopped making out with her boyfriend Luke to dance with Natalie, and Luke grinned and cheered them on. Jill laughed and glanced over her shoulder. Adam, Justin, and their other roommate Ryan were dancing in a small circle and checking out a larger circle of scantily-clad girls dancing near them.

Ryan noticed Jill and she waved. Ryan raised his glass in her direction. "Hey, baby!"

Jill laughed and Adam and Justin turned around to see who Ryan was talking to.

"Hey, where's your beer?" Adam cried, obviously drunk already.

"I'm DD," Jill called back, holding up her keys.

"Damn, that sucks," Adam said, and the boys turned back to the circle of girls, who had noticed them and were moving in their direction.

Jill narrowed her eyes and glared for a brief second at the girls coming up to Adam, then she went back to dancing with her roommates and Luke. Of course he'd rather have somebody slutty and drunk, she thought to herself, annoyed. That's no challenge, and he'll never have to see her again. He's so hot, but he's such a player….Then Jill smiled to herself, because she knew Adam's playboy reputation was part of what attracted her to him. That plus the fact that he looked like a younger version of Brad Pitt. Jill always got bored with boys who made their interest in her too obvious, or boys who were too clingy. She had always told her friends she enjoyed the challenge of getting an aloof guy who loved the single life to commit to her.

However, lately she was starting to wonder if she was actually drawn to boys like Adam not because of the challenge they presented, but simply because of the fact that she wasn't ready for a serious commitment and going after guys who weren't looking for girlfriends made her life a lot more simple, fun, and drama-free. That must be it, she thought to herself, I just want to be unattached and free to do whatever right now. Suddenly she couldn't stand to dance any longer.

"I'm going to the bathroom!" she yelled in Laney's ear.

"All right!" Laney shouted back as she took a long drink of beer and continued dancing.

When Jill left the restroom she looked for an empty table above the dance floor but couldn't find one, so she leaned against the railing that looked down on the dance floor and waited for a table to empty. After a few minutes she saw a group leaving and she hurried to claim the table.

"Hey, Jilly!" Justin said as he plopped down beside her. "Bored?"

"Oh no, I love coming out and not drinking," Jill replied sarcastically. She smiled inwardly though; Justin had a goofy, fun quality to him that always made Jill feel light-hearted. He and Laney had gone to high school together, and although they hadn't hung out much in high school, they had hung out together during the first few weeks of freshman year of college because neither one had any close friends from high school come to Dale. Justin had randomly been paired with Adam as a freshman roommate, just as Laney had been randomly paired with Natalie. Jill and Hilton, best friends since high school, had lived down the hall from Laney and Natalie, and the six of them started hanging out a lot. Sophomore year Adam, Justin, and Adam's friend Ryan had moved into an apartment together, but Ryan had a serious girlfriend from a different school, so he was never around much.

"Yeah, sucks to be you," Justin said, then pointed to the dance floor. "Looks like Adam found his catch of the night." Jill followed his finger and saw Adam making out with a short blonde in a skimpy tank top and a skirt that barely covered her ass.

"Big surprise," she said, rolling her eyes. "What about you?"

"No such luck," Justin said, then, "Wanna make out?" He grinned at Jill and took a swig of beer.

"Right, you can't even get me to make out with you when I'm drunk and you think I would when I'm sober?" Jill laughed and elbowed Justin in the side.

"Hey, gotta try," he replied, then turned away from Jill as three girls in jeans and low-cut tops walked by.

Jill slapped his arm jokingly. "Hey, don't stare at them like that!" she laughed. "You're such a loser."

Justin winked at her and then slid off his stool and followed the girls down onto the dance floor. "Watch, you'll see," he called back to Jill.

Jill laughed and nodded, then watched as Justin approached the girls and tried to start dancing with them. It was always fun to watch him make a fool of himself. It wasn't that he was bad-looking; he was actually cute with his shaggy blond hair coming down to his ears and his baby-blue eyes that had a way of looking so innocent when he flashed a smile. He had a decent body, maybe just a little scrawny, and he was probably about 5'10, Jill guessed. No, definitely not bad looking, just way too obvious when he was drunk and trying to flirt with girls, plus he was a horrible dancer. Girls usually couldn't help but laugh at him when he started trying to dance with them.

Two of the girls looked at each other and giggled when he joined them, but the other girl turned and started dancing with him. He looked at Jill and flashed a huge grin, and Jill raised her eyebrows and gave him a thumbs-up.

As Justin continued to dance, Jill let her eyes wander around the bar aimlessly, then she grabbed her cell phone out of her back pocket to check the time. She was bored and getting really tired, and she hoped Laney and Natalie would hurry up and get wasted so they'd be ready to go home. She knew Hilton and Luke would be ready whenever, because they could only party so long before they wanted to go home and get it on.

Right as Jill lifted her phone from her pocket it started to ring. She smiled automatically when she saw who the caller was and lifted the phone to her ear.

"Hey, hottie! What's up?" she said to Todd.

"Hey, Jilly Bean!" Todd yelled over the background noise. Jill could tell he was out at the bars too. Todd was always partying.

"Where are you?" she asked.

"Tenth Street…I'm not sure…" Todd answered. Jill knew Tenth Street was a street at Eastern Indiana University where several bars were located.

"I just wanted to make sure you're getting *wasted* tonight," Todd continued jubilantly.

"I wish!" Jill moaned. "I'm driving."

"Damn, it's no fun when we're both not drunk! Come on, just get drunk, they'll never know. You can keep it on the DL. Sssssshhhhh."

Jill giggled. "Yeah, that sounds like a good idea. I'll definitely get right on that."

"Yeah, you don't have to drive home. I'll come pick you up. You can spend the night with me."

"Hell yeah, baby, how soon can you get here?"

"What, dude?" Todd said to someone in the background. "What the fuck? That's fuckin' stupid. Okay, okay. Hey, Jill, I gotta go. I'll talk to ya later, okay? Get wasted this weekend." Then he was gone.

Jill shook her head and smiled, and put the phone back in her pocket. 12:33. Hopefully they'd only be here another hour or so. At least the call from Todd had taken up a few minutes.

Todd was her best and oldest friend besides Hilton; she had known him since freshman year of high school. They'd had Advanced English together and had been best friends ever since. Jill had been attracted to him when they first became friends but didn't think he was interested in her, even though he was constantly flirting with her. That was just his personality, and she didn't take it to mean anything romantic or sexual. He was gorgeous and she just assumed he could get any girl he wanted. He was tall, about 6'1 now, with captivating chocolate eyes Jill could get lost in and light brown hair he usually spiked up a little so it looked sort of wild and out of control, and totally sexy. His hair completely fit his personality. He was one of the most fun, laid-back guys Jill had ever hung out with. He was completely down to earth and his main goal in life was to go out and have fun and do whatever he wanted with no regrets.

Jill had been thoroughly intoxicated with him when they first met, and as they became better friends she had tried to be a little more like him. Before they met she had always been fairly cautious and reserved and had taken life and herself very seriously. She was somewhat shy and incredibly naive about boys and relationships. Todd had taught her to loosen up and be more impulsive and less worrisome. Jill knew her friends still thought of her as sensible and even somewhat of a "goody-goody," but she loved the side of her Todd brought out and she loved being around him.

Even though Jill and Todd had gotten along so well ever since they met, the dating aspect had never come into their relationship, which disappointed Jill yet didn't surprise her since she had guessed from the start he didn't look at her that way. With her plain, straight, dark brown hair, skinny, un-curvy figure, and what she had considered average looks in high school, plus her overall inexperience with boys, Jill never thought of herself as the one he would choose. She was the one he wanted as a friend;

when it came to dating he was looking for something completely different…even though she could never figure out exactly what.

Their freshman year of high school she and Todd had hung out a lot in groups, but had never gone on an actual date. Their sophomore year they went to the Homecoming dance together, since neither of them had other dates, but that year Todd grew a couple inches and started working out a lot more, and all the girls began to take notice. He also got some varsity pitching time that year, and by the beginning of the summer after their sophomore year, he had a steady girlfriend.

Her name was Melanie and she was a year behind Jill and Todd in school. She was blonde and cute…skinny but with huge boobs, and two inches taller than Jill's 5'4. She and Jill became friends and even hung out together without Todd sometimes, but Jill knew Melanie never really liked her. She figured Melanie just wanted to keep her close so she could try to make sure nothing happened between Jill and Todd. Keep your friends close, and your enemies closer. Jill knew what Melanie was doing, but she didn't mind because being fake friends with Melanie allowed her to stay close to Todd and involved in his life even though he had a serious girlfriend.

Todd and Melanie broke up once and Todd briefly dated another girl, but then he and Melanie got back together and were still together when Todd and Jill graduated. The summer following graduation Todd, Melanie, Jill, Hilton, and a group of about fifteen others partied and hung out together all summer. Todd and Melanie decided to stay together when he left for Eastern Indiana in August, but by the time he came home for Thanksgiving she had been cheating on him for two months with a boy in her own class and she and Todd ended things for good.

Since then Todd hadn't dated anyone seriously. Jill had dated a few boys in high school, but no one for more than six months, and even though she had gotten over her tremendous crush on Todd, she never stopped being attracted to him. Todd had come to visit Jill and Hilton at Dale several times freshman year and stayed in their dorm room, and Hilton, who had wanted Jill and Todd to get together since freshman year of high school, always encouraged Jill to hook up with him. Jill always blew off the suggestion by saying Todd wouldn't be interested. She honestly believed he wouldn't be, but just in case he was, she wanted to avoid the situation because she knew if she was faced with it she might not be able to resist, and she didn't want to risk ruining the friendship. She was also intimidated by the fact that she knew Todd was a lot more sexually experienced than she was, and she would have been humiliated if they hooked up and he thought she wasn't any good.

Going to a different school than Todd and not being around him on a regular basis had helped Jill find a sense of closure regarding her crush or whatever it had been. During high school and freshman year of college she was always jealous of any other girl Todd dated, but now it didn't even faze her. A couple times he had come to visit her at Dale and made out or hooked up with other girls and she was happy to realize she was fine with it. She still thought Todd was gorgeous, but she had been able to separate that from wanting him. Adam, on the other hand, was a completely different story....

"Hey there, Jill," Adam said as he moved up beside her and rested his elbow on her shoulder.

Jill jumped. "Oh, my gosh, you scared me," she laughed.

"Oops, sorry," Adam said. "Dude, I'm fucking wasted."

"I wish I was!" Jill replied. "But I have to drive....Hey, do you need a ride home? I can take you." It was out of her mouth before Jill realized there was no way she could fit him in her car along with Natalie, Laney, Hilton, and Luke.

"Oh no, that's ok," Adam said, and just as he said it the girl Jill and Justin had watched him making out with on the dance floor came up. She put her arm through Adam's and gave Jill a fake smile that really meant, Stay away from him, bitch. Jill fake-smiled back, and then the girl turned to Adam.

"Ready, baby?" she asked him.

"Yep, let's get the hell out of here." Adam winked at Jill as he headed toward the door with his "catch of the night."

"Thanks, though, Jill," he called over his shoulder.

Jill groaned. "I think I'm going to puke," she muttered to herself.

"What?! You weren't supposed to be drinking; you have to drive us home!" a drunk Natalie cried as she, Laney, Hilton, and Luke stumbled up to the table.

"No, I'm not drinking. Did you see that nasty-ass girl Adam's going home with tonight?" Jill scowled.

"That one he was dancing with?" Laney asked.

"More like getting it on with on the dance floor," Natalie said scornfully. "Can you say diseases? You don't want that shit, Jilly!"

"I know," Jill consented, "but he'd still be fun to at least make out with."

"Come on, let's get the hell out of here," Hilton said impatiently, tossing her long, thick brown hair over her shoulder while she clung to Luke's arm with her other hand.

Jill stood up from the table and the five of them headed toward the exit. As they walked across the parking lot toward her car, Jill saw Adam and the blonde girl crawling into the backseat of a car being driven by one of the girl's friends. Adam's hands were on her ass as she got into the car ahead of him, and Jill could tell she was giggling.

It's pretty pathetic that I almost wish that was me, she thought.

❦   ❦   ❦

On Saturday Jill didn't come out of her room until 1:00 in the afternoon.

"Hey, lazy ass," Natalie teased, a gleam in her bright blue eyes. She was sprawled on the couch in pajama pants and a t-shirt with her long, wavy blonde hair in a messy ponytail, flipping through the latest copy of *Us Weekly*.

She looks so tan and pretty, Jill thought, wishing she could just roll out of bed and look that good. Laney looked cute, too, in an oversized sweatshirt and sweatpants, her shoulder-length black hair pulled into a high, perky ponytail. She was sitting in the chair with her legs hanging over the arm.

Jill yawned and smiled in Natalie's direction as she padded across the living room to the kitchen.

"You had a nice twelve hour sleep," Laney laughed. "How can you still be yawning? We didn't even drink last night!"

"I know," Jill said as she poured herself a bowl of cereal. The girls had stayed in last night and watched movies. "I was just too lazy to get up; my bed felt so nice and warm. Plus I wanted to rest up for tonight so I can be ready to party." She grinned at the girls as she carried her cereal to the table that separated the kitchen and living room. "Woohoo, *Newlyweds*!" she exclaimed as she glanced at the TV.

"Yeah, it's a marathon," Laney said.

"Where are Hilton and Luke?" Jill asked.

"In their room 'watching a movie,' supposedly." Natalie grinned as she made quote marks with her fingers. "Maybe that's what finally woke you up!"

"Nah, I can never hear them," Jill said with a wave of her hand. "Their bathroom blocks the sounds I think. I have heard them in the shower before though…."

Luke was over so often it felt like he lived there, and the girls had begun calling Hilton's room and bathroom "their" room and "their" bathroom. Jill's room was on the same side of the apartment as Hilton's, and her bathroom wall bordered Hilton's bathroom wall. Jill was glad it was set up that way; if it was set up so their beds were just on opposite sides of the wall from each other Jill was sure she would have had to either buy earplugs or shoot herself. But she loved Luke to death, and it didn't bother her that he was over all the time. She had basically considered him another roommate since he and Hilton had started dating freshman year of college, and she had always felt comfortable around him. Luckily, Laney and Natalie liked him too. Hilton had been worried sophomore year when she and Jill moved into the four bedroom apartment with Laney and Natalie. "We really don't know them that well," Hilton had said to Jill before they moved in. "What if they hate Luke or just don't want him over very often? Neither of them has a boyfriend so it might be really annoying having just one guy over all the time." But it had worked out wonderfully and the four girls were still living together now as they neared the end of their junior year.

"How long's this marathon?" Jill asked now as she shoved a spoonful of Froot Loops into her mouth.

"I don't know, probably till four or five," Laney replied.

"Good," Jill said, relieved. "It gives me an excuse not to do anything today."

"I thought you didn't ever do homework on Saturdays," Natalie said.

"I don't, but if there's nothing on TV I feel like I'm just wasting time and I should be doing it," Jill explained. Natalie and Laney

really built in high school when he used to lift weights all the time. Now he had slimmed down a little, but the muscle tone was still noticeable. He had medium-brown hair that came down almost to his ears, but wasn't quite long enough to look sloppy. He usually came off as clean-cut and preppy, and if he was a couple inches shorter, Jill probably would have drooled over him every time she saw him. But being only 5'4, she just never found herself seriously attracted to anyone taller than 6'0 or 6'1.

"So what's the plan for tonight?" Hilton asked during a commercial. She rolled over on her back and glanced from Natalie to Laney to Jill.

"What are Justin and those guys doing?" Natalie asked with a yawn.

"I don't know, but maybe we should find out, 'cause I'm hopefully doing whatever Adam's doing!" Jill said half-jokingly.

"You mean you're hopefully doing Adam," Hilton giggled.

"Shut up, bitch." Jill grinned back at Hilton. "I am not *doing* him. Just making out with him, hopefully."

"Yeah, whatever," Hilton teased. "You know you want it!"

"Yeah, you know my goal," Jill said dryly. "Sleep with at least one guy a weekend and see how many STDs I can accumulate by the end of the year."

"That's kinda funny 'cause that's pretty much how it would be with Adam...the STD thing!" Natalie joked.

They all laughed.

"Well, I'll call Adam or someone in a little bit," Jill said. "First I need some food." She had just realized how hungry she was. As she got up to find something to eat, the apartment phone rang. Jill leaned over the counter and grabbed the portable off its base.

"Oh, it's Adam," she said as she looked at the caller ID. "Hello?....We're not sure yet, what are you guys doing?....Oh, okay, that sounds good….All right, we'll see ya then! Later." She hung up.

"They're having a party at their apartment," she announced.

"Ooooh, perfect!" Laney said and flashed a devilish smile at Jill. "Now it'll be easy for you to spend the night with him."

Jill grinned back at Laney and winked. "Hell yeah, baby," she said with a raise of her eyebrows and a flip of her shoulder-length brown hair. *I hope so anyway*, she thought to herself as she poured a can of SpaghettiOs into a bowl and placed it in the microwave, a small flutter of excitement in her stomach.

The four girls and Luke arrived at Adam, Justin, and Ryan's apartment at about 10:30. There were fifteen or twenty people there already, most of whom Jill knew casually, having met them at previous parties.

Hilton, Luke, Natalie, and Laney had bought two cases of beer and put all forty-eight cans in a large cooler filled with ice, which they had brought over in Luke's car. Jill had opted not to go in on the beer, and she had brought six twenty-ounce bottles of Cherry Coke and a handle of rum that was about a third of the way empty already. She had also brought one of her Turtle cups. She carried her drinks and cup in a small Vera Bradley bag that zipped shut, so she was able to hide her toothbrush and hairbrush and purse inside *just in case* she spent the night. She smiled to herself at the thought and quickly scanned the room for any girls who might be her competition for Adam. To her relief, everyone she saw was at least vaguely familiar, no hot new girls Adam would be interested in, and most of the girls there were already with guys.

Adam walked into the kitchen to grab a beer out of the fridge.

He looks sooooo hot tonight, Jill thought to herself.

He had on baggy jeans that were faded in the front and a white shirt that buttoned down the front and had narrow navy blue vertical stripes spaced about an inch apart. His dirty blond hair was gelled and looked remarkably like Brad Pitt's in *Ocean's Eleven*. Adam was a total Abercrombie hottie, as Jill and her friends liked to say. His sleeves were rolled up a couple times so that his wrists and part of his forearms showed, and on his right wrist he wore a black elastic hair band, like the kind most girls wore and you could get in multi-packs at any store that sold hair products. He always wore it and something about it totally turned Jill on. She imagined it was left in his room by some random girl he had slept with and he found it and just carelessly threw it on, not even knowing who had left it. To Jill it represented his careless, ready-for-anything, bring-it-on attitude towards girls and life in general, and she also loved that he could nonchalantly wear something she considered feminine and look so damn masculine and hot with it on. There weren't a lot of guys who could pull off that look, Jill thought.

"Hey guys," Adam greeted the girls and Luke. "What's up?"

"Not much, man, how's it goin'?" Luke replied.

"Hey, Adam, can I put my bag in your room?" Jill asked. She always did that when the boys had parties at their apartment so her alcohol wouldn't get stolen.

"Yep, go ahead," Adam replied, and as Jill walked by him he mussed up the hair on top of her head. Jill playfully hit him in the stomach with the back of her hand and she could feel his rippling muscles under his lightweight shirt. She felt a little excited flutter in her stomach and once she was alone in Adam's room she allowed a smile to break out. She loved being around him because he was such good eye candy, but sometimes it was hard not to stare. Okay, it was always hard.

Jill did not normally hook up with random guys, or even guys she knew; she had only hooked up with a few guys her whole life and most of her friends admired her for still being a virgin. But every time she was around Adam, she had a small hope in the back of her head that she would get the chance to hook up with him that night. This hope became especially prominent when she was drinking, but tonight it had ballooned into an overpowering feeling of need, accompanied by nervousness that some other girl would get him, because that would be just her luck. She wanted him more than ever and she was determined that tonight was her night. *And I haven't even been drinking!* Jill thought. *This is crazy!*

By about 1:30 in the morning the party had started to die down. Some people had left to go to the bars, and others began heading home or to different parties. Ryan and his girlfriend, who was visiting from another school, were in bed already. Justin, Adam, Natalie, Laney, Jill, and two couples Jill knew through Adam and Justin were playing asshole at the kitchen table. Hilton and Luke were on the couch in the living room watching a rerun of *Entertainment Tonight* and waiting for asshole to be over so they could go home.

Jill was doing very well at asshole; she had been president every hand except for two. The game didn't involve any skill, but she had been getting lots of doubles, and she and Adam had been cheating by trading cards under the table whenever they sat next to each other. He had been flirting with her all night and Jill was almost sure something was going to happen between them.

Natalie laid a king on the table. "You're skipped, drink," she ordered Kate, the girl sitting on her right.

"No way, bitch!" Laney yelled triumphantly. "I laid two kings, you have to beat two."

"Damn it!" Natalie cried. She took back her king and laid a two.

"One, two…" everyone started counting.

Justin let them get to five before he raked the cards in with a grin. The rule was that a two could be played on top of any other card and whenever a two was laid the asshole had to clear all the cards on the table. However many seconds it took to clear them was how many drinks the asshole had to take. Whoever ran out of cards first at the end of each round was president, the second person to run out was vice-president, then secretary, etc. The second to last person to run out was beer bitch, meaning he or she had to get a new drink for anyone who needed one throughout the round, and the last person to run out was asshole. The asshole had to deal the cards and once the round started anyone could tell the asshole to drink any amount at any time. The president of each round got to make a rule. Jill was president this round and her rule was that whenever someone said the f-word, that person had to take five drinks. So far none of the girls had had to drink, but each guy had been caught saying the taboo word at least twice.

Now that the cards had been cleared, Natalie started again by playing her king. Kate laid two sixes, because a pair of anything beat any single card. Jared laid two eights and then Adam laid three aces.

"What the fuck?!" Laney exclaimed. "You fuckin' suck, I never get three of a kind!"

"Hey, drink ten!" Jill said to Laney. "You said the f-word twice!"

Laney groaned and opened the new beer sitting next to her.

"Jill, it's your turn," Natalie said.

Jill grinned wickedly and laid her four tens on top of Adam's three aces. "President again!" she shouted, waving her empty hands in front of everyone.

"Oh that's fuckin' bullshit!" Natalie cried with a laugh. She threw her cards at Jill and Adam. "Y'all are fuckin' cheaters! I'm done!" She laughed and finished the beer she had in front of her as she stood up from the table. "I'm ready to go home and pass out!"

Hilton and Luke jumped up readily. They had been bored and waiting for a while now. "Let's go then," Hilton said.

This was the part of the night Jill had been dreading. She was hoping she and Adam would already have made out so it would be easy to stay without looking stupid, but now she had to think of an excuse to stay.

"Oh come on guys, let's play one more game," Jill said. "Hilton and Luke, you guys should play too." She widened her eyes at Hilton, knowing Hilton would get the hint. "I'm not ready to stop drinking yet! I'm not tired."

"Stay," Adam said. "You can stay here tonight; we'll take you home tomorrow. I'm sure we'll be up for a while, so if you wanna drink some more…."

"Are you sure?" Jill asked, trying to act nonchalant and hide her excitement.

"Oh yeah, no problem," Adam said easily.

"Okay, well I guess I'll stay then," Jill said with a shrug of her shoulders, as though it was no big deal.

"Hey, didn't you leave your apartment key in Luke's car?" Hilton asked. "You better get it in case we're not up when you get home in the morning."

"Oh yeah, good idea. I'll be back," Jill said to Adam and Justin, then followed the girls and Luke outside. She knew she hadn't left her keys in the car, but was glad Hilton had said something because she could hardly contain herself. She waited until they were a safe distance away from the apartment and Luke was unlocking the car, then screamed and giggled.

"Aaaaahhhhh! I can't believe this!" she cried, feeling giddy.

"I know! Woohoo! Finally!" Hilton giggled back.

All four girls were grinning from ear to ear and laughing, partly because they were drunk and partly because they were excited for Jill. Jill was almost bouncing up and down.

"Okay, well you better tell us how it is! Have fun!" Hilton said.

"Yeah, you better come home tomorrow still a virgin," Laney teased.

"Oh, you don't have to worry about that," Jill said confidently, still smiling. "Aaaahhh! Okay, I have to go back inside; I'm freezing my ass off! See you girls tomorrow!"

"Night, have fun!" the girls replied as they crawled into Luke's car.

Jill tried to stop grinning then turned and went back to the apartment.

As she went back inside Kate and Jared and Britt and Park, the two other couples who'd been playing asshole, were leaving. Jill pretended to act disappointed, but she was actually glad. Now if Justin would just go to bed soon….

"Let's play a game, guys," Adam suggested. "Jill said she wants to keep partying! She's not drunk enough yet."

Jill laughed and plopped down on the recliner. "Guys, I'm wasted already!" she said. "But that's okay! Let's play another drinking game." She giggled.

"Well, go make a drink!" Adam said. "What do you guys wanna play?"

They ended up playing a game where they set an empty cup in the middle of the floor and tossed coins into it. Whenever someone made a shot, the other two had to take drinks: one for a penny, two for a nickel, four for a dime, and eight for a quarter. Jill found that, surprisingly, she was better with her left hand, even though she was normally right-handed. She was doing quite a bit better than the boys at the game and was loving it.

"Drunk luck, what bullshit." Justin pretended to be mad and punched the wall. "Fuck, dude, that hurt!" he laughed as he looked at his knuckles to see if they were bleeding. They weren't.

"Well guys, I'm headed to bed," he said. "You kids have fun." He went into his bedroom and shut the door.

"Wanna watch a movie?" Adam asked.

"Sure."

"We have to watch it in my room," Adam said. "We unhooked the DVD player out here and hid it so it wouldn't get stolen."

"I can't move," Jill said, still slumped in the recliner. "Help me up."

"I'll give you a piggyback ride," Adam said, and squatted down in front of Jill's chair. "Get on."

Jill laughed and pulled herself up out of the chair. She put her arms and legs around Adam and let him pick her up and carry her into his room. He turned so his back was to his bed and dropped her on it. Then he went and shut the door and turned off the lights. "I like watching movies in the dark," he announced.

"Me too," Jill said, confident now that there wouldn't be much movie-watching going on at all.

"What do you wanna watch?" Adam asked as he walked back over to the bed. Jill's eyes were still getting used to the dark and she could just see his shadow. He stopped directly in front of her and remained standing, as though waiting for her to choose something so he could get it and put it in the DVD player.

"I don't know, what do you have?" Jill asked, looking up at the outline of his face. She was sitting on the very edge of the bed where he had dropped her and their legs were touching.

"I forget. I don't know where my movies are," Adam said playfully. Then all of a sudden his mouth was on hers and he was standing over her, straddling her legs, which were hanging over the edge of the bed.

Jill felt herself gasp and inhale quickly, surprised even though she had been expecting it. Right away her hands were in his hair then making their way down his back, exploring his incredible body through his shirt. His back arched as he pressed into her, and she responded by drawing her arms tighter around him.

He was a very passionate kisser and he had a larger mouth than Jill had ever realized. It felt like he was devouring her as his tongue wrestled with hers, and Jill hurried to match his fast pace. Now his hands were on her face, then in her hair, and then she was completely lost in him….

When Jill opened her eyes she barely suppressed a moan. Her head hurt like hell and she felt like it would be a huge effort to even sit up, but she had a crystal clear memory of the night before. She glanced at Adam and saw he was facing away from her, his previously gelled hair rumpled and sticking out all over the place. He looked adorable. Jill wasn't sure how drunk he had been the night before, and she didn't want to be faced with an awkward morning-after situation, so she thought she would leave before he got up.

She forced herself up into a sitting position, then had to stop and brace herself on the edge of the bed because her head was pounding from the motion of sitting up. Finally it felt a little better and she got off the bed and grabbed her clothes, which were strewn about the floor. She would hurry and get dressed and then take her bag, go outside, and call Hilton or one of the girls, and wait for one of them to come pick her up.

As she walked slowly to the bathroom to keep her headache from getting any worse, Jill suddenly felt a wave of nausea and realized she was going to throw up. She rushed into the bathroom and shut the door, praying Adam didn't hear her. That would be just perfect, she thought. He'll be completely grossed out and regret ever hooking up with me.

She threw up for about five minutes and finally felt a little better. She hadn't heard Adam moving around, so she was pretty sure he was still passed out and hadn't heard her. She dressed quickly and pulled her hair into a ponytail at the back of her neck, then quietly opened the bathroom door and tiptoed out into Adam's room. She paused to look at his still form for another second, and smiled a small, mischievous smile to herself, then tiptoed out of the room.

Luckily no one else was up yet. She dug in her bag for her cell phone as she walked across the living room and saw that it was only 9:00. No wonder no one was up yet. She walked outside and around the corner from Adam's apartment so she couldn't be seen from the window, then dialed her apartment.

Laney answered on the fourth ring and Jill could tell she'd been asleep.

"Hey, Lane," she said quietly, feeling as though Adam or Justin or Ryan would hear her even though she was away from their apartment now. "Could you do me a huge favor and come pick me up?"

"I thought Adam was bringing you home," Laney yawned.

"He was, but could you just come get me? Please?" Jill pleaded.

"Why, what happened?" Laney asked curiously, a little more awake now.

"Um, nothing really, I'll just tell you on the way home," Jill said.

"Okay, I'll be there in a few minutes." Laney yawned again.

"Thanks so much," Jill said gratefully, and Laney hung up. Jill snapped her cell phone shut and then another wave of nausea came over her and she turned and threw up in the grass.

❦   ❦   ❦

"I feel like shit," Jill moaned as she slid into Laney's car. She moaned and held her stomach.

"Yeah, you were wasted last night," Laney laughed at her. "So, how'd it go with Adam?"

"Oh, it went pretty well," Jill said, trying to be coy but not feeling well enough to really pull it off. She did manage a smile before her head throbbed again.

"So why were you sneaking out of there this morning?" Laney questioned her.

"Um, I just didn't want a weird morning-after situation….because, um…I had sex with him," Jill confessed in a meek voice as though scared Laney would be furious with her, then laughed a guilty but excited laugh. She suddenly felt better.

"WHAT?!" Laney cried, turning to look at Jill. The car swerved and nearly ran off the side of the road.

"Watch out!" Jill cried, clutching her stomach again.

"Sorry," Laney laughed as she straightened the car. She looked over at Jill with wide eyes. "I cannot believe you had sex with him! That's crazy!" But Jill could tell she didn't disapprove; she was just shocked and dying to hear all about it. Laney loved drama and gossip, as long as it didn't have to do with her. She preferred to keep her own life relatively simple, but was always eager to hear or share a juicy story. Jill didn't mind because Laney wasn't malicious with her gossiping, just genuinely interested. Jill probably wouldn't have trusted her with a huge secret though, because even if Laney had the best intentions, she probably would end up spilling to Natalie or someone. It was just who she was. Jill knew it and still considered Laney a good friend. She was an attentive listener and always approachable with a story or problem.

"I know," Jill moaned, covering her face with her hands and slouching in the seat. "I almost can't believe it really happened. But it was *amazing*." She looked up and grinned.

She felt better again and bounced in her seat, giggling. She knew in the back of her head that she would probably feel slutty or something later for what had happened, but right now all she felt was elation and giddiness. The rest of the ride home she filled Laney in on what had happened.

Around 11:30 that morning Laney, Hilton, and Natalie sat in the living room, with the TV tuned to the *Newlyweds: Nick & Jessica* marathon that was on again.

Luke was still in bed and Jill had gone back to sleep when she and Laney got home. She had not come out of her room yet and Laney had been dying for the other girls to wake up ever since she and Jill got home so she could spill the huge news to them. She hadn't been able to go back to sleep so she had pulled her shoulder-length, layered black hair into a ponytail at the base of her neck, made herself a bowl of cereal, curled up in the living room chair in her Dale sweatshirt and Abercrombie beach shorts, and turned on the *Newlyweds* marathon, even though she'd already seen all the episodes.

Natalie had gotten up around eleven and had sat on the couch in her leopard print pajama pants and matching tank top, her long blonde hair mussed from sleep, staring at Laney with her mouth open in shock the whole time Laney told the story.

"I know!" Laney had responded to Natalie's stunned expression. She grinned at Natalie with wide eyes and covered her mouth with her hand, partly to show she was shocked too and partly to suppress a giggle. Natalie wasn't as big of a gossip as Laney and was better at keeping secrets, but she enjoyed a good, scandalous story, and this was definitely the most shocking thing she'd heard lately.

"Well, way to go, Jill," Natalie had replied. "It's about freakin' time!"

"I just can't believe she would do that…after waiting this long…why him?" Laney had whispered, not wanting Jill to wake up and hear them talking about it.

"Who knows?" Natalie had whispered back. "But I'm just glad she did it; she's always such a tease to guys! We have to get Hilton out here and tell her!"

The two girls giggled conspiratorially and tiptoed over to Hilton's door.

Laney knocked quietly. "Hilton!" she hissed.

They could hear Hilton crawl out of bed and a moment later she opened the door wearing gray sweatpants that said Dale down one leg and a black long-sleeved basketball t-shirt from Luke's high school. She yawned and ran her fingers through her long hair. "What's up?"

"Get out here!" Natalie ordered her, motioning excitedly. Hilton had followed them sleepily to the futon, still yawning, but she was wide awake as soon as Laney told her the story.

"WHAT?!" she had cried, about to burst out laughing, then raised her eyebrows as if to say, Oops! She covered her mouth and said more quietly, "I mean, what?" The she had started giggling and rolled over on the futon.

"Oh my gosh!" she cried, pounding the Colin pillow, then kissing Colin on the lips. "Our Jilly! This is so exciting! But so crazy, too!"

Now, a few minutes later, as Hilton, Natalie, and Laney were still talking about it, Jill slowly opened her door and crept sheepishly out of her room.

"Jilly!" Hilton screamed and flung the Colin pillow at her, then jumped up off the futon and hugged Jill, bouncing her around in a circle. Jill had fended off the pillow with a small smile and now she was laughing as hard as Hilton. They both looked giddy dancing around the living room.

"So how was it?" Hilton asked as she plopped back down on the futon.

Jill sank down beside her, still smiling. "Incredible, amazing, wonderful, I don't know."

Hilton laughed happily and bounced on the futon while Laney and Natalie laughed too, as much at Hilton as at Jill's description.

"I just can't believe you guys did it!" Natalie said. "I mean, you're Jill!" Laney and Hilton looked at Natalie and laughed. "What made you decide to do it?" Natalie asked curiously.

"She was wasted!" Laney answered with a giggle, pulling her knees up to her chest and rocking back and forth in the chair because she was cold in her shorts.

Jill smiled a little and shook her head, then lowered it into her hands. "Aaagghhh!" she cried. "Am I just a big slut now? I mean seriously, I can't believe I did it either! What was I thinking?!"

"No, you're not a slut, you're just normal now!" Natalie teased. "As long as you don't get any diseases from him!" she joked. "Did you use a condom?"

"Of course we did," Jill said, as if she couldn't believe Natalie would even ask. "I was maybe drunk, but how could I ever be *that* stupid? He's so dirty. Ugh," she moaned, covering her face again.

"Hey, don't regret it now," Hilton said. "It's all over, and I'm sure you don't have any kind of disease; just because he's a player doesn't mean he's really dirty. And you used a condom anyway! So don't worry. Just think about how fun it was! Didn't it even hurt at all? I guess you were too drunk to notice. That's the way to go!"

"Are you gonna do it again? I mean do him again?" Laney asked with one of her trademark devilish smiles she used whenever she was talking about something sexual.

"I have no idea," Jill said with a shrug. "I mean, I don't even know when I'll see him again. I'm going to visit Todd next weekend and then the weekend after that I'm going home to get everything for spring break."

"Well, he'll be on spring break with us," Natalie pointed out. The four girls, Adam, Justin, Luke, Luke's roommate Ace, and Kate, Jared, Britt, and Park from Adam and Justin's party were all going to Daytona for spring break. They were taking three cars and renting two condos that were next door to each other in the same building. It wasn't really decided who would stay in which condo; they were planning on everyone sharing both of them.

"Yeah, but like anything'll happen there," Jill said dryly. "It's spring break, come on, he's gonna be hooking up with a different girl every night!"

"We'll see," Hilton said with a wink at Jill. "You never know. Maybe you were so good he doesn't want anyone else anymore."

Jill rolled her eyes. "Right!" she scoffed at Hilton, who just laughed and repeated, "You never know!"

When Justin woke up and came out of his bedroom at 1:00 in the afternoon he found Adam sprawled on his stomach on the couch wearing only a pair of red nylon gym shorts and that damn rubber band. His hair was tousled and he looked like he felt like shit.

"Rough night?" Justin laughed at him as he fixed himself a bowl of cereal.

"Dude," Adam replied, then began to repeatedly pound his face into the couch.

"What the fuck happened?" Justin asked, mildly interested. He sank into the recliner with his huge bowl of cereal and shoved an overflowing spoonful into his mouth. He reached down and popped out the bottom of the chair.

"I'm so fucking stupid," Adam replied, lying still on the couch again and staring blankly at the TV, which was showing some weird old movie Justin didn't recognize.

"What the fuck are you watchin', man?" Justin asked, leaning over to grab the remote off the coffee table.

"I don't know, it was what was on…."

Justin wondered how long Adam had been laying there staring at the TV like that. He was becoming more interested now.

"So hurry up and tell me what the fuck happened already!" he said impatiently as he munched on his cereal.

"Jill….I had sex with Jill."

Justin almost choked. "Jill? Jill who was here last night? Jill Sherer?" He took Adam's silence as a yes. "Dude, isn't she a—"

"Yep," Adam cut him off. "She's a fucking virgin. *Was* a fucking virgin." He slammed his fist into the arm of the couch. "What the fuck was I thinking?!"

"I can't believe that," Justin said, still in shock. "Maybe she wasn't a virgin. How do you know she was?"

"You know she was too! We played that damn game of I Never, and she said she never had sex!"

"Well that was a couple months ago; she could've had sex since then."

"With who? I mean we hang out with her all the fuckin' time; does she ever hook up with anybody?"

"Well…" Justin racked his brain. "No."

"Yeah," Adam declared. "I'm a fuckin' dick now. I've gotta start being more careful. I was so drunk last night…."

"I didn't mean no," Justin said, enjoying himself a little bit now. "I meant I don't know. She probably does hook up with guys."

"*Who?*" Adam asked again.

"Maybe Todd," Justin said, trying to sound serious but grinning behind Adam's back. His roommate was such a player and it was funny to see him actually worry about one of his hook-ups. Justin was actually a little surprised Adam felt bad, and was still having a hard time believing the story because he didn't think Jill would randomly lose her virginity to a guy like Adam, considering she saw some of the girls he hooked up with and knew what a player he was. He thought maybe Adam didn't really remember exactly what had happened. But if they *had* had sex, Justin wasn't worried about Jill because she was a smart girl and always knew what she was doing. That was why it was amusing to see Adam so worried.

"Do *you* think she hooks up with Todd?" Adam asked pointedly.

"No," Justin said easily. "You're probably right. She probably doesn't hook up with anybody. She probably never did more than kiss a guy before. You're such a fuckin' prick." He knew Jill had hooked up a little bit with at least two guys last year but wasn't surprised Adam didn't know, since he had such an action-packed sex life of his own and was probably oblivious to anyone else's.

"Oh, fuck you, dude," Adam snapped. "I feel like shit. I think she freaked out too 'cause she left here this morning before I got up. I said I'd take her home but she must've called somebody. So that's just fuckin' great; she thinks I'm a complete asshole now and took advantage of her when she was drunk."

"I doubt it," Justin replied absentmindedly. He was losing interest in Adam's dilemma because he had found *Die Hard* on TV.

They sat in silence for a few minutes, then Adam suddenly pounded his head into the couch again. "Fuck!" he yelled. "I didn't even use a fucking condom!"

For the next couple days, Jill couldn't stop thinking about the fact that she'd had sex with Adam. She replayed everything in her mind several times and was continually smiling and laughing to herself about it. Sometimes it was hard not to sit in class with a huge, stupid-looking grin on her face. She pushed back the few guilty, shameful feelings she experienced and was basically giddy and proud of herself for going through with it and happy she had done it.

But by Wednesday her elation had died down and she experienced almost a complete reversal in emotion. She couldn't believe it had really happened and she felt like the biggest slut ever. Hilton and Natalie and Laney were happy for her, but they must think it was really weird that after waiting so long to have sex, she would lose her virginity when she was drunk, and to Adam, of all people. She really didn't know what she had been thinking and she felt dirty all over. How could she have let herself get so out of control? She had always thought of herself as a smart, sensible person, and she had never imagined anything like this happening. She had wanted to wait to have sex until she was in a serious relationship and in love, and instead she had thrown it all away at a party when she was completely trashed? She felt uncomfortable because it was like she didn't even know who she really was anymore.

There was no way she was going to the Turtle on Thursday because she didn't want to face Adam and have things be awkward, or even worse, see him go home with another girl. She had a hunch that would make her feel even shittier. But she knew if she tried to stay home the girls would make her go, so she decided to leave early to visit Todd at Eastern. She couldn't wait to get away for the weekend and be around someone who didn't know what had happened and with whom she always had fun.

"I can't believe you're leaving early!" Laney cried when Jill came out of her room on Thursday afternoon with her packed bag over her shoulder. "Tonight's your chance to hook up with Adam again!"

"I know…" Jill said, "but I just don't know if I even want anything else to happen, or if the next time we see each other should be when we're both drinking." She hadn't told the girls how she'd been feeling about her hookup with Adam the last couple days, and they were still under the impression she was thrilled about the whole thing.

"True," Laney admitted with a shrug.

"Well he better not hook up with any other girls tonight," Natalie said. "I'll be so pissed. I'll watch him and try to keep him away from girls."

"Oh, don't do that," Jill said, shaking her head at Natalie. "Let him do what he wants. I mean, I don't care if he hooks up with other girls. It's not like we're dating or something. I know how he is."

"Yeah, but still, he better not," Natalie said.

"Whatever," Jill said. "Don't say anything to him if he does. I don't want to be, like, scary obsessed girl who thinks she's his girlfriend now."

"Don't worry, Jilly," Hilton reassured her with a silly grin. "I won't let her say anything. Just go and have fun and don't worry about it!"

Jill grinned for their sakes so they would all think she was fine. "Bye, girls, have a good weekend!"

She walked out the door and hurried to her car, anxious to get away and forget everything for a few days.

❦   ❦   ❦

Jill held her Vera Bradley bag over her shoulder and pounded on the door of Todd's apartment. At first she heard nothing, then finally footsteps coming down the hallway. Todd threw the door open and Jill rushed in and gave him a hug. "Thanks for letting me freeze my ass off for ten minutes out there!" she complained jokingly.

Todd playfully grabbed her ass with both hands and rubbed it. "Nope, didn't freeze off," he informed her with an appealing grin that made him look like a naughty little boy.

Jill laughed and smacked him in the chest, pushing him away. Todd was wearing a big blue hooded Eastern Indiana sweatshirt and white nylon pants that buttoned all the way up the sides. His hair was spiked up all over the place and a little bit longer than usual. He looked completely adorable and sexy at the same time and it had felt so good to hug him and to be in familiar, comfortable arms. He looked so cozy and Jill just wanted to cuddle with him. She beamed at him and realized it was her first genuine smile in a couple of days.

"So what's going on tonight?" she asked, walking past Todd and down the hallway, shaking her butt at him as she went. His room was on the left, off the living room, and she tossed her bag inside the doorway.

"I don't know," Todd said, "but we were waiting for you so we could go get some food." He grabbed a white Eastern hat off his doorknob and put it on backwards. "Hey, man," he yelled down the hallway to his roommate, Conrad. "Jill's here, you ready?"

"Yeah, I'm coming," Conrad called, and a minute later he shuffled out of the living room and down the hall to join them. He was taller than Todd, probably 6'3 or 6'4, and had a lanky build. He had been a star basketball player in high school in Illinois, but had chosen coming to Eastern for its business school over playing basketball at a smaller college somewhere in Illinois. He was dressed almost identically to Todd in an Eastern sweatshirt and hat and nylon pants.

"Hey, Jill," he said, greeting her with a high-five. "What's up?"

"Nothin' much," Jill replied with an easy smile. She really liked Conrad; he was totally laid back and always up for a good time, just like Todd. The two had been randomly paired as roommates freshman year and Jill thought they couldn't have been a more perfect match. "Where are we eating?" she asked.

"Taco Bell!" Todd said as he grabbed his keys off the table beside the door. "Your favorite." He grinned at Jill.

"Our favorite!" Jill corrected, linking arms with Conrad and Todd and walking between them to Todd's truck. "What are you doing tonight, Conrad?"

"Lizzy's coming over; she wants to get wasted here and play poker," Conrad said.

"Sounds good to me, as long as we watch *Friends* first. How come you guys aren't going out tonight?"

"Too fuckin' lazy to change clothes," Todd replied.

Jill laughed. She was glad they weren't going out; she would rather stay in and have a relaxed night and just chill. It was definitely what she needed right now. She leaned back against the seat in Todd's truck and smiled. She was feeling so much better already.

After they ate at Taco Bell, the three of them stopped at the liquor store.

"Beer, Jill?" Todd asked as he hoisted a case of Keystone Light off the shelf.

"No, I think I'm getting some rum," Jill replied and went to pick out a fifth.

"Here, give it to me," Todd said. "I'm buying."

"No you're not," Jill said. "I can buy it."

"Nope, I'm buying," Todd said confidently, grabbing the bottle out of her hand.

"Why?" Jill asked, bewildered.

"'Cause I feel like it," Todd said firmly but playfully.

"He's just trying to get you in bed, Jill," Conrad joked, slapping Todd on the back. "Way to go, man."

"Shut the hell up, dude." Todd rolled his eyes as he stood in line holding the alcohol. "She already sleeps in my bed. And I'm not buying yours so you better get up here and pay for your half."

Conrad laughed and nudged Jill. "See? I was right; he's getting all touchy about it."

Jill laughed and shook her head at Conrad, shoving him ahead of her in line. "Yeah, right," she said.

The thought hit her that a comment about someone trying to get her in bed could have and maybe should have upset her, but it hadn't, and that made her feel good. She always felt good around Todd and was so glad she had planned this visit for this weekend.

Perfect timing, she thought with a smile. *I'll go back to school feeling so much better about everything.*

Hilton, Laney, and Natalie got to the Turtle around 11:00 that night. Luke had opted not to come since he had a physics test in the morning, so it was just the three of them this week. They all got their Turtle cups filled with rum and Coke, then sat down at a table looking out over the dance floor.

"Do you see Adam?" Natalie asked the other two girls as she scanned the dance floor.

"No…." Hilton and Laney said as they looked too.

"He better not be **with some girl** already!" Natalie said, narrowing her eyes.

"No shit," Hilton said. "**I know** he's a player, and I know Jill knows that, and she said she doesn't expect anything to come of it, but I wish it would for her sake. She really likes him."

"Do you think?" Laney asked.

"She wouldn't have had sex with him if she didn't," Hilton said confidently. "I've known her for seven years, trust me."

"Yeah, I'm sure you're right," Laney agreed. "Too bad he's such an asshole."

"It's not too bad," Hilton said. "It doesn't matter. Everything will be fine. We'll just see what happens tonight, if he hooks up with anyone."

Natalie and Laney looked at each other and shrugged. Hilton was always so happy-go-lucky and optimistic about everything working out for the best, and it was hard for Laney and Natalie to just sit back and not worry about stuff.

"Hey, look, there's Justin and Ryan and Park," Hilton said. "Hey, guys!" she yelled as the three boys left the bar. They saw her and headed over to the table where the girls were sitting.

"Hey, what's up," Justin drawled. He pulled out a stool and sat down. Ryan and Park grabbed stools from the next table and the girls scooted around so everyone could sit down.

"Where's Adam?" Hilton asked casually, praying the answer wouldn't be that he was with a girl somewhere.

"He didn't come out tonight," Justin replied, catching Hilton's eye. "Where's Jill?" Hilton immediately understood that Justin was letting on he knew about Adam and Jill, but Ryan and Park didn't.

"At Eastern with Todd," Hilton answered, smiling slowly at Justin. "That's weird that Adam's not out." She gave him a pointed look.

Justin knew she wanted an explanation but he couldn't say much in front of Ryan and Park. So he shrugged. "Yeah, I thought so too, but I guess he's tired or had a test or something."

As the conversation moved on to spring break, Hilton met Justin's eyes again and gave him a small smile, then tipped her mug up and took a long drink.

Later, when they were all dancing, Hilton waited for Justin to go to the bar for a refill, then pointed to her cup to signal to Laney and Natalie she was going too. She caught up with Justin at the top of the stairs and grabbed his arm.

"So what's the deal?" she asked. "Does he just not wanna see Jill?"

"No, I don't think it's that," Justin said as they walked away from the stairs and over near the entrance so they could hear each other over the music.

"He was really weird about it actually. He has been all week. He was freaked out on Sunday and said he needs to be more careful or something like that, and then he didn't talk about it again, but tonight he said he had a test to study for. And you know that's never stopped him from coming out before, so I don't know what his deal is…."

Hilton frowned. "Hmmmm," she said. Then she shrugged. "Who knows? Maybe he really does want to back off and start being more careful or whatever. At least he's not just avoiding her though."

"Well," Justin hesitated, then said, "I think it really threw him 'cause she was a virgin and now he feels really bad…."

"Oh…." Hilton said, looking off toward the bar. "Well, he shouldn't worry about that. Jill knows what she's doing, and she's fine with everything. Tell him that if you want."

"That's what I thought," Justin nodded. "I figured she wouldn't do anything she didn't want to. Okay, well, I'll tell him."

"Good," Hilton said and headed toward the bar. "Jill just wants spring break to be normal and not awkward."

"Oh, yeah, I'm sure it'll be fine by then," Justin said, and he bought Hilton another rum and Coke before they returned to the dance floor.

Jill had borrowed five dollars in quarters from Todd so she could play poker. He kept rolls of them in his room because they played a lot. At one point she had been down to seventy-five cents, but then she won three hands in a row and now she was up to $6.25. They had agreed to stop at 2:00, and it was 1:55. Enough time for one more hand. It was Lizzy's deal.

"Low hold, high spade," Lizzy said, winking at Jill as she started to deal the cards. They always let the dealer pick the game, and low hold, high spade was Jill and Lizzy's favorite. Lizzy dealt two cards face-down and one face-up to each of them.

Jill looked at her cards and could hardly believe her good luck. She was holding the ace of spades in her hand, which meant she automatically won half the pot. The person holding the highest spade won half the pot automatically, and the person with the best five card hand won the other half. They would each have seven cards with which to make the five card hand, and the lowest card each player held in his or her hand was wild for that player. Jill had the ace of spades and the six of hearts, so six was wild for her. In front of her on the table she had the eight of clubs.

Conrad started by betting a quarter. Jill decided to raise right away and threw in fifty cents.

"Someone must have the ace of spades," Todd said sarcastically. It was a huge advantage to have it right away, because now Jill could keep raising every time since she knew she'd automatically get half of the pot.

Jill smiled haughtily at Todd. Everyone stayed in and Lizzy dealt them each another card face-up. Jill's was another ace. Now she might have a chance to win the whole pot, because with her wild she already had three aces. That'd be a nice way to finish the night, she thought to herself.

They bet again and Lizzy dealt again. Jill's next card was a two. Woohoo, she thought sarcastically, and raised the bet again. This time Conrad folded. Jill's next card was a six. Lizzy folded after Jill bet, and Todd raised her. Jill could barely keep her excitement hidden; he thinks he's beating three aces, but there's no way he'll beat four aces, she thought.

"Up or down?" Lizzy asked Jill before dealing her last card. Jill could pay twenty-five cents to have the card dealt down, which could change her wild or give her a higher spade (if she didn't already have the ace), or she could have it dealt up in front of her.

"Up," she said readily. Ace of hearts. Holy shit, Jill thought to herself. Five fucking aces!

"Up," Todd nodded at Lizzy before she asked him. Ten of spades.

Jill looked at Todd's cards. Ten of spades, ten of hearts, queen of hearts, nine of spades, and seven of spades. He must have a straight flush with his wild, Jill thought, 'cause he can see I have four aces now. She bet a dollar, the limit. Todd matched her.

"I would've raised, but what's the point?" he said. "We can split it, since you have the spade." He laid down his cards triumphantly. "Fuckin' five tens, baby!" He had had two sevens underneath, making the seven on the table wild as well, and his three wilds plus the two tens in front of him gave him five tens. Jill was impressed; she had expected the straight flush in spades.

"Good hand," she told Todd.

"Thanks." Todd ruffled her hair as he started to split up the quarters.

"But not good enough." Jill laid her cards down. "Five aces."

"WHAT?!" Todd cried. "That's fuckin' bullshit!" He stood up and threw an empty beer can across the room. Lizzy and Conrad were cracking up. Jill giggled and started counting out her quarters.

"Here's your five dollars back," she said teasingly to Todd.

"Yeah, thanks a lot," Todd said sarcastically, pretending to be mad still. "Bullshit, fuckin' bullshit!" He opened another beer and chugged the whole thing, then took his hat off, turned it around so it was facing forward, and put it back on.

"Nice job, Jill," Lizzy laughed as she stood up and stretched. "See ya tomorrow!" She went into Conrad's bedroom and Conrad stood up to follow.

"Have fun, kids," he joked. "Good luck with him, Jill. You know he's a sore loser." He winked at Jill and went into his bedroom, shutting the door behind him.

Jill finished counting her money and got a Ziploc bag out of the cupboard under the sink to put it in. Todd watched her, shaking his head the whole time.

"Oh, quit being a baby!" Jill teased. She put her arms around Todd's neck and kissed his cheek. "You should be happy for me!"

Todd hugged Jill tightly and playfully shimmied up against her. "I don't know..." he said. "I'm feeling pretty depressed now...maybe we should go in my room and you can cheer me up." He licked Jill's neck and grinned obnoxiously at her.

Jill giggled and twisted her way out of his embrace. "Get off me!" she cried good-naturedly and shoved him away.

"Oh well then, maybe some other time," Todd said with a dramatic sigh as he plopped on the couch, doing a great job of looking completely dejected. Jill bounced onto his lap and put her arms around his neck.

"Oh, poor baby," she said with mock sympathy, then, "Let's watch a movie." She climbed off Todd's lap and walked to the DVD rack beside the TV. After looking through them briefly, she pulled a DVD off the rack and held it up.

"*Dude, Where's My Car?*" she giggled. "We're watching this one; I love it!" She put it into the DVD player and returned to the couch. She grabbed a pillow and smacked it into Todd's lap, then curled up with her feet at one end of the couch and her head on the pillow.

"Sure, you can lay on my lap," Todd said sarcastically, then laughed at her when she gave him a smug smile.

Halfway through the movie Jill fell asleep. She hardly ever fell asleep during movies, but Todd figured she was tired from driving down earlier that day and from drinking. He wasn't uncomfortable with her head on his lap, so he didn't try to move her and he just kept watching the movie, which he always found hilarious. Jill didn't wake up or even shift around when he laughed. Wow, she's completely passed out, he thought, and turned his attention back to the screen.

Jill posed with her arm around Justin's shoulders and they smiled for Ryan's video camera.

"Kiss, kiss!" Hilton chanted with a giggle. Jill found this hilarious and doubled over with laughter.

"Come on!" Hilton encouraged.

Jill turned to Justin and gave him an exaggerated, lingering smack on the lips.

"Whoooooo!" Hilton yelled, throwing her arms in the air. "Hell, yeah!"

Justin smiled, a little embarrassed, and Jill and Hilton laughed uncontrollably, holding onto each other so as not to lose their balance. Unfortunately, someone rushing by slammed into Hilton and she tumbled to the floor, bringing Jill with her. Jill somehow managed to hold her drink upright, and luckily Hilton didn't have a cup in her hand at all. They sat on the floor, laughing even harder now, and Hilton rolled onto her back.

"Hey, get her up," Jill cried to Justin, still laughing. "She has a skirt on…."

"That's okay!" Justin said. "She can stay right there. We don't mind." He and Ryan snickered.

All of a sudden Luke seemed to swoop in from out of nowhere and pulled Hilton up off the floor. Hilton leaned into him as she stood up and grinned sideways at Jill.

"I need another drink!" Hilton announced. "Where's my cup?"

"It's over here," Luke said. "But I don't think you need another drink."

"Sure I do, baby!" Hilton said with a sweet smile. "I'm not as drunk as you yet!" She pulled Luke toward the kitchen with her, and he tripped over someone's foot and fell down with a goofy, drunk smile on his face, and Hilton started laughing all over again.

"Look at my drunk-ass boyfriend!" she yelled.

Jill giggled and put out her hand to Justin to have him help her up off the floor. She saw Todd coming toward her with Kylie. "Hey, there's your sister!" she announced loudly to Justin. "Kylie! Kylie!"

Kylie and Todd came up to them. "I kissed your brother!" she whispered loudly in Kylie's ear. "For the video camera." She pointed to Ryan, standing beside Justin, still taping them.

"Geez, slut, how many guys is that for you tonight?" Todd asked. Then he put his arm around Jill. "Just kiddin'," he assured her. "Just kiddin', Jilly." This statement was overlapped with Todd's voice saying, "Jill!" and his hand ruffling her hair.

Wow, I must be wasted, she thought. I'm hearing him say two things at once….

"Jill!"

She snapped awake and was looking right into Todd's eyes. She realized she was lying on her back with her head still in his lap. "Whoa, that was weird!" she said. "You were in my dream too and I could hear you talking to me but I thought it was in my dream…." She rubbed her eyes and yawned.

"Really, what kind of dream?" Todd asked suggestively.

"Don't worry, not that kind!" Jill said, sitting up and running her fingers through her hair.

"Damn, too bad," Todd said. "Hey, the movie's over. I'm tired; I'm going to bed."

"Okay," Jill said, yawning again as she stood up. She followed Todd into his bedroom and got her toothbrush and pajamas out of her bag, then went into the bathroom to brush her teeth and change. When she came out Todd was lying in bed, but had left the light on for her. She put her clothes and toothbrush back in her bag and turned the light off. When she got to the bed Todd had moved to the middle and was taking up the whole bed and pretending to snore.

"Move over, you jerk," Jill laughed as she climbed onto the bed. Since Todd had a double bed he and Jill always both slept in it so no one would have to sleep on the couch. Todd didn't move so Jill climbed on top of him and laid down.

"Ooooohhhhh, that feels good," Todd moaned, then snickered and moved over to his side of the bed as Jill smacked him and crawled off.

"Night," she said. "Try not to take all the covers."

"Whatever," Todd said in a playful, arrogant tone. Then he laughed and said, "Night, Jill." He turned his back to her and she snuggled under the covers, pulled her knees up to her chest, and fell asleep immediately.

On Friday at 2:00 in the afternoon when Todd came back from class, Jill was still lying in bed watching TV.

"Geez, you lazy ass!" Todd cried when he walked into his bedroom.

Jill grinned at him. "Did you have fun in gym class today?" Todd was studying kinesiology and Jill always teased him about having a blow-off major, even though she knew it wasn't at all. She just did it to annoy him.

"Yeah, we learned how to square-dance," Todd said with a smirk, plopping down on the bed as Jill moved her legs to make room for him. "What the hell is this shit?" It looked like one of those stupid girl shows he hated that Lizzy was always watching on their TV in the living room. It drove him nuts.

"*A Baby Story*," Jill replied, smiling at him innocently as if to say, Why wouldn't you want to watch this?

Todd grabbed the pillow she wasn't using and clobbered her over the head with it. She laughed and ducked, covering her head with her hands.

"I'm taking a shower," Todd said abruptly, standing up off the bed and heading into the bathroom. Jill heard him turn on the water and she could tell when he got into the shower because he started singing loudly for her benefit. His selection of the day was "Piano Man" by Billy Joel.

Jill giggled and rolled her eyes. The first time she had heard him sing in the shower she had made fun of him mercilessly and now he always sang extra loudly and extra badly (if that was possible) when she was around because he found it hilarious. It actually was pretty hilarious, considering he was one of the worst singers Jill had ever heard.

"Get it, William Hung!" she shouted into the bathroom.

All of a sudden her cell phone started ringing and she went over to her bag to grab it. It was Hilton. "Hello?"

"Hey, how's it going down there? You having a good time?" Hilton asked.

"Yeah, it's great!" Jill replied. "Did you guys have fun at the Turtle last night?"

"It was okay," Hilton said. "Luke didn't go 'cause he had a test, so it was just me and the girls….Natalie was supposed to drive but she really wanted to drink so she paid for us to take a cab home and then I had to take her back to pick up her car today. But it was pretty fun."

"Oh…was Adam there?" Jill hesitated to even ask, but she knew she'd be curious about it all weekend if she didn't.

"No, he actually wasn't," Hilton answered. "That's why I wanted to call you. I just thought you might be interested. It was kind of weird. I asked Justin about it and he said Adam freaked out or something because you were a virgin, and he decided he needs to stay away from the party scene for a while and chill out."

"Oh, my gosh," Jill said scornfully. "That's stupid; I can't believe he freaked out about that."

"Yeah, well it's actually kinda decent of him. It's hard to believe," Hilton joked. "But that was just Justin's interpretation. I guess Adam told him he had a test to study for and couldn't go out last night."

Todd suddenly increased the volume of his singing from the bathroom, just as he messed up on the lyrics. "Sorry, Jilly, don't know all the words!" he shouted.

Jill laughed into the phone.

"Oh, my gosh," Hilton said. "Was that Todd singing?"

"You could hear that?" Jill asked. "Yeah, that's his shower singing."

"Wow," Hilton said sarcastically. "That's some good shit."

"Actually it's more like just shit," Jill said.

"Oh, I know," Hilton said assuredly and the girls giggled.

"So what are you guys up to the rest of the weekend? Am I missing anything?" Jill asked.

"I have no idea, but I'm sure you're not missing anything," Hilton said. "I think Luke and I are going on a date tonight, so I have no idea what Lane and Nat are doing. What are you doing?"

"I think going to a party at Lizzy's, and then to the bars probably," Jill said. "Shit, listen to this."

Having struck out with "Piano Man," Todd had moved on to "Paradise by the Dashboard Light" by Meatloaf and was for some reason singing in a horrible falsetto.

Hilton and Jill burst out laughing. Jill had been holding her phone up to the bathroom door so Hilton could hear better and she brought it back to her ear. "Okay, I have to go, and get him to shut up!" she said.

"All right, have a great weekend!" Hilton said. "Bye, babe!"

Jill flipped her phone shut and pounded on the bathroom door with both fists. "You suck!" she yelled. "Booooooooo!"

Todd bellowed out a couple final lines, then turned the water off and a minute later opened the door with a towel around his waist and a huge grin on his face. He looked like a puppy that had just fetched something for its owner and was extremely proud of itself.

"Don't smile at me like that!" Jill said, pretending to be disgusted and backing away. "You are horrible! Are you trying to make me go deaf?!"

Todd pretended to pout. "Well," he sniffed, jerking his head away from Jill. "I can see I am obviously not appreciated around here and neither is my talent."

"It's just that there is no talent to appreciate," Jill teased. "But don't worry, baby, I still love you!" She gave Todd a playful hug.

"Better be careful," Todd warned jokingly. "What if my towel just happened to fall off?"

"I'd probably laugh," Jill said.

"Why's that?"

"A one-inch dick might be a funny thing to see."

"Oh, that's funny. Good one." Todd pretended to be mad. "Whatever, you'd be turned on. I bet you can almost see it now, hanging out the bottom of the towel." He grinned.

"Hahaha," Jill said sarcastically and laughed. Todd reached for his towel as though he was going to unwrap it and flashed Jill a wicked grin, then laughed and slapped her on the butt instead and went into the bathroom to get dressed.

March 2004

The weekend with Todd achieved exactly what Jill had known it would, and she drove back to Dale on Sunday afternoon feeling totally relaxed. She was determined not to let being back at school make her start feeling shitty and slutty and stressed about the Adam situation again.

The next week actually went by quickly and she was able to keep her mind off Adam because she had two tests to study for. Normally when she had something on her mind it was just harder to study because she couldn't concentrate, but her tests were in her two favorite classes so she was actually interested in the material. The first class was business law, which many students found tedious and boring, but Jill's professor was hilarious. He was actually a lawyer in town and often shared stories about his clients and various cases. Jill had learned a lot from him and always had fun in his class.

The second class was criminal psychology. Jill had a double major in pre-law and psychology, and her ultimate goal was to become a forensic psychologist specializing in jury selection, meaning that trial lawyers for either the prosecution or the defense in a case would hire her to look into the backgrounds of potential jury members and psychologically assess them based on the background information she found. Jill would then make recommendations to the lawyers about which members of the jury pool would likely side with them in the particular case, and the lawyers would choose jury members based on her recommendations. She would technically only need the psychology major to pursue forensic psychology in grad school, but she had added the pre-law major in order to familiarize herself with the legal system and therefore know for sure this was what she wanted to do. After taking several classes for both her majors, she was now completely certain she had picked the right field, and had planned to travel to some grad schools this summer and check out their programs in forensic psychology.

She felt she did extremely well on both of her tests, and by Thursday afternoon she realized she had barely thought about Adam the whole week. She knew she would have to decide whether to go to the Turtle tonight, but she didn't want to think about it quite yet.

She and the girls all went out and got Taco Bell and then came back to eat it and watch *Friends*. Since the series finale was coming up in May, there was a countdown of the six favorite episodes of all time for the next several weeks, and tonight was the sixth favorite.

"Aww, it's the one where Monica and Chandler get engaged!" Laney cried as soon as it came on. "I love this one!"

"What do you guys think the favorite will be?" Hilton asked.

"I bet something about Ross and Rachel," Laney commented.

"It better be!" Hilton replied. "If they don't end up together I'll be so upset!"

"Me too!" all the girls agreed. Then as the show came back on after the commercial, they all settled back to watch.

By the end they were all teary-eyed. Hilton wiped her eyes and got up to take her trash into the kitchen. "I cry every time I see that one! So, are we going to the Turtle tonight?"

Laney and Natalie glanced at Jill.

Jill hesitated, then shrugged. "Yeah, I'll go. I don't want spring break to be the first time I see him. If it's gonna be awkward we need to get that out of the way."

"Yay!" Hilton beamed, clapping her hands together. "And Luke said he'd drive tonight, so we can all get trashed!"

Jill smiled back, and hoped she wasn't making a big mistake by going.

As it turned out, she was glad she went. Adam wasn't there, again, and she was able to have a good time with the girls without worrying about him. The only bad thing was it would be awkward on spring break now, because she probably wouldn't see him before that since she was going home this weekend.

"Hey, girlies," Justin greeted Jill and Hilton as he sat down with them. "Where's everybody?"

"Natalie's making out with some guy!" Hilton giggled, pointing to Natalie on the dance floor. She was dirty dancing with a tall, dark-haired guy in jeans and a dark-colored long-sleeved t-shirt. They had been making out, and now the guy was kissing Natalie's neck and she was giggling.

"Get it, Nat!" Justin said, raising his eyebrows and laughing.

"Laney and Luke are in Mike's," Jill added, gesturing vaguely in the direction of the karaoke bar.

"So how was Eastern?" Justin asked Jill.

Jill smiled contentedly. "It was great. I had a lot of fun." She hesitated and her smile faded a little bit. "So is Adam still 'taking it easy' or whatever?"

"Yeah, I guess," Justin said with a shrug. "He said he doesn't wanna go out this weekend 'cause he wants to save money for Daytona and he has two tests next week. But who knows. He's usually not careful with his money at all, and I don't know how he hasn't failed out yet; you know how he is."

"Yeah," Jill said with a small shrug. Adam had a double major in business and econ and she had never known him to stay home and study. She wondered what kind of grades he got. "I hope he's not avoiding me. That should make for a fun spring break." She smirked and rolled her eyes.

"Oh, I wouldn't worry about it," Justin said. "He won't even worry about it anymore by then 'cause he'll just be in party mode all the time."

"Yeah," Jill said. "I guess."

She forced herself to stop thinking about it and helped Hilton pick out a girl for Justin to go hit on. By the end of the night she had pushed Adam to the back of her mind again, but as she got into bed she realized she was a little disappointed with how the night had turned out. She had wanted and needed to see Adam so they could get past any awkwardness. That would have calmed her down because she would know things were okay between them, at least for now, but instead she had another whole week to worry about it before she saw him.

The two-hour drive that weekend to Brinkley, her hometown, gave Jill way too much time to think, and she was worried the whole weekend would be like that. She was glad to get away again though, and knew that in her small hometown of about 15,000 people, she would feel isolated enough from Dale. The isolation might be what gave her too much time to think though....She wished she was from a bigger town with more stuff to do. Probably none of her old high school friends would be home except the ones who went to Dale Brinkley University, one of eight smaller Dale campuses scattered within about a 200 mile radius of the main campus she attended. And none of her friends who went to Dale Brinkley were her really close friends, anyway. Luckily though, there was plenty to do at home to keep her busy. On Friday night her whole family, except her brother Aaron, went out to an early dinner before Aaron's basketball game, and then went to the game to cheer him on. He was a sophomore and played for the JV team, but they stayed for the varsity game as well.

"Jill, are you okay, honey?" her mom asked when they got home from the game. "You look so tired."

"I am really tired," Jill told her. "I had two tests this week, and I've been trying to get ready for spring break and everything."

"Well, make sure you get lots of rest this week so you're not tired driving to Florida next weekend."

"Don't worry, Mom, I'll be fine," Jill said confidently. "I'm used to not getting much sleep." She grinned, because everyone in her family knew she was a total night owl and although she preferred to sleep in, could make do on two or three hours of sleep if she had to.

On Saturday she slept in till noon, then she took her sister Winnie shopping. Winnie was in eighth grade and was looking for a dress for the upcoming eighth grade dance. Jill loved dress shopping and helped Winnie pick out a short purple halter dress with small silver sparkles and silver heels to match.

"You're gonna look so pretty!" Jill gushed to her sister as they drove home from the mall. "Why won't you tell me who you're going to the dance with?" She had been trying to get it out of Winnie all day.

"I don't know yet," Winnie finally admitted with a mopey look. "I really want Croy Davidson to ask me. Jenna said he told Beau that he likes me, but Ashlyn said she heard he was going to ask Brooke."

"Why would he ask Brooke?" Jill asked. "They broke up." She was close with her younger sister and stayed caught up on a lot of the middle school drama and gossip.

"I know," Winnie said. "But he'll probably ask her."

"He'll only ask her if he thinks you won't go with him," Jill declared. "You should tell Jenna to tell Beau you want to go with Croy."

"Maybe…." Winnie said. "But what if he doesn't ask me then, and I'll feel really stupid!"

"Just do it. You really don't have anything to lose. He'll ask you; there's no way he wouldn't wanna go with you."

"I don't know…." Winnie said hesitantly.

"I do," Jill said confidently. "You better say something to Jenna or Beau, or ask Croy yourself, or something, 'cause if you don't I won't get you anything from Florida!"

"Okay, okay," Winnie said. "I'll call Jenna."

Jill waited in Winnie's room when they got home while Winnie called Jenna and asked her to call Beau, who would then call Croy. When Winnie hadn't heard back from anyone half an hour later she became extremely worried.

"See!" she cried. "He probably wanted nothing to do with me, and Jenna felt bad calling me back and telling me so she's stalling!"

Just then the phone rang. Jill and Winnie both lunged to look at the caller ID.

"It's Croy!" Jill cried, tickling Winnie.

"You answer it!" Winnie said.

Jill answered, then said, "Just a minute…." She handed the phone to Winnie.

"Hello?" Winnie said nervously. "Um, okay, sure….Okay, bye." She hung up the phone and whirled around to hug Jill. "He asked me!" she cried.

"Awww, that's so cute that he called to do it himself!" Jill cried, genuinely happy for Winnie. "See, aren't you glad I made you call Jenna?" She winked at Winnie and ruffled her hair.

"Thanks, Jill," Winnie said. "You're so awesome!"

Yeah, I used to think I was kinda awesome too, Jill thought darkly to herself. Just think if Winnie had any idea what I've been up to lately. She felt ashamed and didn't like to think about it, so she just smiled at Winnie and gave her a big hug. "Congrats, little sis," she said.

The next Thursday Jill, Natalie, Laney, and Hilton all went shopping to buy new stuff for spring break. Natalie and Laney bought new beach bags at Abercrombie and Fitch and Jill and Hilton bought beach shorts there. Natalie also got a new swimsuit at Gadzooks and all four of them bought two new pairs of flip-flops at a department store because they were on sale.

Shopping got them even more excited for spring break than they already were, and it finally felt like vacation was here. They were all skipping their classes tomorrow to sleep in and be ready to drive, and a sense of freedom finally hit them all.

"Let's get drunk while we pack!" Hilton exclaimed as she bounced on the front seat of Laney's car on the way home from the mall.

"Yeah, let's make margaritas!" Laney said. "We can stop at the liquor store on the way home. Let's get the party started early!"

They stopped and picked up tequila and margarita mix, and when they got home Hilton and Laney went to work making the drinks in the kitchen while Jill and Natalie went to get out their suitcases and start packing.

"Everybody has to bring all their stuff out in the living room and pack out here!" Hilton shouted. She turned the radio on in the living room and when Jill and Natalie came back out she was dancing around the room, sipping on her margarita. Everyone did as Hilton said and brought piles of clothes into the living room. As they drank and packed and watched *Friends* they modeled outfits and helped each other decide what to take. At 10:00 the phone rang and Hilton twirled over to the kitchen counter to pick it up.

"Hey, it's Adam!" she cried. "You answer, Jill!"

Jill glanced up from her packing and slowly made her way over to the phone. "Hello?"

"Hey, Jill? This is Adam."

"Hey, what's up?" Jill said, trying to sound upbeat and casual. She made a face at her roommates, who had stopped what they were doing to watch and listen.

"Oh, not a lot…." Adam said. "I just wanted to see if you guys are still coming over here tomorrow to leave with us."

"Yeah, we'll be there around 2:45. You wanted to leave at three, right?" Jill screwed up her face at the girls, thinking it was weird for him to call and ask when Luke could easily have worked it out with Hilton, since he and Ace were driving with Adam and Justin.

"Yeah," Adam said. "Okay, well I just wanted to make sure; I'll see you girls tomorrow."

"All right, bye," Jill said, still confused. She hung up. "He wanted to know if we were coming over there tomorrow still, to leave with them," she said doubtfully.

"Hmmm, that's interesting," Hilton smiled. "Since Luke and I just talked about that this afternoon and Luke called Adam and Justin right then to tell them that we were."

Jill smiled a little bit and shook her head. "Well…this should be an interesting trip."

Adam sat in his computer chair and stared at the phone for a minute after he hung up. He had just had to call her and talk to her a little bit tonight before they left, so he would know whether it was going to be awkward or not. He still felt horrible about what had happened, about taking her virginity. He couldn't get over how stupid he had been. But she had sounded fine on the phone, and she hadn't hesitated or acted cold when she heard it was him calling. See, he told himself. She's fine. And even though you did take her virginity, it's not like you raped her. She's a big girl; she knows what she's doing. She's totally cool with it. It'll be fine this week.

An uneasy thought that had been nagging at him all week came back. What if she expects this to be a thing now? What if she thinks we're gonna be together all week in Florida? Is she gonna get pissed if I hook up with other girls? Because even though she was incredibly hot, Adam didn't intend to hook up with Jill again. It was too messy. He also didn't intend to go all of spring break without hooking up with anyone. She'll be fine with it, he told himself again. She's cool, she doesn't care. Then again, he thought, maybe I will hook up with her again, for just that reason. She's cool about it, and she doesn't seem to expect anything to come of it. It would be fun to hook up with her again. He shook his head. We'll just see what happens, he told himself. The most important thing is to have fun 'cause it's spring break. I've gone long enough without partying. Bring it on! He grinned and finally felt better for the first time in three weeks.

The drive to Daytona was pretty uneventful. When Jill, Natalie, Hilton, and Laney went over to Adam and Justin's to leave on Friday Adam greeted Jill casually and she responded in the same way. She tried to treat him the same as she treated Justin or Jared or Park. She was glad once they got in the cars and headed off though, before things had a chance to get awkward.

Hilton drove first in the girls' car, even though they were taking Natalie's car, because she wanted to drive with Luke, and he was driving the boys' car first. Jared drove the first shift in the third car, which included him, Kate, Park, and Britt. They had decided to do roughly three-hour shifts at first and then whoever had to drive twice on the way there would only have to drive once on the way back.

At about one in the morning they stopped for gas somewhere north of Atlanta.

"Jill, wake up!" Natalie said as she stopped the car at a pump. "You ready to drive?"

"I'm awake," Jill said. "I haven't even slept that much."

"Are you okay to drive?" Natalie asked.

"Oh, yeah, I'm good." Jill had volunteered for the shift everyone thought was the hardest because she never had trouble staying up all night. She also knew she would get to drive through downtown Atlanta, which was her favorite part of the drive to Florida. Even though it would be the middle of the night, it was still cool to look at the city. Every spring break for the first eighteen years of her life, Jill had gone with her family to Fort Myers Beach for spring break. She had been back once since graduation; last year she, Hilton, Nat, and Laney had gone there on spring break. Her family hadn't started flying till her sophomore year in high school, and she and the girls had driven last year, so it was a familiar drive. She had never been to the Atlantic coast of Florida though, so this trip would be a little different.

Jill went into the gas station to buy a Cherry Coke. Adam was waiting in line.

"Hey, Jill," he said when he saw her. "You driving next?"

"Yep," Jill replied. "You?"

"Yep, me too," Adam said. "Think you can keep up with me?" He gave her a small smile.

Jill scoffed. "Please. Have you ever driven with me? Natalie probably won't be able to sleep 'cause she'll be scared for her car. She thinks I'm reckless."

Adam smiled, more genuinely this time. "All right, then! Let's go!"

Jill, Adam, and Park cruised at about ninety down I-75 for a couple of hours. Sometime after Atlanta when the drive got boring again, Jill's phone rang. It was Adam.

"Hey, what's up?" she answered.

"Nothin'….I was just having a little trouble staying awake 'cause everybody in here went to sleep and they don't want the music up."

"Oh…." Jill said. "I'm sorry. Hilton's up with me." She glanced over at Hilton, who was drifting off in the passenger seat.

"All right, well I'll let you go then," Adam said. "I just needed to do something to wake me up."

"All right, later," Jill said. She snapped her phone shut and laid it beside the drink holder. "That was weird as hell," she said to Hilton, who had woken up when Jill snapped her phone shut. She explained the conversation and Hilton frowned.

"He is one weird, confusing boy," she mumbled, then closed her eyes again, and Jill continued driving into the dark, with Adam's taillights just visible up ahead and Park's headlights shining bright behind her.

Each of their condos had two bedrooms and two bathrooms and a foldout couch in the living room. The six girls put their stuff in one condo and the six guys put theirs in the other, because they all agreed it would be easier to have two bathrooms specifically for the girls and two for the boys. Sleeping arrangements would be first come, first serve each night though, and all twelve of them would pretty much be sharing both condos.

After hitting the beach for a few hours, they all went out for dinner and grocery shopping. Then Kate and Jared decided to go to bed early, Britt and Park took a walk on the beach, Laney and Natalie made strawberry daiquiris and watched a movie, and

Adam, Justin, Ace, Luke, Hilton, and Jill decided to go out and find a club.

After drinking and dancing for about two hours, they were all exhausted and ready to come home. None of the guys even tried to pick up any girls, and they all walked back to their condos together. Everyone there had gone to bed already and there was only one bed left. Hilton and Luke volunteered to sleep on a couch, so Adam and Justin took the other bed and that left Jill and Ace to sleep on the other couch. Jill passed out as soon as her head hit the pillow, and the next day no one got up before noon.

The next couple nights they continued to go out to clubs. Jill saw Adam making out with a girl one night, but he didn't try to bring her home. She was hanging all over him and he basically shoved her off. Jill was surprised but glad that she wouldn't have to deal with him bringing someone home.

The same night, Laney met a guy at one of the bars they went to. He was from Eastern and his name was Delaney, which was actually Laney's full name too. They danced all night and she ended up inviting him back to the condo. That left Jill, Adam, and Justin to all sleep on one foldout couch. Jill said she would just sleep on the floor, but Justin made her take the couch and he slept on the floor instead.

Jill glared at him as he spread out a blanket and pillow, and he gave her a mischievous grin and a wink.

Justin was asleep almost as soon as he laid down, and Jill felt completely unsure of what to do. She curled up on her side with her back to Adam and pretended to be asleep.

"Jill." She heard Adam whisper her name in the dark. "Hey, are you awake?"

She thought about not answering, but rolled onto her back instead. She glanced over at Adam, who was also lying on his back.

"Yeah, I'm awake. What's up?"

Adam hesitated, then all of a sudden he rolled on his side and put his arm around her waist and kissed her.

Jill froze at first, but he continued kissing her and finally she kissed him back. As soon as he felt her respond he moved closer to her and his kiss became hungrier, more passionate. Her hands moved to his face, then his hair, and she couldn't stop herself. What the hell am I doing?! she thought, and finally she pulled back, holding his face in her hands.

"Sorry," Adam said. "Sorry. I don't know….I just have really wanted to do that again…."

"It's okay," Jill said. "I was just surprised…." She laid back on the pillow and looked away from him.

After a second she felt him start to roll away from her.

"Sorry," he said again.

Jill thought about just letting him roll away and go to sleep, but she could still taste him, and she was totally turned on now. Fuck it, she thought to herself. It's not like I'll be doing anything worse than what I've already done!

She rolled toward Adam and touched his arm. He looked over at her and she leaned in and kissed him as hungrily as he had kissed her.

"I want to do it again, too," she whispered.

Adam grinned, then pulled her on top of him. She straddled him and leaned down to make out with him again. His hands moved down her back and then up into her hair, pushing it back from her face.

"Hey, we're going to wake up Justin," Jill said breathlessly.

"So? Fuck it," Adam said, starting to kiss her again.

Jill pulled back and sat up, crawling off of him. "No, come on," she said, grabbing his hand. "Let's go outside. Bring that blanket."

"Hell, yeah!" Adam said and followed her, grabbing the blanket off the couch as he went.

Jill led him outside, away from the building, all the way down near the ocean. They spread out the blanket and had sex on the beach, and it was even better than the first time. Afterwards they sat and watched the waves coming in.

"Jill, I think I'm really starting to like you," Adam said.

"You don't have to say that," Jill said, laughing.

Adam reached out and pulled her into his lap, and didn't tell her that her comment had made him like her even more.

That was on Monday night, and the rest of the week was a sort of blur. Laying out, swimming, playing volleyball all day, going out to dinner and then a bar or club, coming home and passing out. Fooling around with Adam whenever they had the chance, late at night on the beach, in the shower, in one of the beds while everyone else was at the beach. She had told Hilton and Laney and Natalie about it, but she was sure everyone else knew, too. She and Adam hadn't kissed or anything in front of them, but they hadn't tried to hide it either. Jill was glowing and tan and having the time of her life.

So was Laney, who was spending every minute with Del, as she had started calling him. She whispered to Hilton and Natalie and Jill in the bathroom of Bubba Gump's one night during dinner that they were going to stay together when they went back to school.

"Yay, I'll have someone to go visit Eastern with me!" Jill said.

"What about you, Jill?" Laney asked. "You and Adam. Are you guys, like, together now?"

"Oh, no!" Jill said airily. "It's nothing like that. Just having fun." She beamed at the girls.

"We'll see about that," Hilton grinned back, with a knowing gleam in her eye. "That boy has got it bad for you, Jilly. He hasn't even tried to hook up with anyone else!"

Jill just rolled her eyes and laughed off Hilton's comment. She didn't really want to think about what was going to happen after spring break; she just wanted to enjoy the here and now.

"So what's up with you and Jill, man?" Justin asked as he and Adam walked back to the condos from McDonald's one afternoon.

"Nothin'," Adam shrugged. "Just havin' fun."

"Is the 'fun' gonna stop after spring break?"

Adam shrugged again. "I hope not. She's fuckin' cool as hell."

Justin grinned at Adam. "Ooooooh," he said, dragging out the "o" sound, "so you like her, then?"

Adam didn't laugh, but just kept walking and looking straight ahead. "Yeah."

By the end of the week they were all exhausted, but Jill wasn't ready to go back. She didn't want to give up everything she'd had here, and she knew Laney didn't either, because even though she and Del were staying together, they'd be two hours apart.

They left Saturday around noon, and when they stopped at 6:30 after two shifts of driving, they saw a cute-looking family-owned restaurant across from the gas station.

"Hey, let's eat there!" Hilton suggested, so they did.

Two hours later, Natalie was driving and they were in a huge traffic jam south of Atlanta when Laney grabbed the trash bag they were keeping in the car and threw up in it.

"Ugh," she moaned. "I think it was that fish I ate at that damn restaurant!"

They were two miles away from the next exit and the way traffic was moving, it'd probably be two hours till they got there.

"Good thing for the trash bag!" Hilton joked from the backseat.

It wasn't good after half an hour of Laney puking though. Even though all the windows were down, they could still smell it.

"I'm so sorry, guys," Laney said tiredly.

"It's okay," Hilton said. "Hey, Natalie, try to pull into the right lane and we can dump that damn bag out!"

Natalie finally managed to pull over, and since Jill was on the passenger side of the backseat, she got out and tossed the bag off the shoulder of the road into the grass. All of a sudden she felt a wave of nausea herself, and bent over and threw up in the grass. She was there for a couple of minutes before she finally managed to return to the car. Luckily it hadn't moved.

"I'm so sorry!" Laney cried. "Was it the smell?"

"No," Jill reassured her. "I think it was the food."

"Yeah, we never should've stopped there," Hilton said. "My bad."

Traffic picked up soon after and they made it to the exit in half an hour. Natalie called the boys and told them Laney and Jill had been puking and they needed to stop. The boys called the two couples in the other car and they all pulled into a gas station off the exit. By then Laney was feeling a little better and just went in to brush her teeth and buy a water.

Hilton went into the bathroom with Jill, where Jill threw up a couple more times.

"I'm so sorry," Hilton apologized again. "I feel so bad about picking that restaurant."

"Hilton," Jill said, looking her friend in the eyes. "The food didn't make me sick. I'm pregnant."

＊   ＊   ＊

Hilton went with Jill to buy a pregnancy test as soon as they got home. Jill was extremely grateful for Hilton's reaction to the whole thing. When Jill had told her in the bathroom the night before, Hilton's eyes had widened, and then she had just nodded.

"It's been, what?" she had asked, counting back in her head. "Four weeks? Are you sure?"

"I'm a week and a half late," Jill had replied.

Hilton had just nodded again, then hugged Jill tightly. "Come on," she'd said. "Let's go back to the car. Don't tell Laney and Natalie yet. Let's make sure first. I'll go with you when we get home tomorrow."

Hilton pulled up to the drug store and left the car running. "You stay here. I'll go get it."

Jill nodded, immensely glad she didn't have to go in. That would make it so much easier. Hilton was back in a couple of minutes, and they went to the grocery store to stock up on food before heading home.

Kate hurried out of the drug store, pulling her phone out of her purse as she headed for her car.

"Hey!" she exclaimed breathlessly when Jared answered. "Did you know Hilton was pregnant?!"

"What?" Jared asked. "Are you serious?"

"I was just at the pharmacy getting my birth control," Kate said. "And I saw her buy a pregnancy test. Luke didn't say anything to you?"

"No."

"I wonder if he knows. Maybe you should call him."

"I am not calling him," Jared said, blowing off Kate's suggestion. "It's none of my business. She can tell him if she wants."

"Okay, whatever," Kate said. "I can't believe it though, that's crazy!"

"Yeah, well she's probably not even pregnant," Jared said. "She was just buying a test. Just let it go." He was annoyed with Kate for sticking her nose into someone else's business, like she always did. "Hey, I gotta go. Later, babe." He hung up.

Kate, irritated, snapped her phone shut. She debated calling Luke herself, but decided she didn't want to piss Hilton off and maybe Jared was right….Hilton would tell him if she was actually pregnant. But she had to share the news with someone who would be more receptive than Jared had been, so she dialed Britt.

"Hello?" Britt answered on the second ring.

"Oh, my gosh, you'll never guess who I just saw buying a pregnancy test!" Kate gushed in a gossipy tone.

"Who?" Britt asked.

"Hilton!"

"What?! Hilton's pregnant?!"

"WHAT?!" Kate heard in the background before she could answer. "What the fuck are you talking about?!"

"Oh, shit!" Kate cried. "Is that Luke?"

"Give me the phone!" she heard Luke demand, then, "Who is this?" in a harsh voice into Britt's phone.

"This is Kate," she said meekly, feeling a little bit bad now.

"Well what the fuck are you talking about? Hilton's pregnant? How do you know?!" Luke's voice had a frantic sound to it, and he didn't even seem to be trying to control it.

"Um…." Kate hesitated. "Well, I was just in the drug store, and I saw her buying a pregnancy test."

"Fuck. Fuck. Oh, shit….Did she tell you she's pregnant?"

"No, so she's probably actually not," Kate said quickly, in a dismissive tone. "I'm sure she's just a little late or something, and it's no big deal. You shouldn't even worry about it. Sorry, I shouldn't have even said anything."

"Not worry about it?" Luke asked incredulously. "How am I just supposed to not think about the fact that my girlfriend might be pregnant?"

"Well, don't say anything to her!" Kate said. She didn't want Hilton getting pissed at her for telling Luke. "You should let her bring it up to you if she wants to."

"Whatever," Luke said. "Whatever." Then he hung up.

Kate stared at her phone a moment, then bit her lip as she slowly closed it and tossed it on the passenger seat. She sat back against the driver's seat of her car and smacked the steering wheel. "Shit!" she said under her breath, but she couldn't stop the small smile curling her lips. She loved drama; this was huge!

Luke stared at the phone for a minute, then slowly handed it back to Britt in a trance-like motion. He glanced from Britt to Park, then said, "I've gotta get outta here." He walked out the door of Park's apartment, where he had gone to chill after the long drive home, and crossed the complex to his own apartment. Luckily Ace was in the shower when he walked in, and he went straight into his own room and shut the door, then collapsed onto the bed with his head in his hands.

He didn't even know what to think. He couldn't think at all. Hilton was on the pill; how could she possibly be pregnant? Well, it can happen, he told himself, she could've forgotten to take it one day or something....

Suddenly he wrenched his phone out of his pocket and dialed Hilton's apartment.

"Hey, Luke," Laney answered. "She's not here."

"Where is she?" he demanded quickly and loudly, then realized he should've tried harder to sound normal.

"Um, she's grocery shopping," Laney said, sounding surprised at his tone.

"Great, thanks," Luke muttered, then added, "I'll try her cell," for Laney's benefit before throwing his phone across the room. It hit the wall with a loud thud and he hoped Laney had hung up before she heard that. He had just wanted to know where Hilton had told the girls she was going….he had been sure there would be some other explanation and that Kate must have been mistaken about seeing her in the pharmacy. But if she'd told her roommates she was going grocery shopping…that sounded like a good excuse to use if you were really going to buy a pregnancy test!

Luke threw himself back down on the bed and stared at the ceiling. Jumbled thoughts were racing through his brain and he couldn't separate them and think calmly. *Pregnant, baby, marriage, the end of our college careers, living together, boy or girl?, what will we name it?, my parents will kill me, should I tell her I know?*

Finally his thoughts seemed to untangle themselves a little bit and he found himself thinking about his current relationship with Hilton. They had met first semester of freshman year at a frat party. Unlikely place to meet someone with potential for a serious relationship, he thought now. He had been trying to decide whether to rush and she was out partying with Jill and some other girls from their dorm. He had seen her dancing and thought she was really cute, so he had gone up and started dancing with her. They ended up making out on the dance floor, and she had given him her phone number when she left. He had been impressed that she wasn't as easy as most girls at frat parties seemed to be, and after going to a couple other parties and realizing he was having a horrible time and the fraternity life wasn't for him, he had called her the next weekend. They had gone out to dinner and really hit it off. She was smart and funny and totally laid back, and she was just so different from most of the girls he had met up to that point at Dale. They all seemed so fake, but Hilton was totally down-to-earth and full of energy for life and everything about her seemed genuine. Plus she was gorgeous.

After their first date they had seen each other once a week or so for the next couple of weeks, and then he asked her to be his girl-friend, and the rest was history. They had definitely had their share of fights but had always worked through them and he was sure he wanted to marry her someday down the road. He knew Hilton was in no hurry to get a ring from him, and would proba-bly say no if he asked her to marry him right now. She didn't want to rush into marriage after college because she wanted to travel and be independent and try to make a name for herself as a pho-tographer and have fun before she settled down and started a family, but he was confident she pictured herself ending up with him because they often talked about their future children, where they would live, what kind of pets they would have, etc. He had never worried about their future because he took for granted that it would follow a certain path—they would graduate, he would go to law school while she traveled, he would propose to her a few years down the road, they would be engaged for a year or two, then they would get married and wait a few more years to start a family….

But now that whole plan could be down the drain. Everything he'd taken for granted had in the blink of an eye been ruthlessly ripped out from under him and his solid foundation was com-pletely gone, leaving him sinking into who the fuck knew what.

At some point he must have dozed off because all of a sudden he was dreaming. He knew he was dreaming, but he didn't want to wake up because he wanted to see what would happen.

He was telling Hilton how sorry he was for her because now she would have to give up all her dreams of traveling and starting a career and having time for herself, and she might not even be able to graduate when she had planned. He kept trying to explain to her how he felt like she was losing ten of the best years of her life because she had to have this baby now, but Hilton kept telling him he was wrong.

"Luke, don't you know me at all?" she was saying. "Sure, I would love to travel and do all those things, and that is a kind of dream for me, but my ultimate dream is to have children, to have a family with you. So I'm actually really lucky, because I don't have to wait anymore, and I get to do all that now. I can wait to travel later, and you can come with me and we can take our baby. And I can get a job working for someone else, like a portrait studio or something, until I have time to do some of my own stuff." She was beaming at him, and Luke suddenly felt a total wave of relief and calmness come over him.

"Oh, thank God!" he said, embracing her. "If you're okay with it, then I am too. I can't wait to start a family with you, Hilton. This is perfect, because it's my dream too."

Luke suddenly snapped awake, but continued to lie still on the bed. Just as it had in the dream, a feeling of relief and calmness had come over him. He knew the dream was right; that was the way Hilton would see it. She wouldn't see it as the end of her dreams, but as the beginning of another dream. She was always so positive and able to see the best in every situation. He smiled to himself. He loved her so much, and even though the timing could've been better in his opinion, he knew that if Hilton was pregnant, he was ready to be a parent with her.

He sat up in bed excitedly and reached for his phone again. She should know the results of her test by now, so he would invite her over for dinner and they could talk.

When Jill and Hilton got back to the apartment after grocery shopping, Laney was sleeping on the couch and Natalie's bedroom door was closed. Hilton went into Jill's room so she could be there with her when she took the test. Jill was really only taking it for Hilton's benefit; she already knew what the result would be.

Just as Jill was getting the test out of the bag, Hilton's phone rang. She looked to see who it was and rolled her eyes. "It's Luke. I better answer or he'll just call the apartment and wake everybody up. I'll get rid of him fast. What's up," she said briskly into her phone as she answered it.

"Hey, baby," Luke said. "How are you doing?"

"Fine," Hilton said irritably. "Luke, what do you want?"

"Well, I was just wondering if you'd want to come over for dinner tonight."

He was acting weird, Hilton thought. Hesitant and unsure of himself. No, maybe that wasn't it. He almost was talking in a concerned tone, as though he was worried about her. Oh well, she didn't really have time to think about it.

"Luke, sorry, but I don't have time tonight. I kinda have a lot to do and I'm exhausted from Florida. Could we maybe do it tomorrow or something?"

"Sure...yeah, tomorrow's fine."

"Okay, I have to go," Hilton said dismissively. "Sorry, talk to ya later." She hung up.

"Sorry," she said to Jill.

"No prob. I did the test; I just have to wait now."

"Do you want me to read it for you?" Hilton asked.

Jill smiled. Hilton was so great in situations like this. Well, not that I've actually ever been in a situation like this, Jill thought with a smirk. "No, but thanks though," she said.

Hilton nodded. After a moment, Jill picked the stick up and glanced at it quickly, then averted her eyes.

"Well?" Hilton asked anxiously.

"It's positive." Jill held it out for Hilton to see. Hilton looked at it as though making sure Jill had read it right, then wrapped her arms tightly around Jill.

"I'm so sorry, babe," she said. "But you know, it'll be fine. Everything happens for a reason." She stepped back from Jill and shrugged, offering her a small smile.

Jill smiled back. "I know. I'll be okay."

"What do you want to do?" Hilton asked.

"I think I just need to be alone…don't say anything to Laney or Nat yet."

"I won't," Hilton said. She hugged Jill again. "I love you, Jilly." Then she left Jill alone, closing the door behind her.

Luke's phone call to Hilton had him freaking out again. She had basically blown him off and refused to see him that night. Maybe he had been wrong about what her reaction would be to having a baby with him. He felt like he might cry.

Don't fuckin' cry, dude, he told himself silently. Maybe the test was negative, and she's just still stressed from the whole thing and wants to be alone. But he didn't really believe that, and the more he thought about it, the more worried he got. What if Hilton didn't want to raise the child with him, and what if she ended up backing away from him, from their relationship? No, he chided himself. She would never do that. You freaked out when you first heard, so if she just found out for sure she's pregnant, she's probably freaking out too and just needs a day for it to sink in. Then she'll be fine. I'll just give her the time she needs, and everything will be fine. He still didn't feel much better though, and he flopped back down on his bed, not even sure what to think about. "Fuck! Fuck, fuck, fuck!" He punched his pillow several times. The whole thing was just too overwhelming.

Todd had just finished playing basketball at one of the recreational sports facilities on Eastern's campus. He walked out of the building to his car, and the cold air felt refreshing and welcome. As soon as he slid into his car he checked his phone. "New voice message from Jilly Bean," it said. Todd dialed his voicemail as he pulled out of the parking lot and headed for his apartment.

"Hey, Todd, um…I just need to talk to you, so give me a call, okay? Bye, hon."

She sounded weird in the message, he thought. He hoped nothing was wrong. He quickly scrolled down to her number and pushed Send.

"Hey, Todd," she answered, sounding relieved to hear from him.

"Hey, Jilly! How was Daytona?"

"Oh, it was crazy!" Jill said, and he heard the smile in her voice. "Totally fun, I had a blast."

"Good. Yeah, I had tons of fun at home working, too," he said sarcastically. He had a factory job that he'd worked every summer and Christmas break since graduation. Since he'd had no spring break plans this year, he'd decided he might as well go home and make a little money, but it'd been depressing knowing a lot of his friends were partying somewhere warm while he was stuck getting up at 5:15 every morning and going to work in the unseasonably cold thirty degree weather.

"Yuck, that sucks," Jill said sympathetically.

"So what's up, girl?"

"Um, well I was just wondering if I could come this weekend….Lane met this guy in Daytona who's from Eastern, and they're like, together now or whatever, so she's coming down this weekend."

"Of course you can come, baby!" Todd exclaimed. He grinned. He hadn't seen Jill for almost a month now and he missed her. "We can get our party on," he joked.

He noticed Jill's slight hesitation before she said, "Yeah, that sounds fun. We'll have a good time. I can't wait to see you."

"Yeah, me too. Jill, is something wrong?"

"No," Jill said quickly. "I mean, I just have something I have to talk to you about this weekend."

"What?"

"I'd rather just wait till the weekend and tell you."

"Okay, whatever you wanna do. It's cool."

"All right…thanks, Todd. She paused for a second, then, "Later."

"Bye, Jilly Bean." He heard her hang up and tossed his phone on the passenger seat, frowning. He didn't like how she had sounded when she'd said she needed to talk. He knew something was wrong and was a little scared to hear what it was. She didn't specifically say it had to do with him, but it must if she was acting weird on the phone and coming all the way down to talk to him about it. Well, he told himself, there's nothing you can do now but wait and see.

Jill didn't say anything to Laney or Natalie yet. She needed some more time to think about things before everybody knew about it and was constantly looking at her and talking about it. She stayed in her room most of the night, saying she was tired. She actually was tired, but she couldn't sleep. She watched almost a whole season of *Friends* on DVD, and since she knew the episodes so well, she was able to be aware of what was going on even though she was hardly concentrating. From time to time she would laugh at something in the show, and then she would think, How can I be laughing?! and flop over on her side with her face away from the TV.

Finally she didn't know what else to do, so she prayed. She had always gone to Sunday school growing up and she considered herself a Christian. Part of the reason she had planned on waiting to have sex was because of her religious beliefs, and part of the shame she had felt after losing her virginity while she was drunk was because she felt God would be extremely disappointed in her.

I know I'm a horrible, horrible person, she prayed in her head. I don't even know who I am anymore, and I feel so dirty and awful. Please help me, God; help me get my life in order! I don't know what to do. I'm so sorry for everything I've done wrong and I know I shouldn't even be in this mess, but please help me know what to do now. Please help me to remember that everything happens for a reason, and show me what the reason is for this so I can know what to do! Is abortion murder? Because I can't really imagine doing it, but I don't want to hurt my family or possibly Adam either, and I don't know which would be the worse thing to do....Please just help me.

Jill put her head in her hands. *Abortion?* How could she possibly even be thinking about that? Things were so out of control. She didn't want to consider abortion because she knew the more she thought about it, the more of a realistic option it would become. That was always how it worked with her; she would start with some ridiculous-sounding idea that she didn't believe she would or could ever follow through with, but then the more she pondered it, the less ridiculous it sounded, and the more acceptable it became. That was how it had been with sex. In high school she had planned to be a virgin till she was married, but when she got to college she became a little more open-minded and decided to wait just until she was in love, and then look what had happened. She was completely disgusted with herself, and she knew she had to get the thoughts of abortion out of her head. She smacked the sides of her head as if that would push the thoughts right out or crush them up, and then flopped back onto her bed.

When she finally fell asleep around four in the morning, she had one of those dreams where she thought she was still awake and was having trouble getting to sleep. She was tossing and turning and Adam was in bed with her, reaching out to stroke her hair and tell her that everything was okay and to go to sleep. She reached for Adam but it wasn't Adam after all; it was Todd and he hadn't been touching her hair because he was asleep with his back to her. At this point she became vaguely aware that she had fallen partially asleep and she didn't want to wake up, so she turned on her other side, squeezed her eyes shut, and tried to keep her dream going. But of course that didn't work, and a minute later she was awake and sitting up in bed, frustrated and crying.

On Monday, Luke waited until 4:30 before calling Hilton. He had hoped she would call him about dinner, but she didn't. He was afraid she wouldn't even answer her phone, so he called the apartment and Natalie answered.

"Hey, Hilton," she called. "It's Luke."

"Hey, babe," Hilton greeted him as she picked up the phone. "What's up?"

She sounds much more normal today, Luke thought with a sigh of relief. "Do you still wanna have dinner tonight?"

"Oh, sure, I can do it tonight," Hilton said easily.

"Good!" Luke exclaimed, a little too eagerly. He forced himself to sound normal. "I'll pick you up."

"Oh, no, that's silly, you don't have to," Hilton replied.

"No, I want to. 6:30?"

"Okay…if you want. That's fine."

"Okay, see you then, baby."

"Bye." Hilton hung up and wandered into the living room, where Natalie and Laney were watching TV.

"Luke's being really weird lately," she mused as she curled up on the couch.

"Like how?" Laney asked, turning from a rerun of *Full House* to look curiously at Hilton.

"I don't know, but last night he called me and wanted me to come over to dinner, and got all upset when I told him I didn't want to. He almost sounded worried about me or something. And he just called again and asked me to come tonight, and then told me he'd come pick me up. It's like he thinks I'm mad at him or something; I don't know. He's just acting like he's trying to be extra nice and thinks I'm gonna snap at any minute."

"Huh, who knows?" Laney said, turning back to the TV. Hilton's story wasn't as interesting as she'd hoped. "I'm sure it's nothing."

At 9:30, Jill, Laney, and Natalie were watching *How to Lose a Guy in 10 Days* in the living room when they heard footsteps climbing the stairs and stopping outside the door.

"Luke, what is wrong with you?!" Hilton practically screamed. "Why the hell are you being so weird?"

Laney grabbed the remote and turned the volume down so they could hear better. All three girls glanced at each other and leaned toward the door.

"You won't talk to me!" Luke shouted back.

"What do you want me to talk about?" Hilton yelled, clearly frustrated and annoyed. "You've been asking me all kinds of weird questions all night but you're not really talking to me either! If you have something you want to say or ask about, just fucking tell me!" She grabbed the door handle and started to open the door, but Luke pulled it back shut.

"I just don't understand how you could not tell me about this!" he snapped. "I have a right to know!"

"A right to know WHAT?" Hilton shouted.

There was a short silence.

"Are you pregnant or not?" Luke finally asked, his voice quieter and less heated. Laney and Natalie exchanged shocked stares and Jill's eyes went wide, but she quickly looked down at her lap to avoid Natalie's and Laney's glances.

"WHAT?!" Hilton shrieked. "*Pregnant*? Why the *hell* would you think that? Of course I'm not pregnant!"

"Well then why the hell did you buy a pregnancy test?" Luke shouted, confused and angry again.

Another pause. Jill's stomach clenched. Shit, she thought.

"How do you know about that?" Hilton's voice was low, almost a growl.

"Kate saw you, okay? In the pharmacy. She called Britt to tell her, and I was there, at Park's."

Hilton was silent for a moment and Jill panicked. Her cover was blown now; what was she going to do? How were Natalie and Laney going to react? She wasn't ready for this. Why did Kate have to open her big fucking mouth? Stupid bitch! Jill glared at the arm of the couch.

Then Hilton spoke. "I'm sorry, Luke," she said very coolly and dismissively. "I can't talk to you about that right now." Then she opened the door, closed it calmly behind her as she stepped inside, and walked straight into her room and shut the door without so much as glancing at any of the girls.

❧   ❧   ❧

Laney, Natalie, and Jill sat motionless in the living room, staring after Hilton.

"Should we go talk to her?" Natalie finally asked.

"Do you think she's really pregnant?" Laney replied in a shocked whisper.

Natalie shrugged in bewilderment.

"Let me talk to her," Jill said. "It might be bad if we all go in at once." Before Laney or Natalie could object she jumped off the couch and hurried into Hilton's room, shutting the door behind her.

"Do you think Jill already knew?" Natalie asked Laney.

Laney narrowed her eyes and stared at Hilton's door. "Maybe. She seemed like she did, kinda. She didn't seem that shocked when Luke said it. I bet she did know already."

"So you think she's really pregnant, then?"

"Shhh," Laney said, putting her finger to her lips. "Let's listen."

They crept up to Hilton's door and put their ears up to it. They could barely make out Jill and Hilton talking in low, confidential voices.

"Hilton, I'm so sorry," Jill was saying. "I'm so sorry it turned into such a mess with Luke. What are the chances of Kate seeing you in there? Ugh, I wanna slap her."

"No, it's fine. Luke can just deal with it. I'm not really worried about him right now."

"No, that's not fair to him. You have to tell him the truth now. He has a right to know."

"Not yet. It's not the right time yet, do you think? Maybe after this weekend, when there's been more time to think."

"Yeah, I guess that would be better...if you're sure."

"Oh, I'm sure. Don't worry about it. Luke will be fine."

"Yeah, I just feel so bad...."

"Why should you feel bad? It's actually a good thing Kate saw *me* in there buying that test....Just think how much worse this situation could be right now...."

Then it was silent.

Laney and Natalie looked at each other, then tiptoed back to the couch.

"Well, she's definitely pregnant," Natalie mouthed. "And Jill definitely knew. She was talking about telling Luke the truth, so she obviously has known what the truth is."

"Yeah, but what the hell was that about it being *good* that Kate saw Hilton buy the test?"

"Who knows?" Natalie frowned. "Maybe she wasn't going to tell Luke. Maybe she was gonna have an abortion."

Laney's eyes widened. "Do you think?"

Natalie shrugged. "Who knows? She said the situation would be worse right now if Kate hadn't seen her."

Luke was devastated. Hilton's whole attitude toward the situation was the complete opposite of what he had imagined it would be and he couldn't shake the feeling that something was dreadfully wrong, or that he was missing something. Why would she continue to keep him in the dark and refuse to talk to him after he had told her he knew about the pregnancy test?

He knew he hadn't handled it very well though. He had hoped she would volunteer the information, but when he kept pressing and she kept evading the subject, he had gotten frustrated and annoyed and had blurted out what he should have said calmly and understandingly. Now she probably thought he was freaking out, when he had intended to let her know he was okay with everything and even excited to have a baby with her. The more he replayed the scene outside her apartment, the more he could understand why she had responded as she did. She was probably shocked to find out he knew, and it totally threw her off. Maybe she had been waiting to go to a doctor and verify the results of the pregnancy test before telling him, and so she just wasn't ready for him to know yet.

But he couldn't get over how completely cold she had become toward him as soon as he told her he knew about the test. She had totally frozen, and her anger had turned into an icy indifference that had bewildered him and shut him out completely. How could she show such a lack of emotion?

Luke suddenly froze in horror as a new thought came to him. Maybe she was getting an abortion. It would make sense that she would try not to feel any emotion for a thing she was about to kill. But it was *me* she was so cold toward, he reminded himself. Not the baby. And Hilton would never get an abortion. She thinks everything happens for a reason so she'd believe she was meant to be pregnant. Plus she'd just never be able to go through with it.

Luke pulled into a parking space outside his apartment and shut his car off, then just sat there in a daze. She froze the moment I mentioned the test, he thought. Before that she was just annoyed with me, and even confused, but as soon as she found out I knew about the test, she totally shut me out. Why then? What was it that I said? It flashed through Luke's mind that maybe the baby wasn't his. As quickly as it crossed his mind, he pushed it away, but he felt a brief wave of nausea just at the thought of it.

"No fucking way," he said to himself. "No fucking way. You know that, man." He felt ashamed for even thinking it, but now he knew it would be there, in the back of his mind, until he found out what was really going on. And who the fuck knows when that will be? he thought angrily. I don't even know when she'll talk to me next!

❦   ❦   ❦

Hilton was glad she hadn't come out and told Luke the truth about Jill. But she couldn't stand the thought of him agonizing all week over her being pregnant, plus she didn't want to go all week without talking to him. Finally she thought of a way she could stop Luke from panicking without giving away Jill's secret.

She went to Luke's apartment as soon as she got out of class on Tuesday. She breezed through the door and found Luke and Ace sitting in the living room watching TV. She bent down in front of Luke and kissed him quickly, then grabbed his hand.

"Come on, baby, let's go talk," she said with an eager smile.

Luke, baffled but hopeful by the complete change from the previous night, allowed Hilton to lead him into his room. He sat on the bed without saying anything, and Hilton sat Indian style facing him.

"So," she said, "I'm not really pregnant."

"What?" Luke asked, narrowing his eyes and staring at her in confusion.

"I'm not pregnant. I bought the test because I thought I might be, but it was a false alarm. I'm sorry I was so shitty last night, but it just freaked me out that you knew, because I wasn't planning on telling you about it since the test was negative." She smiled as if asking for forgiveness and reached out to briefly stroke his arm.

Luke was still staring at her with narrowed eyes. "You're sure?"

"Yeah, I'm totally sure."

"So that's it?"

"What do you mean?" Hilton frowned.

"Well...." Luke hesitated. He could tell Hilton was trying too hard to make him believe her, and he knew she wasn't telling him everything. "It just seems like that was a really big deal over nothing."

"Yeah, I guess so," Hilton said. "But we don't have to worry about it anymore, so let's just forget the whole thing. Sorry I was so weird about everything. I love you." She leaned in and kissed him.

Luke reached out to put his arms around her and kissed her back, but he was far from satisfied. Everything she had just said had been a performance, and he knew there was no way she would have frozen like that the night before if the explanation was as simple as the one she had just given him. He was sure she wasn't telling him the whole story, and that scared him more than anything because he was afraid of what the real story might be, and he was also afraid he might never know it.

Hilton left Luke's feeling much more lighthearted. Then all of a sudden for a brief moment she knew what Jill must feel like. It had been bad enough for Hilton having everyone think she was pregnant, because it almost made her feel as if she was. This is what Jill's got coming, she thought sadly. And she'll have to deal with it all the time, not just for a couple days. The full weight of the situation hit Hilton for the first time, and she drove home feeling depressed for Jill. She wondered if Natalie and Laney had asked Jill about last night, and what Jill had told them.

When she walked into the apartment Natalie and Laney were cooking dinner and Jill was nowhere to be seen.

"Hey guys," Hilton said as she kicked off her shoes and glanced through the mail. She saw Natalie and Laney exchange a quick look and knew they had talked about what to say to her.

"So…" Laney said and turned from the stove to face Hilton. "What was the deal last night? What's going on?"

Natalie leaned on the counter to listen to Hilton's answer.

"Oh, nothing really," Hilton said casually. "I bought a pregnancy test the other day because I thought I might be, and Kate saw me and told Luke, and so he thought I was pregnant. But I'm not." She shrugged. "So it was just a little scare is all."

"Oh….well that's good," Laney replied.

Hilton offered the girls a smile and then carried her mail and backpack into her room.

Laney glanced at Natalie. "She's so lying," she hissed.

Natalie nodded. "I know. Last night Jill was talking about telling Luke the truth and Hilton said maybe she would this weekend after she had more time to think about it. Why would she have been saying that if she knew she wasn't pregnant? She definitely thought she was pregnant then, so there's no way that test came out negative."

"Maybe she took another test later, and the second one was negative," Laney suggested in a whisper.

Natalie's eyes widened. "I bet she got an abortion! Or she knows she's going to. I bet that's why she said she needed time to think about it before telling Luke. See, I told you!"

Laney nodded slowly. "And she made up her mind already, so now she can just tell everyone she was never pregnant. We should ask Jill. Too bad she's not here. Of all the nights she would actually go to her movie lab! Damn it, I wanna know!" She giggled and flashed a sly grin.

"I know, me too!" Natalie cried. "I bet Jill went to lab purposely so she wouldn't have to answer questions from us! 'Cause she *never* goes to that lab; she said they don't even talk about the movies in class ever so it's pointless to go watch them."

Hilton came back out of her room with a textbook and notebook and settled down on the couch. "Hey, do you guys know where Jill is?" she asked.

"She's at her movie lab," Natalie said, and she and Laney glanced at each other with small smiles. They waited for Hilton's reaction.

"Oh yeah, I forgot that was tonight," was all Hilton said as she opened her textbook and turned her attention to her reading.

Jill *had* gone to her movie lab to avoid Laney and Natalie. She loved them both, and she and Hilton didn't normally keep secrets from them, but she just wasn't ready to tell them. She needed to talk to Todd this weekend, because once he knew, she felt she'd be more ready to tell everybody else.

Why? she thought to herself now as she slumped in a desk in the almost empty lecture hall and stared blankly at the screen. That's stupid to want to tell Todd first. It's not like he'll know what to do. Nat and Lane would have better advice. And they at least know I had sex. What the hell is Todd going to think?! I never even told him about Adam at all….Maybe I should just go ahead and tell Lane and Nat. But she knew she couldn't…for whatever reason, she had to tell Todd first, even before Adam. Once she told Laney and Natalie, everyone in her circle at Dale would know, and she wasn't quite ready for that yet. Todd was removed from the situation and he wouldn't tell anyone else about it, so he would be able to help her decide what to do, or at least comfort her. She hoped, anyway.

The next question was when to tell Adam. She hadn't talked to him in the two days since they got back from Florida, and she assumed their little fling was over. She missed him, and fooling around with him, but she hadn't expected anything more to come of it and she had bigger worries right now than hoping to get some. She figured it would be best to tell Adam before she told Laney and Natalie too, and then once Adam knew she could tell everyone else. But she dreaded dropping that bomb on Adam, and she wanted to stall as long as she could. Maybe I shouldn't even have told Hilton, she thought. Then no one would know yet and I'd have some more time...but oh well, what's done is done. Why did Kate have to be in that damn pharmacy? Ugh, she just ruined everything!

She sighed and checked the clock. She had no interest in seeing this movie; she couldn't even remember what it was and she wasn't paying attention at all, but she wanted to stay gone from home as long as possible so she didn't have to face her roommates' questions. She felt a little bad for leaving Hilton with them, and wondered what Hilton was telling them. Maybe she wasn't home either. Jill felt even worse about how Hilton had left things with Luke last night, because she felt it was really unfair to Luke to make him worry like this, and something this huge could have a serious effect on Hilton and Luke's overall relationship. I can't let that happen, she decided. I'll tell Hilton to tell him, and just ask him to not say anything, and if he does, then I guess there's nothing I can do about it. But that's the only option, because he doesn't deserve to be thinking Hilton's pregnant.

Jill got up to leave the lecture hall and call Hilton right then to tell her to tell Luke the truth, and just as she was walking out, her phone started vibrating. She was surprised to see it was Adam, and wondered a little bit nervously what he was calling to say.

"Hello?"

"Hey, Jill! What's up?"

"Not much, what's up with you?"

"Oh, nothin', we're just havin' some people over here tonight to play some cards and drink a little; I was just wondering what you're doing."

"Oh, well I'm not really doing anything; I'm at a class right now but I could come over for a while I guess...." Jill immediately wondered if that was smart, but she wanted to see him, plus it would keep her out of the apartment.

"Okay, awesome," Adam said, and he sounded genuinely glad she was coming. "See ya soon, then."

"Yep, later." Jill hung up and frowned at the wall, then shrugged and smiled a little. At least he wants to still see me; he's not avoiding me! she thought. She dialed Hilton's cell.

"Hello?" Hilton said.

"Hey," Jill replied. "Are you at the apartment?"

"Yep. We're just watching TV and I'm doing some reading for sports photography....Okay, now I'm in my room. What's up?"

"Have Nat and Laney asked any questions about last night?"

"Yeah, they just asked what the deal was and I told them it was a false alarm; I bought the test 'cause I thought I was pregnant but I turned out not to be. I actually told Luke that earlier today too."

"Oh, good!" Jill breathed a sigh of relief. "I was really worried about that whole Luke thing. I'm glad you thought of something to tell him. I was calling to tell you to just tell him the truth."

"Nope, I got it covered," Hilton said with a smile in her voice.

Jill smiled too. "You're awesome, thanks so much," she said gratefully. "So Adam just called me."

"*Real*-ly?" Hilton said in a teasing voice. "Woohoo! What's up with that?"

"Well he invited me over to play some cards and drink; he said some people are coming over tonight."

"Are you going?"

"Yeah, I said I would....It should be interesting I guess."

"Yay, that's good!" Hilton said. "See, that boy really has a thing for you! He can't even be away from you for two days!"

"Yeah, we'll see about that," Jill said doubtfully. "But I'm glad he called....Who knows, right? Wanna come?"

"Yeah, I'll come," Hilton said. "You wanna meet there in like fifteen minutes?"

"Sure," Jill said. "Invite Lane and Nat too; you almost have to, right?"

"Yeah….They probably won't come though. But if they do it's not like we can talk about any of this while we're over there at the boys', so at least they can't ask more questions."

"True," Jill said. "All right, see ya there."

"Okay, bye babe."

Hilton smiled as she hung up from Jill. She really wanted more than anything for things to work out between Adam and Jill, because she knew Jill really liked him and it would at least make the situation a little better for Jill if Adam liked her back. She had gotten the impression in Daytona that Adam did really like Jill, because he was the biggest player ever and he hadn't even tried to hook up with anyone else. Plus just the way he looked at her….Hilton had been sure she saw something there. But she had been worried whatever it was would be gone when they got back from vacation, and when she had found out Jill was pregnant she had hoped more than ever that she had been right about Adam really liking Jill. There would still be no guarantee he would want anything to do with her once he found out about the baby, because this thing between them had just started and that was a lot of responsibility to drop on a guy who was the complete opposite of responsible and commitment-oriented, but still, it would help if he at least cared for her. And it probably will help too that they've been friends for a couple years now, Hilton thought. He has to at least care about her as a friend, and he's a decent guy, even though he's got a bad track record with girls. He'll want to do the right thing. But Hilton didn't want him to just be "doing the right thing." She wanted him to fall in love with Jill. She really thought he might, if there was more time. She wished Jill didn't have to tell him about the baby so soon….Oh well, she told herself as she threw on a sweatshirt and some tennis shoes. Everything happens for a reason and everything works out for the best…so there's nothing I can do about any of this. I can just be there for Jilly.

She went out into the living room. "Wanna go to Adam and Justin's?" she asked Laney and Natalie, who were doing homework and watching *One Tree Hill*.

Laney looked up, surprised. "Sure, I'll go! I've had enough chemistry for one night. I can't wait till this damn class is over. What the hell does it have to do with accounting? I don't know. Plus I'm like the only non-freshman in the whole class. It's great. Stupid core requirements." She dumped her book and lab manual on the coffee table, flashed a sarcastic grin, and jumped out of her chair to go get shoes. "What's going on at the boys'?" she called from her room.

"Playing cards and stuff."

"Was that who just called you?" Natalie asked as she tied her shoes, leaving her unfinished sketches on top of her huge fashion portfolio on the couch. She was a fashion design major and had been building up a portfolio of her own designs over her three years at Dale. Hilton glanced at the top sketch and saw a short V-neck dress with a tight bodice and loose, flowing skirt.

"I love that dress," she said. "But no, it was Jill; we're meeting her there. Adam called her." Hilton smiled suggestively at Natalie, hoping to lighten the awkward tension that had hovered over the room all night, ever since Hilton had come home. She had tried to act normal, but the girls had hardly talked at all the whole night, which was unusual for them.

"Oooh," Natalie said, and grinned back. "I see!" They all giggled.

Good, they're being pretty normal now, Hilton thought. I hope they believed me earlier. She wasn't sure if they hadn't believed her, or if they just hadn't known what to say to her and therefore left her alone. But as long as she could keep a normal conversation flowing now, things should be better. Hopefully.

When the girls got to the boys' apartment, they pulled up and parked next to Jill, who was waiting in her car, and they all went in together.

Thank God Kate's not here! Jill thought as she quickly surveyed the room. Just Britt, Park, Adam, Justin, Ryan, and two guys from the apartment across the hall.

Jill saw Britt throw a quick glance at Hilton, and Hilton met her look and smiled brightly at her. Jill smirked to herself.

"You guys wanna get in? We're playing asshole," Adam said.

"Sure, I'm in," Hilton said.

"Grab a beer out of the fridge," Justin invited her. "Anybody else?"

Jill saw Natalie and Laney narrow their eyes at each other and watch Hilton get a beer. They didn't believe her, Jill realized. They still think she's pregnant. I wonder what they'll think now.

Laney and Natalie joined in too.

"Jill?" Justin asked.

"Um, do you have anything besides beer?" Jill asked. She was thinking she could pour a mixed drink but not actually put any alcohol in it, and nobody would know she wasn't drinking. She didn't want to arouse any suspicion.

"No, I don't think so. Sorry." Justin said.

"Okay, well I'll just watch then. I'm not in the mood for beer."

"Well, pull up a chair," Adam said. "Here, come sit by me." He scooted over to make room for her.

After a few rounds of asshole, Hilton had finished five beers already, and Jill wondered what Natalie, Laney, and Britt were thinking.

Adam was flirting with Jill a lot, and kept asking for help with his cards. He had her hold them for him and asked her to arrange them in order when a new hand was dealt. He had his arm around her most of the time, and Jill wondered how drunk he was. She had no idea how long he'd been drinking before she got there, but she didn't mind the attention.

"I need to get going," Laney said, standing up from the table. "I still have to finish my pre-lab for chem."

Natalie stood up too, and they waited for Hilton.

"Are you coming, or do you want to come with Jill?" Laney asked.

"Oh, well I think I'm leaving now too," Jill said quickly. She started to stand up.

"Why?" Adam asked, pulling her down on his lap. "You should stay."

Jill smiled. "Well…"

"Come on, stay," Adam pleaded with a grin. "It'll be fun, I promise."

"Yeah, Jill, stay." Justin winked at her and laughed. "It'll be fun!"

Jill glared at Justin teasingly, then said, "All right, I guess I'll stay for awhile. Is that okay, guys?" she looked at her roommates.

"Yeah, it's fine!" Natalie exclaimed. "Don't worry about it. Just have fun!" She smiled knowingly at Jill. Hilton finally got up and the girls said goodbye and left.

"Have fun, Jilly, yay!" Hilton whispered on her way by Jill, squeezing her shoulder.

"Hey, Jill, you wanna go in my room with me?" Adam whispered in her ear with a big grin on his face.

Jill giggled. "Sure, why not." She stood up and helped pull Adam up too.

"Piggyback ride?" Adam asked.

"You'll drop me," Jill laughed at him. "You're drunk!"

"No, no, I won't, I promise. Come on." Adam leaned forward so Jill could climb on his back.

Jill shrugged and shook her head at Justin, laughing. Justin had a big, drunken smile on his face too. She jumped onto Adam's back and he half-ran, half-stumbled across the living room into his room, with Jill giggling the whole way.

"Yeah, baby!" Justin called after them. "See you guys in the morning!"

When the girls got back home, Hilton went right into her room to call Luke. After she had shut the door Natalie went into Laney's room and sat on her bed. Laney was at the computer seeing if Del was online.

"So I guess she's definitely having an abortion then!" Natalie said, referring to Hilton's drinking.

"I guess…." Laney frowned. "I just can't believe she would do that. I mean, it's Hilton. You know how she is. I can't picture it. Maybe she was telling the truth. Maybe it was really a false alarm." She shrugged and started to check her e-mail.

"Oh, my gosh," Natalie said suddenly. "What if it's Jill?"

"What?"

"Yeah. Holy shit, it is. It's gotta be Jill." Natalie nodded as everything started to make sense. Laney had turned from her e-mail and was looking at Natalie with utter confusion.

"She went shopping with Hilton Sunday," Natalie continued. "Hilton could've been buying the test for her. It makes more sense it'd be Jill anyway, 'cause Hilton's on the pill, and Jill's not. And think about it. How long ago was it that Jill had sex with Adam? It was like, exactly a month ago I think. Or maybe five weeks, something like that. But it's about the right timing." Laney's green eyes had widened and Natalie kept talking as more thoughts came to her. "And then Kate saw Hilton and told Luke, and Hilton couldn't tell Luke the truth 'cause only she and Jill know, so she made up that story about it being a false alarm. And that's why Jill went right into Hilton's room to talk to her last night before we had a chance. And she was telling Hilton that Hilton had to tell Luke the truth and Hilton told her to wait till after the weekend when there was more time to think about it….It makes a lot of sense. That's gotta be it! And Jill didn't drink tonight!"

Laney just shook her head. "I don't know….I just can't imagine that. The first time she had sex and she gets pregnant? That would suck so bad! Do you really think?" Then a thought struck her. "Hey, Jill drank all the time on spring break though. Wouldn't she have at least been suspicious by then?"

Natalie frowned. "I don't know…maybe not because maybe she wasn't late until the last couple days….Do you know if she drank much those days?"

Laney shrugged. "I thought so; I mean we were going out every night. But I was with Del….I wasn't paying that much attention to her I guess."

"Yeah, me either," Natalie said. "I did see her with drinks in her hand though, but I bet she just realized it at the end of break."

"Shit, this is huge," Laney said, shaking her head in disbelief. "You almost have to be right though."

Natalie nodded, and both girls were silent for a minute. Then Natalie said, "I wonder when she'll tell us."

"I wonder what Adam will do," Laney replied, and the girls looked at each other gravely.

❧   ❧   ❧

"Jill, come back to bed," Adam complained playfully, stretching out his arm toward her as she came out of the bathroom the next morning.

"I can't," Jill said, smiling at how cute he looked with his hair all rumpled from sleep. "I have to go to class."

"Who gives a shit about class? You can skip it."

Jill leaned over Adam and gave him a lingering kiss. "Nope, I have to go," she said as she stood up again. "Sorry!" She grinned teasingly.

Adam grabbed her arm. "Do you wanna go out to dinner on Friday or something?"

Jill tried not to show how shocked she was that he was asking her on an actual date.

"I can't Friday; I'm going to Eastern for the weekend with Laney." *Why did I say 'with Laney?'* she wondered immediately. *To downplay the fact that I'm visiting Todd? Why should that matter?* She shook it off.

"Let's do it tonight then," Adam said, still holding Jill's arm.

Jill raised her eyebrows. "Okay….Yeah, I guess I can do it tonight."

"Don't sound so excited," Adam pouted playfully.

"Of course I'm excited." Jill smiled and ruffled his hair. "I'm just surprised."

"Uh-huh, yeah, whatever," Adam said, pretending to be miffed. He rolled over and faced the wall. "I really like you but you're just using me for sex."

Jill giggled and jumped on top of him, giving him a long kiss. "You're right, I *am* just using you," she said haughtily as she climbed off and headed for the door. "But I might as well get a free dinner out of it, right?" She blew him a kiss and quickly shut the door behind her.

What the hell? she thought, but she couldn't stop smiling. She had never expected him to ask her on a date; she had thought it was nothing more to him than casual sex. She had actually been surprised he wanted more after spring break, but now she didn't even know what to think. He had said he really liked her, and even though he had been joking around when he said it, he must like her a little at least since he'd asked her out to dinner.

Jill tried to wipe the huge, silly grin off her face as she got into her car. She wanted to stop thinking about it because she didn't want to get her hopes up and then have it turn out to be nothing. She was afraid to even let herself start to picture how perfectly it could all turn out if he really did like her a lot and they got involved in an actual relationship....

Jill couldn't concentrate in class all day because she kept playing the date out in her mind. She imagined hypothetical conversations she and Adam might have, where they might go to dinner, and what she should wear. She was somewhat nervous because she was afraid they wouldn't have anything to talk about and it would be awkward, and end up ruining everything. If the date didn't go well, the sex was probably done too and she could just imagine Adam trying to avoid her and ignore her at parties and bars for the rest of the year. Ugh, she groaned and rolled her eyes at the ceiling of the lecture hall. This has *got* to work out. She wondered briefly if maybe she should've said no, because what they had was so fun and great, and this could really fuck everything up. No, she finally convinced herself, you had to say yes to the date. You have to at least see what happens. It's better than never knowing, because maybe you'll come out of this with a lot better situation than what you have right now. If it's meant to be, it'll work out. But no matter how certain she became that she was doing the right thing by giving this whole date thing a chance, she couldn't shake the feeling that it *wouldn't* work out in the end, because there was no way she and Adam were meant to be together. It's *Adam*, she reminded herself, shaking her head. You actually think you might end up in a relationship with him? Get a grip, Jill! You know how he is….

She shook her head viciously to clear all her thoughts of Adam, tapped her pen on her paper, and squinted at the overhead projector, trying to focus. She realized she was three pages behind in the notes packet she had printed out and quickly flipped the pages to catch up.

As it turned out, Jill had worried over nothing, because the date went better than she could ever have expected. Adam picked her up at 7:30 and they decided to go to Logan's Roadhouse, one of Jill's favorites.

Jill had decided to wear a pair of low-rise jeans and a black V-neck, off-the-shoulder shirt with three-quarter sleeves. She wore her dark brown hair down and spent longer blow-drying it than normal so it would look full and the layers would be accentuated, even though they were almost grown out.

"Hey, gorgeous!" Adam had grinned and raised his eyebrows as soon as she opened the door.

"Did you expect anything less?" Jill teased as she glided past him out the door. She glanced back over her shoulder and smiled warmly. "You look pretty good yourself!"

He had on dark jeans and a lightweight red shirt that buttoned up the front. It was his trademark outfit; almost every time she saw him at a party or a bar he had on a shirt like that. He always rolled the sleeves up a little too, and she smiled to herself when she noticed the ever-present hair band on his wrist. His normally gelled hair was slightly tousled and looked incredibly sexy. He took her breath away.

"Good, maybe I can get a good-night kiss or something then," Adam joked as they headed for the stairs. Jill started down in front of him and he touched his hand lightly to the small of her back as he followed. Jill practically melted; that was one of the things that turned her on the most.

When they got to the landing between the second and third floors Jill turned back to face Adam, stopping him abruptly. "Maybe you can get a kiss right now," she said in a low, silky voice, and then pressed into him with her arms loosely around his waist and started to kiss him deeply, but pulled away quickly to leave him wanting more. "Come on!" she said with a mischievous smile, grabbing his hand and leading him down the second flight of stairs.

At Logan's they were lucky enough to get an intimate corner table and they talked non-stop throughout the meal. It wasn't uncomfortable, fill-the-silence kind of conversation like Jill had imagined in some of her hypothetical scenarios; it was easy and natural. They talked about their mutual friends, school and future jobs, funny stories from childhood and high school, and finally, how much fun they had both had on spring break.

"I was really surprised," Jill admitted. "I didn't even think we'd hook up again after the first time."

"Why not?"

"I don't know....I just figured it's spring break, ya know, and there would be other people to hook up with there."

"Yeah, I thought that too," Adam said, looking straight into her eyes. "But I couldn't help myself that night on the couch....I just wanted you so bad." He glanced away and laughed. "Sorry, that probably made me sound like an asshole, but I'm serious. And then, after that…" he grinned with a devilish-little-boy look on his face, "well, let's just say it was a fun week."

Jill grinned back and nodded. "Yeah, I'd say it was fun."

"Can I just say something?" Adam asked.

"Sure," Jill said, a little bit anxious about what it would be.

"I really like you, Jill." He was looking right at her now, and his tone was serious. Then he looked a little embarrassed and said in a lighter tone, "I wasn't going to ask you out because I know you probably don't like me and you think I'm a player and pretty much a fuckin' asshole to girls and this is probably just a pity date." He looked back at her and smiled jokingly, but she could tell he was anxious for her reaction.

"Well…" she said slowly, raising her eyebrows and looking at him with her best sassy smile, which was a mixture of a challenge and a tease, "like I said earlier, I *am* just using you for sex, and I was afraid if I said no to the date the sex might end, so I guess it's not technically a pity date…." Then she laughed and shook her head, grabbing one of his hands off the table and interlacing her fingers with his. "Just kidding," she said. "I actually really like you too." She smiled genuinely at him. "And of course it's not a pity date; I can't believe you would even say that!" She kicked him playfully under the table.

Adam smiled back at her. "So you really like me, huh? So maybe we could do this again sometime?"

"I can't wait," Jill replied truthfully, barely able to contain herself from squealing in delight and bouncing up and down.

When Adam walked her to the door, Jill turned to face him. "I would ask you in, but I'm not the kind of girl who does that on the first date." She flashed him an innocent smile. "Sorry, baby."

"Well then I guess we'll just have to make out." Adam moved in quickly and smashed his mouth to hers, pinning her back against the door with his hand above her head. "How was that?"

"Wow," Jill breathed with a dreamy smile. "You take my breath away, Adam!" She giggled and batted her eyelashes.

Adam laughed and tousled her hair. "See you tomorrow at the Turtle? You guys going together, or you wanna ride with us?"

"Oh, we'll just all go together probably. We can work it out tomorrow." Jill smiled and put her hand on the doorknob. "Night, Adam. I had a really great time. Thanks."

"I did too. And remember, you promised me another date." Adam grabbed her face in his hands and kissed her quickly. "Night, Jill."

Jill stepped into the apartment with a huge, irrepressible grin on her face. Laney and Natalie were sitting in the living room and looked up from their homework. As soon as they saw Jill's face they couldn't help but smile too.

"So I guess it went well?" Laney said excitedly.

"Oh, yeah," Jill sighed, flopping down on the couch next to Natalie. She looked from one girl to the other, practically glowing.

"So, tell us about it!" Laney exclaimed.

Right then Hilton hurried out of her room and joined them. She giggled and tucked her feet up under her as she dropped onto the futon.

"So?" she asked expectantly and all three girls leaned toward Jill, eager to hear about the date.

As Jill described it, Laney and Natalie shared a secret pleased glance. Since they thought Jill was pregnant, they were both hoping for her sake the date would be perfect. All four of them were relieved and ecstatic for the same reason—now that the date had gone well maybe Jill and Adam would actually start dating and end up raising the baby together—but Jill and Hilton had no idea whatsoever that the other two girls had guessed at the truth.

The next night everybody went to the Turtle and Adam came back to Jill's apartment for the first time. At first Laney and Natalie were surprised to see Jill drinking, but, "Did you ever hear her order a drink?" Natalie asked. "I bet she was just ordering Coke or something."

"Maybe," Laney agreed.

They wondered when Jill would tell them and then decided she probably wanted to see how things developed with Adam so as not to drop the bomb on him right away, and she probably wanted to tell Adam before she told them.

On Friday afternoon Laney and Jill drove to Eastern. Laney felt awkward because she was afraid she didn't sound normal, even though she was trying to make "normal" conversation. She didn't want Jill to know that she and Natalie knew. Finally, hoping for a little bit of information and curious to see Jill's reaction, Laney said, "Isn't that crazy that Hilton thought she was pregnant? Can you imagine if she really was?"

Jill knew Laney was digging for information, but she assumed Laney didn't believe Hilton's story about a false alarm and thought there was more to it. She still didn't guess that Laney had realized it wasn't Hilton at all.

"No, I can't….That would be weird," Jill said, and left it at that.

When Laney dropped Jill off at Todd's, they agreed to meet at Don Pablo's for dinner at 7:30, and Jill quickly grabbed her bag and shut the door. She had been nervous the whole way down, and now she felt a little nauseous. Maybe it's because you're pregnant, she thought sarcastically. But she was pretty sure it was because she didn't have any idea how she was going to tell Todd, or what he would think. And she desperately needed his support and friendship if she was going to get through this whole thing.

She sighed and rested her hand on her churning stomach as she approached his door and knocked.

Todd was nervous too. Ever since Jill had called him earlier in the week, he had been anxious about what it was that she needed to talk to him about. It definitely hadn't sounded like good news, and this assumption was reinforced when he answered the door. Her gorgeous, usually lively brown eyes had a dull, almost dejected look in them, and she was a little slumped over.

"Hey, Jilly," Todd said, trying to sound normal, and she stepped through the door and into his arms, hugging him tightly and holding on for a little while. It wasn't one of their usual hugs where they playfully swayed from side to side or Todd picked her up and whirled her around; this time she just stood still and clung to him. Todd was somewhat surprised; maybe he had been wrong about her being mad or upset with him. Now he was even more confused.

When Jill finally pulled back, she looked more relaxed and she offered him a genuine smile. "Hi, Todd."

"Hi, Jilly Bean." Todd smiled back at her and ruffled her hair. "Wanna put your stuff down?"

They walked down the hallway and into Todd's room. Jill tossed her bag against the wall and plopped onto Todd's bed. "So how've you been?"

"Oh, you know, fuckin' miserable, but now that you're here everything's good in my life again," Todd joked, hoping to lighten the mood and help himself relax.

Jill laughed. How ironic was it that Todd would jokingly describe exactly how she felt about him at that moment? She felt ten times better now that she was with him. She still had to tell him, but she had decided to do it after dinner so the meal wouldn't be weird, and so the pressure was gone for a little while at least.

"So…." Todd sat down on the bed beside Jill. "What was it you wanted to talk to me about this weekend?"

Jill shook her head, blocking his question out and refusing to think about it. "Let's just talk about it after dinner. We have to go to dinner with Del and Laney. Del, you know, the guy she met in Daytona."

"Yeah, okay," Todd agreed, trying to push it out of his mind as well so he wouldn't drive himself crazy wondering what it was. "So what do you wanna do now?"

"Can we take a nap?" Jill asked, curling up on her side. "I'm exhausted."

"Sure," Todd said, "but only if we can spoon." He flashed Jill a wicked smile.

"Okay," Jill giggled, moving over so Todd could fit in behind her. Suddenly a shocking realization came to her and she literally flinched, then pretended to just be adjusting herself. This might be her last weekend here with Todd like this, because who knew what would happen once she told everyone about the pregnancy. Her life was going to change completely, and one of the things she would have to give up would be her playful relationship with Todd.

He won't even want to flirt with me anymore when I start to show, or when I'm a *mom*, she thought. He'll be so freaked out by it. Plus I won't be able to come visit anyway once I have a baby to take care of! Where will I even be living? I'll probably have to live at home and go to Dale Brinkley! And what about grad school? Aagghh! she screamed silently. My whole life is ruined…and what's sad is of all those changes like where I'll go to school and stuff the one I'm most upset about is that I won't be able to be as close to Todd anymore.

Jill squeezed her eyes shut and snuggled closer to Todd, enjoying his arm around her waist and his body against hers because she felt protected. *I am going to make the most of this weekend, since it's probably the last one like this,* she promised herself.

Dinner was fun, and Jill got to know Del a little bit better and decided she really liked him. She had been distracted in Florida and hadn't ever really talked to him much. He was tall with short brown hair and he seemed like a bit of a metro, very preppy and clean-cut. He was easy-going and friendly, and Jill found that he was easy to talk to. He and Todd got along well too, which would be nice for future visits to Eastern. *Oh, never mind,* Jill realized gloomily, *like there will be any more of those!*

After dinner they went to see *The Butterfly Effect* and everyone loved it, Jill especially, since it was a sort of psychological thriller. That was her favorite type of movie, which she figured made sense, since she was studying psychology and was fascinated by the workings of the mind, especially the abnormal workings.

Del invited Jill and Todd to come back to his apartment and play euchre or something after the movie, but Todd declined, saying they were supposed to meet Conrad and Lizzy back at the apartment. Jill could tell Laney and Del were actually glad they turned down the invite. She was sure they wanted to be alone, since their private time was so limited anyway.

Jill talked about the movie the whole drive back to Todd's apartment, partly because she was still intrigued by it but partly because she wanted to avoid the other subject a little longer.

When they got back no one else was home. Todd went in and dropped his keys on the table, then headed to his bedroom without bothering to turn on any lights in the apartment. He turned on the one in his bedroom and turned on his TV, then sat in his computer chair. Jill sat on the bed and leaned back against the wall.

"So...." Todd said hesitantly. "You wanna talk now?"

Jill shrugged and hugged her knees, and Todd saw all the light and energy drain from her face. She looked like she had when he first opened the door that afternoon.

"Jill, what the hell is it?" Todd asked anxiously, reaching out to touch her arm.

"I have no idea how to say this..." Jill began, "and I don't know what you're going to think, but...." She paused and took a deep breath. Todd leaned forward and tried to look into her eyes, but she stared at her knees. "I'm pregnant," she said, in a voice barely louder than a whisper.

Todd's hand dropped from her arm and he jerked away from her. "What?! How long have you known?"

"About a week or so...." Jill looked up tentatively and saw his stunned expression. He was completely shocked, as she had expected.

"But...wh-...how...I mean, how far along are you?"

"Um, a month, five weeks, something like that."

"A month? Are you sure? Have you been to the doctor yet?"

"No...but I know because I took a pregnancy test and it has to be about a month because I had sex about a month ago." Jill gave him a weird look. "Don't you want to know how it happened, who the father is?"

Todd had been staring blankly at the wall. He started, then leaned toward her again.

"What? Yeah, of course....I'm sorry....I just don't know what to say...." He seemed to realize he was handling this terribly and stood up and pulled Jill into his arms. "I'm so sorry, Jilly," he said softly. "I love you so much. I'm so sorry."

"Stop apologizing," Jill said with a small laugh. "I'm trying to be positive about the whole thing...."

"Oh, shit, sorry. I mean, I'm not sorry. So tell me about it." Todd released Jill but still held onto her shoulders, rubbing them briefly then moving his hands down her arms. He pulled her onto the bed and sat next to her and held her hand.

Jill was surprised he was still even touching her; she had thought he'd be freaked out and not want to come near her. Thinking about it now, she wasn't sure why she had predicted that reaction, but she was extremely glad she'd been wrong because she needed this closeness; it was incredibly comforting.

"So...it's Adam," she confessed, looking at Todd with an almost scared expression, as though she was afraid he would be mad. His whole face tightened and he squeezed her hand harder.

"Adam? That fuckin' prick?"

"Todd! He's not a prick. We're actually kind of dating...well, we might be; I'm not really sure what's going on."

"You mean he won't even date you now that you're pregnant? I'll fuckin' kick that bastard's ass!"

"No, no, he doesn't know yet!" Jill cried, grabbing Todd's other hand and turning to face him more directly. He wouldn't look at her so she grabbed his face and turned it toward her own. His eyes were blazing and he was shaking his head in anger.

"I fucking HATE that asshole!" he yelled, standing up suddenly and moving to the other side of the room. He ran his hand through his hair and then saw Jill's devastated expression. He rushed back to her and pulled her into his lap. "Jilly Bean, I'm so sorry. Damn it. I didn't mean it like that. I just never really liked that dude and now he did this shit to you."

"Todd, seriously, it's not like that. I had sex with him at a party, the weekend before the last time I came here, and I wasn't expecting anything more out of it because I know he's such a player. But then in Daytona we ended up being together all week kinda, and then a couple days ago he asked me on a date, and it was amazing, and he told me he really likes me. So, maybe it will work out. I don't want to tell him yet though because I want to see what happens between us."

Todd looked a little more relaxed now, and he rubbed Jill's back. He was still staring off into space though and wouldn't really look at her. Then suddenly he stopped rubbing her back and stared at her again.

"Was that…the first time you had sex?" he asked, scrunching up his face in what Jill assumed was sympathy for her having such bad luck her first time.

Jill nodded. "You know I was a virgin."

Todd nodded slowly and started to rub her back again. "Well I hope it works out for you two then," he said in a slightly dismissive tone.

Jill chose to ignore the tone and smiled gratefully and kissed him on the cheek. "Thanks, Todd. I love you too."

"I probably shouldn't even ask you this 'cause it's none of my business, but why did you have sex with him?"

Jill wasn't surprised or offended by the question; she still wondered that herself and tried not to feel guilty about it. But hearing the question made the guilt and shame she had pushed away start to come back and she felt sick to her stomach.

"I don't know," she said softly, staring at the floor over Todd's shoulder. "I really don't. I feel so cheap and slutty." She felt tears coming and continued to stare at the floor. "I try not to think about it like that, you know, but then it will just all come back. I mean, I'm supposed to be the good girl, you know, the virgin, and now I'm pregnant because I got drunk at some party and fucked some random guy. Well not random, but still…." She burst into tears and covered her face with her hands, rocking back and forth on the bed. "My whole life is ruined now!" she wailed. "I don't know what I'm gonna do. I won't be able to finish college and I've already signed a lease for next year, and my parents are going to kill me. What the FUCK was I thinking?! My whole life is completely ruined! I hate this!" She fell backwards on the bed and curled up in a ball, sobbing uncontrollably.

Todd could barely understand her through the hysterical tears. He had no idea what to even say to her. He was still shocked by the revelation and was trying to figure things out in his head. He also felt overwhelmingly depressed all of a sudden, and felt almost as though his future had abruptly become bleak and hopeless as well. He understood Jill's desperation without trying; it just became a part of him. Without really knowing what he was doing, he laid down facing Jill and pulled her into his arms. She was still crying and had her hands over her face, but she had stopped shaking and they just laid there diagonally across the bed with their legs touching and his arms around her and her face and hands buried in his sweatshirt.

When Jill woke up she was lying in Todd's arms and was snuggled up against his chest. Their legs were intertwined and Todd was sleeping. The light and TV were still on and Jill glanced at the clock over Todd's head. It was four in the morning. Her eyes still felt puffy from crying and she was sure she looked horrible. She thought about waking Todd so they could lie down normally in the bed, but decided not to because she really just wanted to be asleep again where she didn't have to deal with her problems or start thinking about them again. She pulled her legs out from between and under Todd's and got up quietly to shut off the TV and light. Then she laid back down and snuggled up to Todd again because she was suddenly freezing.

Now, of course, she couldn't go back to sleep. She tried to change her position a little, but couldn't really get comfortable again. She wished she'd never gotten up to turn off the light and TV because she'd been fine before that. And now all she could think about was what a horrible mess things were. Tonight had been the first time she had really broken down because up until now she'd been pushing all the bad thoughts back and not allowing herself to realize how completely her life was going to change. Then it had just all come out at once and she felt bad because she had put Todd in the uncomfortable position of feeling like he should comfort her but not knowing what to say. The longer she lay there awake and thought about how ruined her life was, the more she couldn't bear it, and the thought she had repressed the most pushed its way to the forefront of her mind. It was like a big, dark storm cloud, but it also had a silver lining because it could end this whole fucked-up mess. She looked at the clock again. 4:45.

"Todd." Jill shook his arm gently and he turned his head a little but didn't wake up. "Todd!" She shook him harder.

"Huh? What?!" Todd jerked awake and blinked a couple times before focusing on her. "What? Is something wrong?"

"Todd," Jill said, with her hand on his arm but her eyes looking into the darkness behind him, "do you think I should get an abortion?"

Todd blinked again, then shook his head viciously, trying to clear it. "What?! No! No! You can't get an abortion." He rose up on his elbow to stare at her.

"Why not?" Jill asked, sounding truly curious.

Todd was completely awake now. "Jill! Are you serious? I mean, I guess I have no right to tell you what to do, but I just can't see you doing it. I think you'd always regret it."

"Yeah, but what the fuck else am I supposed to do?" Jill burst out, sounding like she was going to cry again. "Todd, seriously, I know it's horrible, but I'm seriously thinking about it now. Things would be *so* much easier. It's, like, my only option! I don't know what else to do! I'm so lost, Todd!" Her voice was trembling and her hand fell off his arm as she let herself drop on her side. She stared blankly into Todd's sweatshirt.

Todd reached out and wiped tears off her face, then laid down next to her again. "Jill, I really don't even know what to say. I'm lost too…and I obviously don't know anything about pregnancy or abortions, but I just don't know. I mean, don't take my advice I guess. Just do what you want to do. But at least think about it some more before you do it, okay?"

Jill nodded slowly, then looked up at him and ran her hand through his hair. "I'm so sorry, Todd. Ugh, I know you don't even want to be hearing about any of this and I'm just bugging you with all my troubles and this is the last thing you want to be doing right now, listening to all my shit. I'm so sorry. I feel so bad. I won't talk about it anymore." She started to roll away from him.

"Damn it, Jill!" Todd grabbed her arm forcefully and pulled her back. "You know that's fuckin' bullshit. I care about you so fuckin' much and now you're acting like you're some fucking burden? Fuck that, Jill."

Jill was surprised at his anger but she knew he was right. She felt even worse now. "Damn it, Todd, you're right, I'm sorry." She hugged him as best she could with him lying on his side. "And you've been so great. That was really shitty of me. I love you so much. Please don't be mad." She hugged him tighter, managing to get both arms around his neck and pressing as close to him as she could. "Please don't be mad. I don't know what I'd do if you were mad at me; that's the last thing I need right now." She kissed him on the tip of his nose, trying to be silly like they usually were.

Todd grabbed her around the waist and kissed her on the lips. Jill started to giggle, relieved that everything was normal between them again, but then Todd whispered, "Jill," and kissed her again. This time it wasn't one of their friendly little smacks, it was hungry and passionate. Jill was too dazed to move and she let him kiss her.

Then, just as fast as he had kissed her, Todd pulled away sharply and flew off the bed as if it was on fire. "Fuck!" he cried, running his hands through his messy but adorable hair. "I'm so sorry; I don't know what I was thinking." He disappeared into the bathroom.

Jill quickly went after him and found him leaning over the sink in the dark with his hands on the counter, taking deep breaths. She hesitated in the doorway.

"Jill, I'm so sorry," Todd said huskily, staring into the sink. "You probably hate me; I'm such a fucking asshole. I don't even know what I was doing." He shook his head.

Jill went behind him and put her arms around his waist and leaned against his back. He didn't move. "Todd, don't worry about it," she said quickly. "It's not a big deal."

"Yeah, right," he said in disgust. "You're like counting on me to be a friend and I go and fuckin' do that."

Jill squeezed his waist and then started to rub his back. "Todd, please don't be mad at yourself. I swear I'm not mad at you! Who knows why you did it, but it's a weird night, right?" She peered around him and looked at him in the mirror with hope in her eyes, but both their facial expressions were masked by the darkness.

Todd finally stood up and walked past her out of the bathroom. "I guess so," he said, but he didn't sound too convinced.

Jill stormed out of the bathroom after him and stood with her hands on her hips. "Damn it, Todd, I will be mad if you keep fucking acting like this! Please just forget about it!" The anger in her voice diminished and she sounded brokenhearted instead.

Finally Todd turned to face her. "Okay, you're right, I'm sorry. I didn't mean anything by it, and it is a weird night."

Jill smiled in relief and stood on her toes to hug him. "Thanks, Todd. Okay, I'm exhausted now; I have to go back to sleep." She grabbed one of Todd's sweatshirts out of his open closet because she was still cold and then flopped onto the bed, not bothering to get her pajamas out at this point.

"I'll sleep on the couch," Todd said. "So you can be comfortable."

"No, Todd!" Jill cried, sitting up and reaching out for him. "I need you to sleep in here with me. Please?" She made a pouty face and stared at him with puppy-dog eyes.

Todd ran his hand through his hair and sighed. "Okay," he said. He laid down beside her on his back, praying she wouldn't want to cuddle or anything, but she did. So he spooned with her until she fell asleep, then rolled away from her immediately to face his computer. He wanted her so badly right now and was pissed at himself for losing control earlier and kissing her. He didn't want to be in his bed with her because that made it so unbelievably hard to just lie there.

What in the fuck is wrong with you, dude? he asked himself. How can you even be thinking about her like this, especially right now? She's gonna fuckin' hate you in the morning when she thinks about it. At the moment, Todd hated himself. He lay there miserably, unable to fall asleep and unable to think about anything except how much he had wanted to keep kissing Jill.

"Who knows why you did it?" she had said, and then she'd attributed it to the whole night just being weird. Shit, Todd thought, if she only knew how long I've wanted to do that. And of course I go and pick the worst fucking possible time. But it was probably the only fucking chance I had left now. He felt an over-whelming hate toward Adam and realized unhappily that it was because he was losing Jill to him. Losing her? You never had her, you fucking pussy; maybe you should've done something sooner and this never would've happened!

Todd frowned at the path his thoughts were taking. He had thought he wanted Jill sexually, but if that was it, then why was he so upset now? He could find tons of other hot girls if he tried. He shouldn't feel like someone had just dropped a brick on his heart or taken him deep-sea diving and not given him enough oxygen. He imagined himself struggling to push his way upwards through the dark blue water, but it felt as thick as syrup and he was losing his strength….

At that point Todd flipped onto his stomach and pounded his face into the pillow and forced himself to think about his upcoming anatomy test and go over everything he knew for it in his head, because he was scared of what he might have to admit to himself if he kept thinking about Jill.

On Saturday morning around ten, Jill woke up and had morning sickness. She had been experiencing it on and off; some days were better than others, and she didn't always get it at the same time of day.

She was in the bathroom for half an hour, and was glad to see Todd was still sleeping when she returned to bed. She was still tired and wanted to sleep more. She hoped he wouldn't still act freaked out about last night. She was surprised he had kissed her like that, but didn't think much of it. She assumed he had felt sorry for her and just wanted to show sympathy and affection, and had gotten a little carried away, or caught up in the moment, or something like that. And I was worried he wouldn't even want to come near me! she thought to herself with a small laugh as she crawled back into bed.

She sat there for a moment watching Todd sleep. He was so adorable. He still had on his sweatshirt and jeans and he was lying on top of the covers, as she had been. He was on his stomach and his face was turned away from her. Even in his baggy clothes, Jill couldn't help thinking he looked hot and imagining his well-toned body underneath.

Damn it! she thought. I wish he would've kissed me some other night, in some other situation! But of course that's just my luck….Oh well, it never would've happened another night any-way because he doesn't even think about me like that; he only did it last night because it was a weird situation and he wasn't even thinking clearly…and he obviously didn't enjoy it too much! Jill smiled a little ironic smile to herself and laid back down facing away from Todd. She wasn't going to let any of it bother her too much because there was nothing she could do about it and she had other things to worry about.

When Jill woke up again at two in the afternoon, Todd wasn't in bed anymore. Jill changed out of her jeans into a pair of cotton Dale shorts and wandered out to the living room. Todd was lounging on the couch in a pair of pajama pants watching TV and eating a bag of chips.

She crawled onto the couch beside him and tucked her legs up under her.

"Lazy ass," Todd said without looking at her.

Jill smiled. "Oh, shut up. I was up till five!" She grabbed some chips, and then got up to fix herself something to eat.

Todd glanced at her while she had her back to him, making pancakes. Her hair was messy from sleeping, and the ends of it disappeared into the hood of his sweatshirt. It was his baseball sweatshirt from senior year, with his name and number on the back. He hated the fact that he loved seeing her in it because it was *his*. He knew there was no way he could sit here and just chill with her all day.

"Do you wanna go play miniature golf or something, when you're done eating?" he asked.

"Sure, is it nice outside?"

"I think so," Todd said. He had no idea.

"Yeah, that would be fun!" Jill didn't want to just sit around all day either because she wanted to try to keep busy for awhile after the emotional turmoil of last night.

She wore the damn sweatshirt golfing, and Todd wasn't sure if he was glad or not. He was reminded of how he used to like Melanie wearing his jerseys or sweatshirts to school and to games. He didn't want to be thinking about Jill in a girlfriend type of way, though, and he had never felt this way before when she wore his stuff, which was all the time. This was just fucking great.

I'm probably fucking in love with her, he thought irritably, and proceeded to putt the ball so hard it skipped up over the little bricks surrounding the green and went into the water. He threw his putter and Jill burst out laughing, thinking he was joking around.

That night Jill decided she wanted to go out. She couldn't take any more sitting around feeling down and after how last night had turned out with Todd, she decided it would definitely be better to go out and be around other people. Todd was relieved; he worried Jill wouldn't have much fun since she couldn't drink, and he thought she shouldn't be around the smoke, but as soon as she said she was sure she wanted to go, Todd didn't ask again because he didn't want her to change her mind. Another night like last night and he thought he'd completely lose it and who knows what the hell he might end up saying or doing.

They went to Tenth Street with Conrad and Lizzy and met up with Laney and Del. They bar-hopped for a couple hours and Jill always ordered Cokes, telling everyone else it was rum and Coke. She still wasn't planning on telling anyone else until she had told Adam.

Laney guessed at what she was doing but didn't say anything, not even to Del. She hadn't been able to resist telling Del that she and Natalie thought Jill was pregnant, but she had warned him against saying anything in front of Jill.

Laney also was sure that Jill had told Todd last night. She could feel a weird kind of tension between them, and Todd was acting almost protective of Jill, buying all her drinks and not letting her out of his sight; however, Jill and Todd weren't being as flirty as they usually were and they barely touched the whole night. Laney wondered if things would be awkward between them now. She assumed that eventually they would grow apart because of this, because obviously Jill's life was going to change a lot and she and Todd wouldn't be visiting each other at school all the time and stuff.

That's too bad, she thought reflectively. I always thought they'd end up together. But look at them; they won't even look each other in the eyes or touch. If they've fallen apart this much already they won't be so close for much longer. Laney shook her head sadly as she watched them sit there and talk to Del but not to each other, and then she downed the rest of her drink.

Todd was wasted by the time they got home at two in the morning. He stumbled up the sidewalk, pulling Jill after him, and she pretended to trip and giggled loudly for Conrad and Lizzy's benefit, since they thought she'd been drinking all night.

Jill was extremely glad they'd gone out and been around other people, but she had still noticed the weirdness between herself and Todd. He had refused to let her buy any of her own drinks and had stayed by her side all night, but he hadn't said two words to her, really. He had talked to everyone else and so had she, but Todd had avoided eye contact with her all night and hadn't put his arm around her or anything, and he was usually pretty touchy-feely in a friendly, flirty way. Now she was surprised that he had grabbed her hand, and she was afraid of what he might say or do in his drunken state once they got inside. She just hoped he wouldn't say anything in front of Conrad and Lizzy.

Luckily Conrad and Lizzy went straight into Conrad's room when they got inside, and Todd, still holding Jill's hand, led her into his room and shut the door loudly. He could barely walk in a straight line and Jill groaned inwardly as he fell onto his back on the bed. Maybe he'll just pass out, she thought hopefully.

She took her toothbrush and pajamas and headed into the bathroom to get ready for bed.

"Jill!" Todd called a minute later. "Jill, where are you?"

Jill rolled her eyes at her reflection in the mirror. "In the bathroom," she replied in a patient tone a kindergarten teacher might use with students.

"Come out here."

"Hold on, I'll be out in a minute." When Jill finished in the bathroom she went and stood near the bed, looking down at Todd with her arms folded across her chest. "What?"

"Jill." Todd gave her a pleading look with his chocolate-colored, puppy-dog eyes. "Help me up." He held out his hands.

Jill rolled her eyes again and reached out to pull him up, but he pulled her down on top of him and started laughing.

Jill rolled off quickly and sat up beside him. "What do you want, Todd?"

"Jilly, I'm sorry." That damn puppy-dog look again that was so irresistible. Then his expression became more serious. "I mean I'm sorry about everything. Last night. I fucked up."

Jill felt a small smile of forgiveness coming, and she reached out to stroke his hair. "I just don't like how things were weird between us today. I just want to go back to normal, if we can."

"Me too," Todd said. "Me…fucking…too." He shook his head. "Jill," he said suddenly in a conspiratorial whisper. "Did you know I've always thought you were hot?"

Jill frowned and leaned away from him. "You have not, Todd. You're just drunk."

Todd shook his head again. "I swear. Always. I have always thought you were hot."

"Yeah? You've thought I was hot for how many years, like seven, and never tried anything with me? Yeah, right!"

"No, I mean, I don't know why I never tried, but I swear, I've always wanted to."

"Please, Todd," Jill said, refusing to believe him.

"Fine," he said, acting miffed. "Don't believe me. But I just thought you should know."

"Why?" Jill asked, and then wondered why she had even asked. He was trashed and she should have just let it go.

Todd shrugged, still on his back looking up at her. "I don't know. I just can't stop thinking about you. Damn it, Jill. I'm so fucking drunk right now."

"I know, hon," Jill said, smiling down at him. "Obviously you're wasted or you wouldn't be saying any of this."

"Probably not. But I should have said it a long time ago. Okay, honestly, just answer a question for me. If I would've tried something with you, like in high school, or in college, would you have done anything with me?"

"I have no idea," Jill lied. "I mean, in high school you were always with Melanie so I never really thought about it."

"Well, what about college then?"

"I honestly don't know, Todd. I just never really thought about it because I never thought you were even attracted to me so I never thought of it as an option." No, I only obsessed over it all through high school and part of college too, she acknowledged silently.

"Well, fuck, I guess I missed my chance to try," Todd said gloomily.

"Todd, come on," Jill said. "You don't even want me. You're just drunk."

"Whatever you say. If that's what you want to think."

"Well, I just think if all that was really true, you definitely would've tried something with me by now."

"Yeah, well, I don't know why the hell I haven't. I just know I'm fucking pissed at myself for it now. 'Cause I'll never have another chance now."

"You don't know that," Jill said, thinking, What the hell are you talking about, Jill?! "Who knows what'll happen in the future?"

"Well, you'll probably fuckin', like, be in love with Adam, so I know I sure as hell won't have a chance with you," Todd stated sullenly. "Not like I ever would've anyway."

"Oh, Todd, shut the hell up," Jill laughed. "Of course I would've given you a chance."

"Whatever, you're just saying that now 'cause you know you won't ever have to give me one now."

"I am not! Why are you being like this? You're just drunk." Jill said for about the millionth time. She was getting more and more confused as the conversation went on. She wasn't sure where this talk from Todd was coming from, and she wasn't sure why she hadn't put a stop to it yet. All she knew was she had an inescapable urge to figure out where it was leading.

"Oh, yeah, I'm so fucking drunk," Todd said irritably. "And I really don't mean any of this."

"Well, you wouldn't be saying it if you were sober!"

"Probably not, but I should 'cause maybe then you'd believe me. But whatever."

"Stop being all pouty!" Jill practically yelled, throwing her hands up in the air. "I don't know why you're saying I never would've given you a chance. I'm sure I would have, Todd."

"Whatever, you said you've never thought about me like that."

"Well, I haven't, really, but I mean, I've always thought you were good-looking and stuff…."

"Good-looking? Wow, thanks."

"Oh, shut up! You're hot, okay? I think you're hot."

"Really?"

"Yeah, really."

Todd raised his eyebrows and nodded slowly. Then in a less pouty, more that's-how-it-goes voice he said, "Well, fuck then, I guess I really should've tried something earlier. Damn." Then he rolled away from her as though he was going to sleep now.

There was no way Jill was leaving it at that. She was way too intrigued now. "Todd!"

"Jill."

"So what the fuck was this all about?"

"Wanna make out?" he asked, still facing away from her.

"What?!"

Todd rapidly turned around and sat up all in one motion and grabbed the back of her head, pulling her lips to his. It was a hard, sloppy kiss, and Jill loved it. Her stomach got that fluttery feeling in it, and she didn't even try to not kiss him back; she just went along with it, trying to match his fast pace as his tongue moved quickly yet almost carelessly all around the inside of her mouth.

"Yep," Todd said, pulling back. "I really fucked up, 'cause you're a really damn good kisser, Jill." Then he flopped on his side again, facing away from her, and left her gaping at him and trying to savor the taste of the best kiss she'd ever had.

On Sunday Todd was back to his normal self, somewhat. Jill thought it was partly an act, but at least he was trying. He didn't say anything about the night before, and Jill wondered how much he even remembered.

They slept in till noon and went to Taco Bell for lunch with Conrad and Lizzy. Todd was back to joking around with Jill and she felt an enormous sense of relief. She was still not over the jolt Todd had given her with that kiss last night, but she didn't want to think about it until she was away from him. And maybe not even then because she was scared where those thoughts might lead. She'd spent so much time, so many *years*, getting to the point where she could be around Todd without wanting to get on him or wishing he was her boyfriend. This was *not* the right time for all that to go down the drain!

Laney called and said she'd pick Jill up around four, so after lunch Jill, Todd, Conrad, and Lizzy all went back to the apartment and laid around lazily watching *Best in Show*. It was the type of Sunday afternoon Jill loved and she didn't want it to end.

When the movie was over, it was almost four and Jill went into Todd's room to gather up her stuff. Todd followed her in and stood there watching her, running his hands through his hair.

"So, unfortunately," he said with a wry grin, "I remember most of last night, I think…."

Jill looked up with a hint of a smile around the corners of her mouth and waited.

"Yeah, so I'm really sorry about that. I was obviously wasted."

Jill laughed. "It's okay. I kept telling you that you were only saying that shit because you were drunk!"

"Yeah, well, I'm not sure I remember everything I said, but it's probably better that way. I do remember kissing you though, and I know I wasn't lying when I said you were good." He gave her a half-smile, half-challenging-stare.

Jill shook her head and smiled, looking away. "Well, thanks, I guess."

"Well, anyway, Jill," Todd said, holding his arms out for a hug. Jill got up and went over to him, knowing it might be their last hug for a while, because she wasn't sure when she'd see him again. "I'm sorry I was shitty about Adam," Todd continued. "I really do hope it works out for the two of you. Just call me if you need anything. Seriously. Like if you need me to come beat his ass for you." Todd grinned and ruffled Jill's hair, pulling back and looking her in the eyes. "But seriously, you know I'm here for you."

"I know, Todd, thanks so much. You've been so great." Jill hugged him again and held on tightly for a minute. When she finally backed up and let him go, her smile was sad, but not as bad as it had been on Friday when she first got to Eastern. She patted his arm. "Bye, Todd."

"Bye, Jilly Bean."

Her phone rang and it was Laney. She was outside.

Todd carried Jill's bag out to Laney's car and after saying goodbye to Lancy he gave Jill a quick kiss on the cheek and opened her door for her. She waved at him and he gave her a small smile. As Laney turned her car around and started for the front of the apartment complex, Jill looked over her shoulder back toward Todd's apartment to see if he was still there, but he was already gone.

🍁   🍁   🍁

Todd went straight to his room when he got back inside and shut the door. He collapsed in his computer chair and stared at the ceiling. He felt like he was going to burst. It had taken more self-control than he'd known he had to act normal and goof around with Jill today. He had tried to make last night into a joke, when it was about the last thing he could imagine finding funny. He remembered more than he'd let on to Jill, and he knew it hadn't just been him being drunk and horny or whatever. Everything he'd said to her was true and he'd known it was his only chance to get it out. Jill's refusal to believe him and the way she had laughed off the whole thing had killed him inside.

She had kissed him back though. At least he had that little satisfaction. He wasn't sorry at all for having kissed her, because after she denied ever having thought about him that way, well now that should give her something to think about at least. Plus he had just needed to kiss her. Just to know for sure. He'd been right, of course; it'd been amazing. Even though that knowledge made it even harder not to be able to have her, he was still glad he'd done it.

You fucking idiot! he repeated over and over to himself. You probably made the hugest fucking mistake of your life by not doing anything sooner! He couldn't remember ever feeling so shitty or hating himself so much.

It was a pretty quiet drive back to Dale. Laney talked about Del a lot at first, then mentioned to Jill that she'd noticed Jill and Todd acting "weird" around each other last night. Jill explained in a voice that sounded tired and confused that things had been uncomfortable because Todd had kissed her and she had no idea what it meant and thought he might have been embarrassed about it. She didn't tell Laney he had kissed her again after getting home from the bars last night.

Laney was shocked by this tidbit of information and wondered if she had been wrong about Jill telling Todd about the pregnancy. The kiss would have been more than enough to explain their awkward and unusual behavior toward each other. Laney didn't have much insight to offer Jill about what the kiss could've meant, and when Jill said she was sure Todd had just been drunk, Laney agreed that was probably it. She didn't think about the fact that Todd had been out with her and Del all night on Friday before kissing Jill and hadn't had anything to drink at all.

After that Jill dozed on and off the rest of the way home, and Laney wondered silently if Todd really had a thing for Jill. She knew Jill had always had a little bit of a thing for Todd, and she wondered how much this could mess up things with Jill and Adam. What a fucking soap opera! she thought, not afraid to admit to herself that she was as interested and amused as she was sympathetic for Jill, and she couldn't wait to see what would happen next.

April 2004

That week Jill went on another date with Adam on Tuesday night. They went to O'Charley's and then watched a movie at his apartment, and Jill spent the night. On Thursday she went to the Turtle with the girls and Adam came home with her. On Friday Adam, Justin, and Ryan had a party, so Jill spent the night there, and on Saturday everybody went out to the campus bars together. "Everybody" included Jared, Kate, Park, and Britt. It was the first time Jill or Hilton had seen Britt since that night at Adam's when everyone still thought it was Hilton who was pregnant. They hadn't seen Kate since spring break. Hilton was casually polite to Kate and Britt, but basically ignored them and spent her time with Luke and the girls, taking at least one shot at every bar they went to and always going to the bar with Jill when she needed another drink so no one else could hear her order a plain Coke or cranberry juice. Jill and Hilton both noticed Kate and Britt watching Hilton take shot after shot and whispering, and Hilton gave Jill a private little grin that said, Those stupid bitches have no idea! Jill laughed back, and Hilton was glad to see a twinkle in her eyes.

Things with Adam were looking more serious, and Hilton was relieved and excited for Jill. She told Luke she wanted to have a double date with Jill and Adam, so on Sunday night Luke and Hilton cooked at Luke's apartment, and Jill and Adam came over for dinner. They had spaghetti, and afterwards they all sat around and played euchre. Jill and Hilton won every game they played and gave the boys hell about it. After Jill dealt Hilton a loner in the second game, Luke said sarcastically to Adam, "Dude, can't you fucking control your girlfriend?! She's stackin' the deck over there!"

Jill's eyes flashed to Hilton's, then down to the table. "I'm not his girlfriend," she said quickly, afraid Adam might freak out if he thought people saw their relationship that way. She didn't want him to think she'd given Hilton and Luke the impression they were together. Damn it, Luke! she shouted silently.

But Adam just smiled nonchalantly and said, "Dude, what can I do? She's too damn good."

"I don't cheat, by the way," Jill said, narrowing her eyes at Luke, hoping to get the message across that he'd said a stupid thing.

But he didn't seem to get it. He just grinned at her and said, "I know, Jilly, just kiddin'."

Jill glared at him a moment longer, then looked at Hilton and rolled her eyes, but Hilton had a sly smile on her face, as though pleased with Luke. She gave Jill a very slight shrug of her shoulders as if to say, Oh well, what can you do?

By the time Jill and Adam left, Jill was feeling really happy about the way the night had gone, because it would be great to have another couple to hang out with. Another couple?! she thought suddenly, taken aback. Slow down, girl, you don't even know how long this is gonna last! You're not even part of a couple yet, so you don't really need other couples to hang around with! She hoped Adam wasn't freaked out about what Luke had said, and she tried making conversation on the way home so he wouldn't think about it.

"Hey, Jill," Adam cut her off as he pulled into a parking space in front of her apartment building. "Can we talk for a sec?"

Shit! Jill said silently while saying, "Sure," aloud and managing to sound a mix of curious and cheerful.

Adam pressed a hand to the top of the steering wheel and stared straight ahead. Jill's heart sank.

"So…" Adam finally started, "when you said you weren't my girlfriend, did you just mean that you aren't, or that you don't want to be?"

"What?" Jill asked, flustered. "I mean, I just meant that I'm not. I like how we are right now…." She had no idea what kind of answer he was looking for and she was sure that wouldn't be it. Adam turned to face her, keeping his hand pressed to the steering wheel. He looked almost…nervous?

"So I guess what I'm asking," Adam continued, "is would you ever be interested in being my girlfriend?"

Jill still had no idea what kind of answer he was looking for, so she decided to just be honest. "Well, yeah, I would definitely want to be your girlfriend. But don't feel pressured or anything, because like I said, I like how things are right now and I'm fine with just seeing how things go and what happens." She felt like she had a scared puppy-dog expression on her face but didn't break the eye contact. He was still staring intently at her, as though trying to read her.

"Well, I really like you, Jill, just so you know." He glanced away quickly and Jill thought he took a deep breath before turning back. "And I know I'm not the kind of guy you would probably pick for a boyfriend, and you probably can't even imagine me with a girlfriend, and I'll be honest; I didn't get into this looking for a relationship." He paused and Jill held her breath. "But fuck it, I just can't stop thinking about you and I would totally understand if don't feel the same way or just don't want me as a boyfriend…but I'd really like it if you were my girlfriend."

Jill hoped the darkness hid her gaping mouth. *Say something!* she reminded herself after staring at him speechlessly for a moment.

"Um, wow," she stuttered. "Yeah, I am really surprised that you want a girlfriend, and I never expected that out of this, but I really like you too." She leaned over and kissed him, cupping his face in her hands.

Adam grinned and touched his forehead to hers. "So was that a yes?" he asked teasingly.

"Yes," Jill said, grinning back at him. "Yes!" She giggled and then kissed him again, longer and deeper this time.

"Wanna come in?" she asked him between kisses.

"I can't; I actually have homework and shit to do tonight. 'Cause I've been with you every other night and I really need to get at least a 2.0 this semester!" he added teasingly. "But I could spare a few more minutes in the car…."

Fifteen minutes later when Jill finally extracted herself from the car, she blew him a kiss and winked before shutting the door. "Night, boyfriend!" she called with a silly, teasing grin, and Adam grinned back at her.

"Night, girlfriend."

Jill flew up the steps to her apartment, digging her cell phone out of her purse as she went. She stopped just outside her door and leaned back against the wall while she called Hilton. She had to tell her first, before Nat and Laney.

"I have a boyfriend!" Jill practically screamed as soon as Hilton answered, and giggled uncontrollably as she heard Hilton's giddy shriek in return.

"Woooooo! Hell yeah, get it Jilly!" Hilton exclaimed. "I knew it'd work out!"

"Oh, my gosh, I am still in shock!" Jill cried. "Thanks, Luke! Aaahhh!"

Hilton giggled. "I thought that comment from Luke might help things out!"

"Did you tell him to say it?"

"Maybe…." Hilton said mischievously.

"That was risky, Hilton!"

"Yeah, but it worked! See, I know what I'm doing!" Both girls started giggling and screaming again, and finally Jill hung up and went into the apartment.

"I have a boyfriend!" she yelled as she walked in, and Natalie and Laney ran out of their rooms to hear the story.

"Awww, that is so cute!" Natalie cried.

"Woohoo, we both have a boyfriend now!" Laney exclaimed, hugging Jill.

"Yeah, now I'm the only single one! That blows," Natalie said, laughing. "I have yet to meet a college guy that would make a good boyfriend! How do you guys all find them?" Natalie had been single as long as Jill had known her, and although she'd had a serious boyfriend in high school, she had never shown a real interest in having one in college. It wasn't that she was against having a relationship; she would if she found the right guy, but she liked being single and felt that a lot of college boys weren't ready for serious commitments anyway, so she might as well have fun while she could. Jill had always identified with Natalie prior to this whole Adam thing.

Jill could barely keep from bouncing up and down, and after about five minutes of trying to watch a movie with Laney and Natalie she went into her room where she could dance around some more and grin at herself in the mirror. Maybe things would actually work out now; this was better than she could ever have imagined! She still had to tell him, but this was a major step in the right direction and she was closer than she'd been before. She refused to think anything negative about what could happen when she told him, and focused instead on how amazing this whole night had been. My prayers worked! she thought, blowing a kiss skyward. Thank You, God! I guess this is how things were supposed to turn out! Maybe Adam and I *are* meant to be together! She twirled around and around in front of the mirror, never wanting the blissful moment to end.

It was the same party at her apartment, and Adam was leaving with the cute brunette in the off-the-shoulder top who'd been hanging all over him the whole night. Jill looked quickly away and pretended not to see, not in the mood for sympathy from Laney or Hilton, with whom she was dancing. She hoped they hadn't even seen because she just wanted to have fun tonight. But how could she now? Even in her drunken state, she felt her mood darken and she tried to block it out by flashing a smile at the girls and dancing faster, trying to lose herself in the music.

Justin walked by with a shot, and Jill grabbed it out of his hand and swallowed it quickly.

"Yeah, Jill!" Justin nodded and grinned, starting to dance behind her.

"Hell yeah!" Jill screamed, but her voice got lost in the music and the swirl of other voices. Then Todd stepped in front of her and she was dancing with both him and Justin. She ran her hands over Todd's ass jokingly and he turned around, grinning, to dance face to face with her.

"Yeah, baby," he said as he shimmied up against her and they grinned drunkenly at each other. He ran his hands down Jill's sides playfully.

Jill hadn't even noticed Justin was no longer behind her, but now she saw him dancing with Laney. Out of the corner of her eye she saw Hilton watching her and Todd and smiling. She rolled her eyes at Hilton, because she knew Hilton wanted her and Todd to hook up, but this was just like so many times before. But since Adam was with that other girl, she might as well enjoy this! She lifted her arms above her head and suddenly Todd grabbed her around the waist and dipped her back. They both almost fell, but Todd managed to keep her in his arms and they both came back up laughing hysterically.

"Was that your *Dirty Dancing* move?" Jill giggled, with her arms sloppily around Todd's neck.

"Hell no. You wanna see my *Dirty Dancing* move?" Todd asked with a teasing challenge in his eyes. With his arms still around her waist, he threw her head and shoulders back and moved her upper body in a circle before bringing her back up again. She whipped her head up so that it came up inches from his face.

"Sexy," she breathed in a fake seductive voice.

"Hell yeah it is," Todd said arrogantly, then started kissing her sloppily, running his tongue all over the outside of her mouth.

Jill giggled and leaned away. "Yuck, Todd! My face! You're a sucky kisser!"

"Oh, yeah?" Todd eyes glinted impishly as he grabbed her again and kissed her for real, hard and deep with his tongue roaming the inside of her stunned mouth. "Don't even try to tell me you didn't like that," he said confidently when he pulled back from her.

"Oh no, baby, I loved it," Jill said sarcastically, running her hands through his hair in an exaggerated manner. "Give me more! Please! I can't wait!" She sank into him, and to her surprise and secret delight, he kissed her again, and this time she kissed him back.

"Get it, Jill!" she heard Laney yell, and then she didn't hear anything; all she could feel or think about was Todd and his body and lips pressed against hers.

Jill awoke with a start and sat straight up in bed, taking a minute to get her bearings. When she did she was pissed. What the fuck?! she thought. Why do I have to dream about Todd now? This is not good….I actually got what I wanted and Adam is my boyfriend and he's who I should be with anyway…well, okay, who was I kidding earlier, maybe not who I *should* be with or was meant to be with but who I am with now because I got myself into this situation, and plus, I really like Adam; it's not like this situation is the only reason I'm with him….But, damn it, why do I have to think about Todd?! Why did he have to kiss me last weekend? Ugh, he was so fuckin' good….Jill could still taste the kiss from the dream; it had been so real and she hated that her first emotion upon waking up had been disappointment that it was a dream.

But it *was* just a dream, she told herself now, lying back down. It was just a dream, and tomorrow I won't even think of it anymore because I'll be with Adam, my *boyfriend*! She smiled giddily into her pillow at the thought and drifted back off to sleep, with Todd for the moment pushed out of her mind.

That weekend Adam went home with Jill for Easter. She had been thrilled when he invited himself. If he wanted to meet her family he must be really serious about her. She hadn't been planning on telling her family she was pregnant until she was home for the summer, and now this was the perfect chance for them to meet Adam and hopefully love him to death, which would, with any luck, soften the blow when she told them, because at least it wouldn't be as if she was pregnant by some random guy. She had been thanking God all week for the fact that Adam was now her boyfriend, because that would put things on a totally different level when she told her parents.

She had told her family she was bringing a "surprise" for them, because they were laid back enough that she knew they wouldn't mind having an unexpected guest all weekend.

She called Todd on Friday afternoon before she left for home because she knew he was going home for the weekend too. She'd been so busy with Adam and school that she'd hardly been on AIM lately, so she hadn't talked to him since she'd been at Eastern two weeks ago.

"Todd, guess what!" she gushed. "Adam asked me out, like, he's my boyfriend now!"

"Wow, well congratulations; that's good for you guys, then," Todd said, sounding vaguely surprised and not at all overjoyed.

"Oh, come on, Todd, I know you don't like him, but it really is a good thing for me, and I really think he's serious about this, and about me, 'cause he's coming home with me today. And it was his idea. So I think he really wants to meet my family and stuff, so that sounds pretty serious, right?"

"Yeah, it does," Todd said, and he sounded a little more like he was happy for her. "Sorry I'm not the biggest Adam fan, but I'll try. I'm really happy for you, Jilly Bean."

Jill smiled into the phone. "Thanks so much, Todd," she said sincerely. "I love you so much. You're so great. I'll give you a call this weekend, okay? Agh, I really hope my parents like him....I'm not telling them till the summer so this really needs to go well."

"I'm sure it will; don't worry about it," Todd said.

"Yeah, thanks, I'll try," Jill replied. "Okay, well I gotta go, but I'll call you; have a good drive home."

"You too, Jill."

"All right, bye, Todd."

"Bye, Jilly."

Jill smiled and pressed her phone to her heart for a moment as she hung up. *I love Todd to death; he's such a sweetie!* she thought.

She hopped off her bed and picked up her bag, swinging it over her shoulder and grabbing her purse and keys as she headed out of the bedroom. She said goodbye to Natalie, who was the only one who hadn't left for the weekend yet, and headed out to pick up Adam. She couldn't wait to spend the whole weekend with him.

As Luke threw some clothes into a gym bag to take home for Easter, his mind drifted to the question that had never been answered and had remotely bothered him for the last couple of weeks. He still had no idea what the real story was behind Hilton's pregnancy test. She had been back to her normal self ever since she'd told him it'd been a false alarm, but he didn't buy that story for a minute. He'd known her for two and a half years now, and he was confident that meant he knew her pretty damn well.

After she'd first told him the false-alarm story, he'd felt that her normal behavior was all an act she was putting on for his benefit, or more for her own benefit, he thought bitterly, because it sure as hell didn't benefit him any.

But as her behavior had remained normal over the past couple of weeks, he had started to forget his suspicions, because it honestly didn't seem like she was being shady. Whenever the false-alarm story would pop back into his head, he would do a double-take and wind up more confused than he'd ever been. Maybe I don't know her at all, he thought to himself now, as he signed off AIM, shut down his computer and tossed an extra pair of shoes into his bag. I was so sure that story was a lie, but I really don't think the way she's acting now is fake. Could she really lie like that and then blow it off so easily that she doesn't even feel guilty around me? What the *fuck* was the deal with that pregnancy test? He had to know. It was driving him crazy, and Hilton had no idea, because he was putting on an act too. That thought made him feel a little proud of himself, in an ironic and sickening sort of way.

"I guess I can do it too, if you can," he muttered disgustedly.

But he really couldn't go on like this; there was no way. It was about time he got this bullshit figured out. He told himself determinedly that he would ask Hilton about it on the drive to his house today, since she was going home with him for Easter, and he wouldn't let her get away with any more of her shitty, fake, beat-around-the-bush, flat-out fucking lies.

It did not go well. Hilton seemed confused when he first asked her about it, confused as to why he would bring it up again. When she realized he had never believed her, the confusion changed into bewildered surprise, which slowly morphed into all-out fury when he got kind of shitty with her about it and still refused to believe her.

"How could you possibly think I'm lying?" Hilton screamed. "What other fucking explanation could there possibly be?! I thought I was pregnant, took the test, and I wasn't! What do you *want* to hear? Do you want me to be pregnant? Fine, I lied, I am pregnant!" She stared at him with wide brown eyes. Luke had always found her eyes mesmerizing. The color was like a mix between caramel and chocolate. He looked away quickly and focused on the road.

"No, I don't want to hear that you're pregnant. I want to hear the fucking truth! Don't fucking bullshit with me anymore, Hilton. I know you and I know you were lying about it being a false alarm."

"Oh, my gosh, I don't even know what to say. This is the stupidest argument I've ever had! You apparently believe me that I'm not pregnant, but you don't believe it was a false alarm. That doesn't even make any fucking sense, Luke! What the fuck else could it be besides one of those two things?!" She felt like pulling her hair out. It didn't even occur to her to just tell him the truth about Jill; she was just pissed at this point that he was being so ridiculous and that he had waited however many weeks to bring it up again.

"I don't fucking know what else it could be, Hilton. That's what I'm asking you! But it's obviously something pretty damn bad that you don't wanna tell me about."

"What, do you think I fucked another guy? I fucked another guy and thought I was pregnant from him?" Hilton yelled in frustration. "Maybe that's what you think!"

Luke felt a wave of nausea beginning. "So is that it?" He couldn't even bear to think that it might be.

Hilton was speechless. She stared at Luke with her mouth hanging open, not really seeing him.

"Well?" he asked coldly, not taking his eyes off the road.

Hilton suddenly felt empty inside. She turned away from him and faced the passenger-side window, folding her hands in her lap. "Yeah, that's it," she said dispassionately, and it sounded to her as if someone else was saying it. Her voice sounded strange and hollow and she couldn't even believe she was having this discussion.

A moment later Luke punched the steering wheel and the car veered to the side a little, but Hilton didn't move. She just stared out the window at nothing.

"Well, you can take me back if you want, since we're not too far from school yet," she said uninterestedly a minute later. "I'll give you some gas money."

"No, I'm not fucking taking you back. You're coming home with me," Luke snapped, and even though Hilton didn't turn to look at him, she could tell he was still staring straight ahead. She thought about arguing with him, because it was going to be one hell of an uncomfortable weekend now, but she changed her mind because she didn't feel like wasting the energy.

❧   ❧   ❧

Todd was bored out of his mind. He'd sat at home all night Friday and it looked like it'd be the same way tonight. He knew some of his friends from high school were home for the weekend too, and a couple of them had called to invite him to a party. He had planned on going, but he just didn't feel like it now. He felt like lying around on his ass and feeling sorry for himself.

While he was playing a video game, his mom had come down to the basement and asked him why he wasn't going out with Jill tonight, and Todd had dully responded that she'd brought her boyfriend home. His mother's face had fallen and she had given him a sympathetic, all-knowing look that pissed him off.

"Don't give me that look. It's no big deal. Why would I care about her boyfriend? It just sucks having shit to do all weekend." He turned his attention back to the game and refused to look at his mom again, because that damn look almost made him feel like crying. He hated that somebody else could spot his vulnerability.

Get a fuckin' grip, man! he scoffed at himself. What the fuck is your problem?! He shook his head and continued to stare at the TV screen, trying to force everything but the game from his mind.

When his phone rang he heard it somewhere in the back of his mind, and it didn't really register with him until it rang again right away and then someone left a voicemail. He figured it was his friends wanting him to go to that party, so he didn't check it right away. Finally when he got to a break in his game he shuffled slowly over to the table where his phone was to listen to his message. It was Jill saying, "Damn it, Todd, why aren't you answering your phone? I need your help; I really want you to come out with me and Adam tonight 'cause I'm gonna take him to a couple bars, 'cause he wants me to, but he's gonna try to buy my drinks and I won't be able to drink them! I don't know how I'm gonna pull that one off, because my freakin' parents actually offered to pick us up so we could both drink! Plus you should come so you and Adam can hang out 'cause I really want you to like him. Todd, you know how much it means to me; please do this for me! I'll love you so much for it! Call me back; bye, babe."

Todd hung up and went back to the TV without returning her call.

She called again at nine, but he didn't answer. He knew she was getting ready to go out and would just beg him to go, and that was the last thing he wanted to do. The thought of it almost made him sick.

Finally at ten he got sick of video games and decided he had to do something other than sit around all night. He called Dirk, one of his baseball buddies from high school, and said he'd decided to go to the party. He quickly took a shower and then headed out to Dirk's to have a couple beers before hitting up the party.

By 12:30 he was pretty wasted. He'd had four beers at Dirk's, and at least six or seven more since they'd gotten to the party. It was mostly all the guys he'd hung out with in high school, and a couple of their girlfriends. One of the girlfriends had brought a hot friend Todd had never seen before. Her name was Mandy and she seemed a little out-of-place and bored, since everyone else knew each other.

"Dude, get on that shit!" a drunken Dirk urged Todd, laughing. "Seriously, man. I would, but Hillary's on her way." He grinned at Todd and punched him in the shoulder.

Todd grinned back, then ambled over to where Mandy was standing off to the side of a group of people.

"Hey, I'm Todd." He offered his hand and she shook it. "You look bored. Here, let me get you another drink."

Mandy smiled and let him lead her into the garage where the keg was set up. Twenty minutes later they were making out in a shadowy corner of the garage when Todd's phone rang. He ignored it, but when it rang again immediately Mandy backed up a little bit and said, "You better answer that."

Todd groaned and pulled his phone out of his pocket. He glanced at the screen. Just as he'd thought. "I don't fuckin' wanna talk to her," he muttered.

Mandy peered at the phone. "Who's 'Jilly Bean'?"

"Just my friend, Jill." As the phone started to ring a third time, Todd rolled his eyes and finally answered. "Hello?"

"Todd!" Jill squealed giddily. She was obviously drunk. Todd blinked. Wait, she couldn't be drunk….

"You finally answered; I'm so happy!" Jill cried. "Where the hell are you?"

"At a friend's," Todd replied dully. "Look, Jill, I'm kinda busy…."

"Jill?" asked Tyler Bennett, whose house it was, as he walked past. "Jill Sherer?"

Todd nodded with a sinking feeling in his stomach.

"Tell her to get the hell over here!" Bennett yelled, then came up and grabbed the phone out of Todd's hand.

"Jill, sweetie, hey! Why aren't you here?…He didn't tell you?" Bennett gave Todd a weird look, then said, "Oh…I see. Well you guys should come on over for awhile! Everybody's out here. All right, awesome, see ya."

He handed the phone back to Todd and narrowed his eyes at him. "Why didn't you tell Jill, man? Hey, she and her boyfriend are gonna stop by, hope it's not a problem." He clapped Todd on the shoulder and headed into the house.

Todd glared after him as he shoved his phone back into his pocket.

"So what's the deal with your 'friend Jill'?" Mandy asked, putting her arms around his waist.

"Nothing, she's just an old friend," Todd said, lowering his lips to Mandy's.

When Jill hung up from Bennett, she smoothed her hair in the mirror of the bathroom and left to go meet Adam outside the bar, trying not to show how irritated she was. Why was Todd being so weird? She was pissed he hadn't called her back earlier and that he had blown her off just now. If Bennett hadn't heard Todd say her name, she never would've found out about the party. Couldn't he at least give Adam a fucking chance?

"Hey, do you care if we go to a party for a little bit?" she asked Adam casually. "It's a bunch of people from high school, and I want you to meet them."

"Sure," Adam said. "That's cool." They headed toward Jill's car. She had finally convinced her parents that she would just drive, so they would stay home and she'd have an excuse not to drink.

Adam was pretty drunk, and he joked around with Jill most of the way to the party. She laughed with him, but didn't really feel it. She couldn't get over Todd being shady.

When they got to Bennett's, Bennett and Dirk and some of the other guys came up to her right away and wanted to meet Adam. Jill started to feel a little better because she loved showing him off, and Dirk's girlfriend Hillary whispered, "He's *sooooo* hot!" and winked at Jill, which brought out a genuinely happy smile from Jill.

Bennett went to get Adam a beer, and Adam and Jill approached the bonfire where Todd was standing with some girl Jill had never seen before. She hated the instant feeling of jealousy. You're being ridiculous! she snapped at herself.

"Hey, Todd," she said carelessly as she and Adam walked up. "You've met Adam."

"Hey, man," Adam said, reaching out to shake Todd's hand.

"What's up," Todd responded, shaking Adam's hand casually. "This is Mandy. Jill, Adam."

"Hi, guys," Mandy said, putting her hand through Todd's arm. Jill hated her immediately, but plastered on a fake smile anyway.

"So did your parents bring you here?" Todd asked Jill, taking a swig of beer. "I thought they were driving so you could drink."

Jill stared at him, narrowing her eyes a little bit. He refused to acknowledge her look. "Um, no, I decided I didn't really want to drink tonight," she said finally.

"Oh, why not?" Todd asked, taking another drink of beer and putting his arm around Mandy, drawing her up against him.

"I don't know," Jill said, trying not to show how pissed she was now. "Just didn't really feel like it, and I thought Adam and I would have more fun if my parents weren't out with us." She grinned at Adam and gave him a long kiss, hoping that would piss Todd off, since he apparently hated Adam so much.

"Well, we're gonna go inside," Todd said, leading Mandy toward the house. "Catch you guys later."

"Later, man," Adam said.

Jill turned and kissed Adam again to suppress her anger, and then led him over to talk to Hillary and a group of her guy friends who were standing around a little ways away from the fire. She smiled and joked around with them for half an hour or so. At one point Dirk said, "Hey, where are Todd and that chick? Uh-oh...." He winked at Jill and grinned. "He's gettin' some ass!"

Jill giggled in response and said, "Hell, yeah, he is!" She clung to Adam as an automatic response to the unbearable and unacceptable jealousy and hurt she felt, and Dirk had no idea anything was wrong. Hillary, an old best friend who knew Jill had been obsessed with Todd in high school, gave Jill a curious look, but Jill pretended not to notice. When she and Adam left fifteen minutes later, Todd and Mandy hadn't come back from the house and Adam had no idea anything was wrong either.

Adam was still drunk and was all over Jill on the way home. By the time they got back to her house she was feeling much better because she was thinking about Adam and how hot he looked right now in his green and white striped shirt and faded jeans, and the ever-present black hair band, of course. Jill smiled to herself as she thought of that, and after she parked in the driveway, she and Adam made out for a couple of minutes. He tasted good even though he'd been drinking all night, and Jill loved his tongue because it was so long and seemed to just devour her.

"Hey, come to the basement with me," Adam whispered loudly to Jill as they went inside. "Ssshh, your parents will never know." He gave her a silly grin and put his finger over his lips.

"Okay," Jill grinned back devilishly. "But we have to be quiet."

"OKAY," Adam replied in an exaggerated whisper. Jill giggled and led him down to the basement, where he was sleeping in the guest bedroom for the weekend. She shut the door behind them and turned off the lights.

"Come over here," Adam said from the bed, and Jill went.

Because Adam was drunk, he was sloppier than normal, and Jill loved it because it felt almost animal and the raw, hungry passion thrilled her. It was some of the best sex she and Adam had ever had. Jill cuddled with him afterwards until he passed out, which wasn't long, then went upstairs to her room feeling relaxed and lazily content.

The next morning at church Jill felt extremely happy and proud to have Adam there, but it also made her feel like a hypocrite. All these people probably think it's so nice I brought my boyfriend home from college and he's going to church with my family, she thought sourly. But what would they think if they knew I was pregnant? I guess they will know sooner or later…and he will too, she thought dejectedly. Things were going so well this weekend and she hated that it had to end and she had to face the reality of telling Adam, then all her friends and her parents. This was her last chance to enjoy her hometown as Jill Sherer, the smart, innocent, perfect daughter and citizen, etc. Next time she came home she'd be Jill Sherer, who had gotten pregnant before she even graduated college, and who wasn't even planning on getting married. What a shame for such a good girl to turn out like that. Her poor parents.

Jill rolled her eyes. She knew that's what everyone in town would say and think, and it really upset her because she had always enjoyed being liked by everyone, including all the adults, and had enjoyed her reputation as a smart, nice, good-girl who had so much potential. Damn small town, she thought to herself. I hate how they'll all gossip about me. Suddenly she was really angry. This is 2004, she thought. It's not like it's a big scandal to have sex before you're married, or even to be pregnant before you're married. But that's how all these people will see it, because they're so close-minded.

Then all of a sudden she felt extremely sorry for her parents, and even more so for Aaron and Winnie, whose friends would give them tons of shit about their sister being in college, unmarried, and pregnant. Not only did I screw up my own life, I screwed up theirs, too. This was something that hadn't really occurred to her before, and she really hated herself now. She sat through the rest of the church service unable to concentrate, but after she took Communion she prayed hard for God to forgive her for being so selfish and to please not make it too hard on her parents and

Aaron and Winnie, and for the people in her town to be more open-minded and less gossipy. Afterwards, as she introduced Adam to people, she felt like she was lying to their faces because she was pretending to be innocent or something.

When her family got back home they did an Easter egg hunt around the house, and Adam had a basket too, because Jill and Winnie had made one for him yesterday when they were dyeing eggs. Enjoying such a childish pleasure made Jill feel even more hypocritical because she was acting so silly, as though she was ten again, but she was hiding the secret that proved she was definitely not a wholesome little girl anymore. She didn't know how she'd ever manage to tell her family. It was too frightening to even think about anymore. Maybe if she stayed at school for the summer, and then had the baby and gave it up for adoption, her parents would never know. When she realized she was seriously considering this idea she thought she might be losing touch with reality completely and felt as if she was in a dream. Wished she was in a dream, actually. *Needed* to be in a dream, and for all of this not to be real. She felt panicky.

Later, before she and Adam left to head back to school, Jill's mom told her how much the whole family liked Adam. "We're so happy for you, Jill," she said genuinely. "I've heard you talk about him before and I know you liked him, so way to go!" She laughed and hugged Jill, who hugged her back half-heartedly. "What's wrong?"

Jill shook her head quickly. "Oh, nothing, I'm just afraid it won't work out and I really like him…."

"Oh, don't think like that," her mother said. "It'll be fine. He likes you so much; it's obvious. Winnie is so jealous," she added with a smile. "She thinks he's so hot."

That got a smile out of Jill. "He *is* hot," she said, raising her eyebrows as if to say, how could you question that?! "Brad Pitt, baby!" She and her mom grinned at each other.

After the blow-up in the car on the way home, Luke's weekend with Hilton went a hundred times better than he would've expected. Hilton had barely said two words to him the rest of the three-hour drive down, but as soon as they got to his house she jumped out of the car with her usual energy and ran in to greet his parents excitedly. He knew his family had no idea anything was wrong, because around them Hilton was always smiling and joking around and holding Luke's hand, and at their Easter picnic she had played Frisbee with his younger brother and the family dog, then run over to where Luke was sitting with his parents and thrown her arms around him happily and easily. They were outwardly the perfect couple, as they'd always been.

But whenever they were alone, which wasn't often because Hilton managed to avoid that situation as much as possible, she barely acknowledged him. It was the first time she was glad of his parents' rule that she got the guest bedroom while she was there, and instead of sneaking into Luke's room late every night, she went to bed when his parents did, and when he tried to kiss her in private once, she leaned away and said, "Don't touch me," in a cool, quiet voice.

On Saturday night they went out with Luke's friends to a bar, and Hilton was basically the same way she'd been around his parents, acting as though she and Luke were fine. She wasn't as all-over him as she normally would've been, but she didn't ignore him or shove him away when he touched her. She danced with him and got drunk with him, but still went right to the guest room as soon as they got back to his house.

The ride back to school Sunday afternoon after the picnic started out in complete silence, with Hilton staring out the window again, and finally Luke couldn't stand the silence anymore.

"So what the fuck is your deal?" he asked, irritated as hell with her. "You can manage to be nice to me and act like you like me in front of other people but when we're alone you can't even talk to me?"

"I didn't want to embarrass you or hurt you in front of your family," Hilton said, still looking out the window. "I didn't think it'd be right to have a scene in front of them, and I really like them. I wasn't faking having fun."

"But you were faking when you hugged me in front of them, and acted like we were okay?"

"I guess. Yeah, I was. I thought it was the best thing to do."

"So what now?"

Hilton turned to face him with a look that said, What, you don't know?

Luke sarcastically imitated her look and then faced the road again.

Hilton sighed sadly. "Well, I'm assuming nothing's changed since Friday and you still don't believe me about the pregnancy test?"

"No, it hasn't." Then Luke sighed too, and his shoulders slumped. He glanced over at Hilton. "Look, Hilton, you have me so confused. You're right, I haven't changed the fact that I don't believe your story, but just seeing you with my family this weekend, and how perfect you are with them, and how much I love you….Hilton, you're so perfect for me. And I don't believe your story and I want to know the truth but damn it, I just love you so much." He stared out the front window.

Hilton felt herself melt a little bit, and smiled at his profile, but it was a sad smile. "Well," she began. "What if I told you you were right; I did lie about the pregnancy test; it wasn't a false alarm but I'm not pregnant either, but I still can't tell you what the truth is right now? It doesn't even have anything to do with you or me, but I can't tell you right now?"

Luke shrugged his shoulders disconsolately. "What the hell is that supposed to mean?" he asked.

"Well, it means I can't tell you but you don't need to worry about it because it doesn't have anything to do with me or with you at all. So you've been worrying over nothing."

"Oh, that really helps," Luke muttered, starting to get pissed again. "If it's really not a big deal, and isn't anything I should worry about, why can't you tell me? I'm sorry, Hilton, but I can't live with something like that between us in this relationship. I don't need any big fuckin' secrets."

Hilton glared at him. "That's the exact reason I can't tell you, Luke! Because it's not about this relationship! It's not about you!"

"So who is it about? Some other guy?"

"Oh, my gosh, are you really fucking serious? We're back to that now? Did you actually just say that? You know what, Luke, I think maybe we shouldn't see each other for a while."

Hilton breathed out slowly, shocked at her own words.

Luke looked as though he was starting to say something, then stopped for a minute as though he'd changed his mind, then finally snapped, "Fine, since that's obviously what you want."

"Of course it's not what I want, Luke! But you don't trust me, you don't believe me, you won't stop making shitty comments about other guys who don't even exist....I just can't deal with this shit! So I think we shouldn't be together right now."

"You're right," Luke said dismissively. "I don't believe you and I don't trust you. So it's probably better if this is over."

Hilton thought about saying something, but decided to end it there.

Luke was waiting for her to respond, and was furious when she didn't. She was just going to leave it like that? What a bitch.

The rest of the ride went in silence, with Luke fuming and Hilton staring out the window seeing nothing. When Luke pulled up to her apartment Hilton climbed out and grabbed her bag from the backseat without saying anything. Luke couldn't believe she wasn't even going to say goodbye or try to talk it out.

"Well, have fun fucking your other guy," he said coldly without thinking, and regretted it immediately.

Hilton pressed her lips together and shook her head. She thought about flipping him off or slamming the door, but she just tossed her bag over her shoulder, shut the car door, and turned her back on him, walking up the stairs without glancing back. She was relieved no one was in the living room when she went into the apartment and she went straight to her bedroom, shut the door behind her, and collapsed on her bed in sobs.

"Thanks so much for coming home with me," Jill said in the parking lot outside Adam's apartment. "It was really fun, and my family loved you. Winnie thinks you're hot." She grinned mischievously.

Adam laughed. "Yeah, I had a really good time," he said. "You better be nice to me or I might have to give Winnie a call." He grinned and ruffled her hair, then kissed her and climbed out of the car. "I'll give you a call tonight."

"Okay, sounds good. See ya, babe."

"See ya." Adam shut the door and Jill backed out of the parking spot, smiling a little to herself. He was just so cute.

But now it was back to reality, and she knew she had to tell him this week. She had a doctor's appointment tomorrow, her first one. She knew she should've gone a long time ago, but she'd been really busy with schoolwork and honestly, just scared to go. But she figured she'd make sure everything was going well and then let Adam know. She drove home with depression and nervousness setting in.

When she got home the apartment was quiet. She didn't think Nat or Laney was home, but Hilton's door was shut. Jill went over and knocked quietly. "It's Jill."

"Hey, come in," Hilton said in a tired voice. Jill opened the door to find her sprawled on the bed. Her eyes were red and Jill could tell she'd been crying.

"What's wrong?!" Jill exclaimed, rushing over to sit on the bed beside her.

Hilton buried her face in her comforter. "I think Luke and I broke up," she mumbled into the bed.

"What?!" Jill cried. "Oh, my gosh, Hilton, I'm so sorry. What happened?" She rubbed Hilton's back.

"He was just being a fucking dick all weekend," Hilton moaned. "He brought up that pregnancy test, and said he didn't believe me it was a false alarm, and he thinks I was taking it 'cause I thought another guy got me pregnant!"

"Oh, my gosh, are you fucking serious? Oh, my gosh, Hilton, this is all my fault! Why didn't you just tell him? Oh, I feel so horrible now!"

"No, it's not your fault, babe. I told him it didn't have anything to do with me or him but I couldn't tell him what it was and he just needed to trust me, and he couldn't do that, and he just kept bringing up that other guy shit. So I told him we should take a break, and then he said it was best if it was over or something. So I don't think it's a break, it's more like a complete breakup." She buried her face in her arm.

"Oh, I'm sure it's not a breakup," Jill said comfortingly. "Come on, Hilton, do you really think an argument like that is gonna end you guys' relationship? That's crazy. You guys will be fine. And you can tell him about me whenever you want. I have a doctor's appointment tomorrow, and then after that I'm gonna tell Adam."

"Awww…." Hilton gave Jill a sympathetic look and sat up to hug her. "Don't worry about it, Jilly. It'll go fine. Did things go well with Adam this weekend?"

"Yeah, it was almost perfect. Except for Todd; he was a complete asshole and wouldn't even return my calls and he was a dick to Adam when we saw him at Bennett's party." She wrinkled her nose in disgust.

"Oh, Bennett had a party? I'm sorry I missed it! I can't believe Todd was such an ass; guys suck, don't they?"

"Well, at least Adam was great. And my family loved him." Jill tried to smile hopefully, but didn't really pull it off.

"Yeah, it'll all work out. Fuck Todd. Hey, do you want me to go to the doctor with you tomorrow?"

"Yeah, if you want. That'd be great. Fuck Luke, too."

"Okay, I'll come with you. Hey, you wanna go get some ice cream or something? I've gotta stop this shit. I need to get out of here."

"Sure, sounds good to me!" Jill agreed with relief.

Jill was dreading her doctor's appointment because she had no idea what to expect, and she was also sure she would get chastised about not having come sooner. When she made her appointment at Dale's student health center she had requested a female doctor, thinking maybe a woman would be a little more sympathetic. Luckily, the doctor was very understanding and told Jill everything looked great. She asked about the father, and Jill admitted she hadn't told him yet and had been waiting until after this appointment.

"When do you think I'll start to show?" Jill asked, hoping it wouldn't be until after finals so it wouldn't be obvious when she was walking around campus.

"Most women start to show around the beginning of the second trimester," the doctor informed her. "But it's different for every woman; I can't say exactly what week of your pregnancy it will be noticeable. If you wear baggy clothes, it may not be noticeable for several months yet."

Jill nodded, biting her lip.

"I'm going to do an ultrasound. Would you like to listen to the heartbeat?"

Jill nodded eagerly. She waited excitedly to hear what it would sound like, and as soon as she heard it a wave of emotion came over her. This was really real. There was something growing inside of her. She raised her hand to wipe tears from her eyes and returned the doctor's smile. "It's amazing," she breathed.

"Do you want to know the sex?" the doctor asked with a smile.

"You can tell already?" Jill asked, surprised.

"Yep, sure can."

Jill returned the doctor's smile but shook her head quickly. "No, I don't want to know, at least not yet."

When Jill walked back out into the lobby, Hilton jumped up anxiously. "So, how was it?"

Jill smiled. "Really good, actually. She said everything's fine, and I got to hear the heartbeat. Hilton, it was so amazing."

Hilton bounced up and down and hugged Jill tightly. "Awww! You should've let me come in with you!"

"I know," Jill said. "But I just didn't know how it would be, and all that."

"I know," Hilton said understandingly. "It's okay. So do you know if it's a boy or girl?"

"No. She could've told me, but I didn't want to know…not yet anyway. Maybe I will later. I don't know. I haven't decided yet."

Hilton smiled jubilantly. "Jill, this is so exciting! I mean, I know it's not the ideal situation or whatever, but aren't you a little excited at least?"

Jill smiled softly. "I have to be now. I mean, it didn't even really hit me until I heard the heartbeat. But now I love it, Hilton. It's mine, you know. I created another living thing! It's just so weird."

"You and Adam created it," Hilton corrected. "You guys are gonna have a damn good-looking kid!"

Jill smiled half-heartedly. "Yeah, me and Adam….Well, I'm gonna tell him tonight. So we'll see how that goes."

Hilton put her arm around Jill as they walked to the car. "Well, I think it will end up being great. But if it's not, I'm here for you, hon. So don't worry."

That night Jill went over to Adam's, to "study and watch TV," or so he thought. They watched *Fear Factor* in the living room with Justin and Ryan and half-heartedly worked on a little home-work, and then Jill suggested that she and Adam go in his room.

"Yeah, baby," Justin teased with a wink.

Jill smiled, and felt sick to her stomach with nervousness. If only Justin had any idea how far from the truth he was about what would be going on in Adam's room.

"What's wrong?" Adam asked as he flopped on the bed and Jill sat anxiously on the edge of his computer chair, staring at him.

"Um, well, I have something to tell you about." Jill was relieved he had asked what was wrong and forced the discussion because otherwise she wasn't sure she would've been able to start it.

"What is it?" Adam raised his eyebrows expectantly and laid on his side facing her.

Jill ran her hand through her hair. "Well...I don't really know how to say this to not freak you out...but I'm pregnant." She automatically winced and ducked her head a little bit, scared of his reaction.

For what seemed like an hour, there was no reaction at all except for a slight widening of his eyes. Then he threw a book so hard Jill was sure there would be a dent in the wall. But she couldn't take her eyes off Adam to look; she was frozen in fear, waiting to hear what he would say.

"Fuck!" he shouted, and Jill felt like covering her ears, but she couldn't seem to move at all. She felt her heart drop with a thud.

Adam was lying flat on his back now, staring at the ceiling. "It was that first fucking time, wasn't it?" he snapped coldly. "We didn't use a condom. I knew it. I was telling Justin the next day how we didn't use a condom." He turned to face Jill. "Was it that first time?"

Jill nodded meekly.

Suddenly Adam sat up and glared at her accusingly. "How long have you known about this?"

Damn it! This was what she'd dreaded. "Um, like a couple of weeks?"

"Bullshit, Jill. That first time we had sex was two months ago, I bet. There's no way you've only known for two weeks. Why didn't you tell me sooner?"

"I don't know. I was scared to, and I felt like it'd just be too much, too soon; I wanted to wait till we were together longer...." Her voice faded as she saw it wasn't working.

"Too much too soon?" Adam asked, shaking his head in disbelief. "It's not that now? We've been together how long? And you knew about this for a long time. That's probably the only fucking reason you're even dating me. You thought it was just a one night stand, but then you found out this shit, so you just drug me along with you and you got just what you wanted, didn't you? And I bet you thought everything would be all perfect now, and I'd never figure it out, and we'd just be a perfect little family." He was still glaring at her.

Jill was sobbing. She could hardly even see Adam's face through the tears. "You know that's not true!" she cried desperately. "Okay, so I've known about it since spring break, but I really like you! That's why I'm dating you, not because I'm pregnant. Even if I wasn't pregnant, I'd still be dating you! I've always liked you. Come on, Adam, you know that! Just ask any of my roommates, or Justin; I'm sure he could always tell."

"Please, Jill. That's bullshit. How do you think this makes me feel? I really liked you; you're the first girl I've actually wanted to date in I can't remember how long, and look what happens! I guess I had the right idea before, never getting serious with anyone. I've gotta get the fuck out of here!" He leaped off the bed and grabbed his coat off the floor and stormed out of the room, slamming the door behind him and leaving Jill sitting in his computer chair, sobbing hysterically.

When she finally was able to stop crying, she could barely think. After the doctor's appointment had gone so well, she had felt a little more hopeful about the whole thing, and now she had no idea what to do. This was by far the worst she'd ever felt in her life. She was so lost and felt completely alone in the world. Her only thought now was that she wished she hadn't heard that damn heartbeat so she could still have an abortion!

She quickly gathered her coat and prayed Justin and Ryan were in their rooms so she wouldn't have to face them on the way out. She practically ran out of the apartment and to her car. Once she was in her car she felt more secure, but after she sat there a minute the sobs came again. She started to feel sorry for her baby and protective of it. That fucking asshole doesn't even want his own kid! she thought furiously, forgetting how she had been wishing five minutes ago she could still get an abortion.

Still sobbing, and hiccupping now, she dug her phone out of her purse and started to call Hilton, but dialed Todd instead. He already hated Adam, and right now what she needed was to talk to someone who hated him as much as she did. She knew hearing Todd's anger would make her feel better.

When he didn't answer Jill frantically called again. She didn't know what she'd do if she couldn't talk to him right now.

When Todd came out of his group meeting at 10:30 he had four missed calls, all from Jill. What the fuck? he thought. He figured she was just calling repeatedly to be annoying, and he wasn't really ready to talk to her and face up to what an asshole he'd been this weekend.

He was in his car on the way back to his apartment when she called again. He felt like throwing the phone out the window, but instead he pushed Send and snapped, "Look, Jill. I don't know why you keep calling; I'm assuming you wanna know what the hell was up this weekend, and basically, I'm in love with you. So there it is. That's why I can't stand being around Adam, or you, and I'm sorry but that's just how it is. I know you want me to be a friend right now and I tried, but I just can't fucking do it. So sorry. I guess I'm not as great as you thought I was. So please stop calling me, because I don't want to talk to you and I think it'll just be best for both of us that way." Still fuming, he jammed his thumb down on the End button before she could say anything.

He expected it to ring again right away but there was just silence. He continued to grip his phone in his hand, waiting. When nothing happened, he flipped the phone angrily onto the passenger seat. "Fuck!" He couldn't believe he'd just said that to her. What a huge fucking mistake. He felt guilty as hell for letting her down, but he also believed it was the right thing to do, for both their sakes. Okay, so it was for my fucking sake, he relented irritably. He was in a horrible mood and didn't think he'd ever felt so pissed off at Jill, himself, or the world in general.

When someone knocked on the door of Todd's apartment he was sprawled on the couch pretending to watch *The Boondock Saints* with Conrad.

"Who the fuck is that?" he asked crossly as he glanced at the clock and saw that it was midnight.

Conrad paused the DVD and went down the hall to answer the door. Todd didn't move; he just stared blankly at the blurry picture on the screen. All of a sudden Conrad came back into the living room and said quietly, "Hey, man, I think it's for you."

Todd stared at him impatiently, but Conrad settled back into his chair and started the movie again. Finally Todd rolled off the couch and dragged himself to the door. Conrad hadn't even opened it yet, but Todd didn't have the energy to look through the peephole. He exasperatedly threw the door open and started to give whoever was outside an annoyed look, but the look was wiped off his face the instant he saw her, and his hand fell slowly from the doorknob.

She stood motionless, with her long brown hair hanging messily around her tear-streaked face and her red, shiny eyes looking at him pitifully. She was wearing an oversized black Dale hooded sweatshirt and a pair of gray cotton pants, and she clutched her cell phone close to her stomach in her right hand. Her left hand fell dejectedly at her side. She stared into his eyes, and he couldn't have looked away if he tried.

"I told him," she said simply and tragically after a moment. "And you were right." Her mouth formed into a small, unconscious pout and her shoulders slumped. Then, without ever taking her eyes off his or changing her tone, she added, "And I think I love you too, Todd."

Todd stared deep into her eyes for another endless moment, and then opened his arms to her without a second thought. It was the obvious and natural thing to do. All his anger and hurt was forgotten, and as she stepped into his embrace and buried her face in his shoulder he felt like he had found what he'd been looking for his whole life. This was perfect; Jill was perfect for him.

As Jill clung to him he affectionately brushed the hair away from her face, and when she looked up at him he kissed her softly on the lips.

"Jill," he whispered huskily, staring into her heartbreaking brown eyes, amazed at how beautiful she was. They reached for each other's hands at the same time and Todd led the way into his bedroom, shutting the door quietly behind him.

When he turned back to her, their bodies melted slowly into each other, and her hands covered his face and then ran through his hair as they shared a long, slow, tender kiss. This was so different than their other kisses, but just as passionate and even more fulfilling because of the emotion that was finally out in the open. There was no longer anything to hide and they both poured everything they had into this moment.

They moved unhurriedly toward the bed and Todd pulled Jill's sweatshirt over her head. His jaw dropped when he saw she had nothing but a bra under it, and he ran his hands over her cool, bare skin. "Wow," he breathed. "Wow."

Jill smiled a little as she pulled his t-shirt off, and they fell onto the bed together as they kissed again.

Todd's lips moved to her neck, then her shoulder. "Jill, you're so gorgeous," he whispered, then his mouth was moving over her again and she sighed deeply and contentedly.

Todd wasn't rough and hurried as he'd been the times he'd kissed her. He took his time because he wanted to enjoy every part of her incredible body. She responded naturally and effortlessly to him, as though this was something they'd done a thousand times before. It felt so damn good….it felt perfect.

"Todd," she sighed. "Todd, I love you."

When it was finally over they lay facing each other with their legs intertwined and Todd's arm around Jill, grinning at each other.

"Wow, Jill," Todd said. "I don't even know what else to say. That was the best sex I've ever had." Then his eyes lost some of their twinkle and his face became more serious. "And I really do love you. I love you so damn much. I don't think you have any idea."

"I do," Jill said softly, "because I love you, too. Funny how I didn't realize it until you said that on the phone."

She smiled and kissed him, and he grabbed her and pulled her back on top of him, squeezing her as tightly as he could. Jill giggled and playfully bit at his nose but he caught her in a sudden kiss instead.

He thought he could never get enough of her….

It was one of those dreams where Jill knew she was dreaming and didn't want to wake up because it was such a great dream. She had just had sex with Todd for the first time and they were lying in her bed, cuddling and lazily making out. It was one of the best feelings Jill had ever had; she felt warm and contented and happy. Forget Adam, this was what she really wanted; this was a dream come true.

❦   ❦   ❦

Suddenly her eyes fluttered open and she glanced around the dark room. She was lying on her back and she saw the clock to her left that said 5:12 in huge red numbers. Slowly a satisfied, cat-like smile spread across her face as she realized where she was and she turned to her right. Todd was sprawled on his back with his face toward her. His hair was messy as usual and his hand was resting casually on his chest. It wasn't a dream! It was real. Jill couldn't stop smiling to herself. She kicked her legs a little out of excitement and squirmed under the covers and Todd stirred. When he opened his eyes and found her staring back at him he grinned automatically and reached out to pull her up against him. He threw his leg over hers and snuggled up to her.

"Hey, Jilly."

Jill was still grinning. "Hey," she said softly.

"So, that was amazing," Todd said in a half-silly, half-serious voice, as though pointing out the most obvious fact in the world.

"Yeah." Jill reached up and ran her hand though his adorable hair. It was so soft. She couldn't get enough of it, of him.

"Seriously," Todd said, still in the silly, serious voice. "That was, like, the best night of my life."

Jill grinned at him. "It was for me. It went from the worst to the best. Wow. This is so crazy. I'm so glad you said that on the phone."

"It's true. I love you." Todd looked deep into her eyes.

"I know. I love you, too."

Todd leaned down to kiss her, and then pulled her even closer. She lay contentedly in his arms as they drifted back off to sleep.

❧   ❧   ❧

When Jill woke up again it was 8:30. She had class at noon, so she needed to get going in the next hour or so. She hated to leave; she wished she could stay here forever. Fifteen more minutes, she told herself and closed her eyes blissfully, snuggling closer to Todd. When she finally made herself get up, she tried to wiggle out of Todd's arms without waking him but it didn't work.

"Jilly, where are you going?" he asked sleepily as he pulled her back down.

"I have class," she said. "I have to go."

"Just stay here with me all day. We'll skip class. Come on."

"I really can't; I have a test on Thursday in criminal psych so I have to go to it today...." She gave him a glum look.

"Okay...." Todd pulled her close and kissed her, then watched as she climbed out of bed and gathered up her clothes from the floor. She went in the bathroom to freshen up a little, and sighed as she looked at herself in the mirror. How were they going to leave this? She wasn't sure what to say to him when she left. She wished she could just be with him and not have to worry about Adam and the baby. She decided to not bring it up and wait and see what Todd said. She hoped it wasn't too awkward. Before leaving the bathroom, she couldn't help but flash herself a giddy smile in the mirror. No matter what happened now, this had been incredible and she didn't regret it at all.

When she went back into the bedroom, Todd was still sprawled out on the bed. Jill climbed in beside him and kissed him. "I was serious, you know," she said, pushing her hair back as it fell between their faces. "That was the best night of my life."

Todd smiled and his eyes twinkled. "Yeah, me too. Definitely the best sex I've ever had." He grinned and pinched her ass. She giggled and squirmed.

"Jill," he said suddenly, more serious. "I don't know exactly what happened with Adam last night that made you come here, but don't ever think I was just taking advantage of you. I love you, and last night was about you and me. And I don't know if you and Adam are still together, but I will always be here for you, and I would love to be with you and raise your baby with you." He reached out and stroked her hair.

Jill melted inside. Nobody had ever said anything that sweet and loving to her before. She felt tears in the corners of her eyes. "Thank you, Todd." She tenderly ran her hand over his cheek, staring into his solemn brown eyes.

"Do you want to know about Adam?" He nodded, and so she told him. She was crying by the time she was finished and Todd was rocking her in his arms.

"Baby, I'm so sorry," he whispered, his mouth against her hair. "What a prick."

Jill looked up at him, wiping her tears with one of her sweat-shirt sleeves. "When I started driving here last night it was because I needed to be around someone who hated him as much as I did. And I kept trying to call you and you didn't answer, so I just decided to come. But then after I called you again and you said all that, it wasn't even about Adam anymore. It was all about you. I just knew; I knew I loved you too." She smiled through her tears. "And I don't know what to do now; I mean, I would love for you to raise my baby with me; that would be so perfect. It's only three and a half weeks till finals are over, and hopefully I can get things with Adam figured out by then and then you and I will be home for the summer and we can be together. I mean, I don't even love Adam and I never did, but I wish he would at least want to be a father, you know?" She shook her head helplessly, crying again, and Todd pulled her close to him, kissing the top of her head.

"Shh, Jilly Bean, it's okay," he soothed. "That's fine. You get things worked out with Adam, and I'm sure he'll come around some. What kind of fucking asshole wouldn't even care about his own baby?" He felt anger boiling up inside him even as he said it. Why couldn't it be his baby? Or why did she have to be pregnant at all?

"Three and a half weeks isn't that long," he continued. "But remember, if you need anything before then please let me know. You can come here or I'll come there to be with you; I promise." He tipped her chin up so he could look her in the eyes and repeated, "Promise, Jilly? Call me or whatever. I'll do whatever you need."

Jill smiled and kissed him. "Thank you, Todd. You're so great. I love you."

"I love you too, Jilly."

Todd walked Jill out to her car and they shared a lingering kiss before she got in.

"I'm so glad I came," she whispered with a delighted smile.

"Me, too. I'm so glad I made a complete ass out of myself on the phone," Todd joked, then kissed her quickly and patted her head as she lowered herself into the car.

"Bye!" Jill called as she backed out of the parking spot, and grinned and waved at Todd as she pulled away.

Watching her drive away, a little bit of Todd died inside. Unless Adam was really the world's biggest fucking jerk ever, he would come around and Jill would try to work it out with him. Jill had said she'd call if she needed anything, but she wouldn't need anything.

Nevertheless, he would never regret last night and he knew she wouldn't either. He was so glad he'd finally told her how he felt, because one perfect night with her was better than nothing. He smiled to himself a little as he walked back inside. Fuckin' bittersweet, he thought.

As soon as Jill got on the road she called Hilton, who she knew would be in the Union on a break. "Hilton," she gushed as soon as Hilton answered, "I had sex with Todd."

"*What*?!" Hilton practically screamed. Jill knew Hilton wouldn't even care if everyone in the Union started looking at her, and she laughed.

"Yeah," she said. "Yeah. I'm on my way back from Eastern right now."

"Holy shit!" Hilton cried. "I can't believe it! Finally! But wait, what the hell happened?! I thought you were going over to Adam's last night!"

"Yeah…." Jill paused, then launched breathlessly into the whole story, not pausing till she was finished. As she talked, her mind whirled continuously. She was ecstatic about last night, but she also felt like it was so unfair that this had to happen when she was pregnant. Why couldn't it have happened sooner, and this be Todd's baby? Or why did she have to be pregnant at all? "Because I'm fucking careless!" she reminded herself and Hilton. She wished she'd never slept with Adam, because then she could be with Todd. But, she realized, if this whole thing with Adam never happened, Todd might not have even known how he felt about me. She frowned. Is that what made him realize how he felt? Or has he felt this way longer? She had no idea. This definitely explained that weekend when he had kissed her though. Todd, she thought. Todd loves me. I never, ever thought this would happen; it's what I've always wanted, and now that I have it I can't do anything about it! Ugh! Life was so unfair. Was it bad to be kind of hoping in the very back of her mind that Adam wouldn't come through at all so she could just be with Todd? Yes, she realized with a sudden jolt. That is bad. Just because Todd said he'd raise the baby with you doesn't mean you should dump that on him. He might think he wants to now, but it would ruin his life and he might regret it later….Jill's heart sank as she rambled on to Hilton, who listened silently. Even if Adam didn't come through, how could she let Todd do this for her? It would be so selfish….She wasn't even sure how she felt about Adam now either. She knew she was telling the truth when she told Todd she'd never loved Adam, at least never the way she loved Todd. But if Adam did come around—and she had no idea what the chances were on that—would she even be able to be happy with him now? Because she had *been* happy with him, before Todd. They had a lot of fun together and he was gorgeous and funny and laid back and they had never fought before last night, and she knew Hilton had liked them together. Jill shook her head fiercely. There was just no way she'd know until she saw him, and who knew if he'd even call her, so whatever. She'd just have to wait and see. What she was more focused on now was how devastated she was that there was no way she could take Todd up on his offer, because she'd already fucked up her own life and Adam's but there was no way she'd do that to Todd, the person she loved most. She reached up absent-mindedly and brushed away a tear, not even realizing she was crying.

"But I don't regret it, no matter what," she told Hilton assuredly. "It was unbelievable. Un-fucking-believable. I guess I'm done. I don't know what else to say."

When Jill finished Hilton burst out laughing. "Holy mother of Buddha, Jill!" she giggled. "That's freakin' crazy! I don't even know what to think. I'm so happy about you and Todd though.

But you're probably right, you can't necessarily just take him up on it….I wouldn't decide anything right now though. Just wait till you get back and see what happens with Adam. You never know. And don't worry about it too much because whatever happens is for the best. So just go with the flow. You did last night, and look how it turned out!" She laughed again. "Wow, wow, wow, Jill! Hey, I have to go to class, but I'll see you tonight, okay? And if you ever start to feel bad about this, just remember, I would've been pissed at you if you pussed out with Todd; that was an experience you couldn't turn down! You did the right thing."

"Thanks, Hilton; I feel a lot better. Hope I gave you some good entertainment over lunch!" Jill laughed. "See you tonight."

"Bye, babe!"

Jill hung up with a relieved laugh. She was so glad she'd called Hilton and gotten her perspective on the whole thing, because Hilton always had such a positive way of looking at things, and Jill knew she would've been pissed at herself if she hadn't taken advantage of last night too. She wasn't worried about ever regretting what happened between her and Todd. No matter what happened, that was the one thing she was sure of, the one right choice she knew she'd made.

Jill went straight to criminal psych when she got back because she didn't have time to stop at her apartment first. It was the first time in her life she didn't even think about the fact that she probably looked like shit. Surprisingly, she was able to focus well in class and totally block everything else from her mind. After that class and one more, in which she also concentrated fervently, she headed home, exhausted but fairly upbeat, still riding the high of last night. Adam was sitting on the steps outside her apartment. He jumped up when he saw her.

Jill sighed and stopped at the bottom of the stairs. She looked up at him and waited, not in the mood for this at all. What a buzz-kill.

"Jill," Adam said, sounding unsure of himself, but determined. "Jill, please hear me out. I'm so sorry about last night. I said a lot of shitty things that I had no right to say. I was just surprised and I didn't handle it well at all. I'm so sorry about saying that's the only reason you were dating me; I wanna shoot myself for saying that. Please. Can we talk? I want to hear about the baby and how you're doing. I want to stay together, Jill. I really do like you a lot, and I just freaked out because I wasn't expecting it at all. I'm sorry." His eyes pleaded with her as he stood there nervously.

Jill gazed at him for another moment, squinting her eyes as though trying to gauge whether he was telling the truth or not. Suddenly she felt completely drained and the heartbreaking realization came back to her and hit home hard that she couldn't count on things to work out with Todd; she couldn't just say fuck Adam and dump this all on Todd. She owed it to Adam, and probably to Todd, to give this another chance.

Finally she walked up the steps and sat down beside where he was standing. She wasn't overly friendly toward him, but she wasn't cold either, and they talked. She told him about how she got sick on the way home from spring break, and about how she'd had some morning sickness on and off, and about her doctor's appointment the day before. He asked a few questions but was mostly quiet and listened to her talk. When she finished he asked her to come over to his apartment but she said she was exhausted and just needed a long nap. She said she didn't want to pressure him, and he should think things over and make sure he was sure, and that she had a test on Thursday so she would be busy studying but he could call her tomorrow night if he wanted. He thanked her profusely for giving him another chance and promised her he was sure. "Well then," she said matter-of-factly, "I'll talk to you tomorrow night," and then she stood up and walked inside.

When Jill woke up from her nap it was four hours later. She blinked at the clock, surprised she'd slept so long. She had passed out from sheer exhaustion the moment her head hit the pillow, but she still felt tired. That was the worst part about taking a nap; it was always so hard to get up. She dragged herself out of bed and into her bathroom, turned on the hot water, stripped, and stepped into the shower. She let the warm water cascade over her as she turned her face up into it, refusing to think about anything except how good it felt.

She felt much more awake after her shower, and went out into the living room to eat dinner. Natalie was watching TV and she said Hilton was at a group meeting and Laney was sleeping. Jill started some Hamburger Helper and then sat down with Natalie to watch TV. She had considered telling Laney and Natalie tonight, but she decided she would wait till Thursday because that way her test would be over. She knew once she told them it'd be the focus of the whole rest of the night and she wouldn't get anything else done, and she really needed to get this test over with before being distracted again. Right now she was doing a really good job not thinking about anything. Thank You, God! she breathed, rolling her eyes heavenward.

After dinner she hit the books and was actually able to study hard for a couple of hours. Criminal psych was really interesting but her professor was so disorganized and she hated that he didn't put the notes online. He never even used PowerPoint or the overhead; he just made random scrawls on the board and everyone was always racing to write down what he was saying. At least it was interesting, because if it wasn't Jill was sure she would've shot herself by now. This test was basically over psychopathy, and as Jill poured over her notes she didn't even realize how much time was going by. She was surprised to see it was almost ten already, and she was extremely pleased with herself for getting so much done, since her test wasn't for two days still.

She decided to stop for the night and put in a *Friends* DVD instead. Just then Hilton knocked on the door and poked her head in. "Hey, just wanted to see how you're doing."

Jill rolled her eyes and sank back against her pillow. "Oh, my gosh, Hilton," she moaned, and told her about Adam. "I mean, I think I have to give him another chance to be fair to all of us…me, him, and Todd. If it's not meant to work out it won't, right? And if it is meant to work out with Todd, then that will happen eventually?"

"Yes, definitely," Hilton said. "Don't worry about it. I think you had to give Adam another chance. And if you're not happy in a week or two with him, then just break it off. At least you'll know for sure."

"Hey, whatever happened with Luke?" Jill asked.

Hilton shrugged and rolled her eyes exaggeratedly. "Haven't even talked to him. He didn't even try to call me or anything yesterday, but today he's left me two messages. I haven't listened to them yet."

"Hey, if you want, you can go ahead and tell him. I'm gonna tell them after my test Thursday." She motioned her hand toward the living room.

"No, that doesn't even matter," Hilton said. "It's not the issue anymore; he just apparently doesn't trust me. But, wow, will he feel like such an ass when he finds out. He'll owe me big time, and he'll owe you, too! But I'm in no hurry to tell him; he's being such an asshole I don't even want to talk to him."

"So you think you guys will get back together now? You didn't sound too positive the other day?"

"Oh, probably. I just want him to learn his lesson...but who knows; I mean he's being so weird lately I'm really not sure what to expect at all. So we'll just see...." Hilton's voice trailed off, and she looked a little glum. "Everything works out for the best, right?" she added with an encouraging smile.

"Right," Jill assured her, and they grinned at each other, then Hilton left and closed the door behind her.

Jill felt better for awhile as she settled back against her pillows and watched a few episodes of *Friends*, because she was able to push Todd out of her mind. But eventually all her thoughts kept drifting back to her situation and everything in the episodes she was watching seemed to remind her of it. Jill burst into tears and buried her head in the pillow. It was so unfair! She felt an overwhelming sense of anger toward Adam. I just want to be with Todd! she cried silently and despairingly. Why does it have to be like this? Why, why, why? She sobbed and sobbed, her whole body shaking as she lay there miserably.

The next night Adam called Jill around eight and she agreed to go over to his apartment to watch *The O.C.* and take a study break. She had been in her room all night and just needed to get out. It went pretty well, but how badly could things really go when two people sat there and watched a TV show? After the show Jill said she had to get back to studying. She had tried to act slightly distant all night because she definitely wasn't going to give him the impression they could go right back to where they'd been before. She had sat at the opposite end of the couch during *The O.C.* and she didn't want to stay and really have a chance to talk. He'd have to earn that, and she was testing him to see if he'd stick around.

He asked her to stay and seemed disappointed when she didn't, and Jill was ashamed to admit to herself she wished he would just give up on her. She just wanted to be with Todd. Stop being so selfish! she scolded herself. You *know* that can't work out! But no matter how many times she told herself, she just couldn't get it out of her head, and later she cried herself to sleep for the second night in a row.

On Thursday she aced her test, which made her feel temporarily better. She was proud of herself for being able to block everything out and really focus. She had always done well in school; at least there was one thing that hadn't changed. When she got home later that afternoon she went right into Hilton's room.

"I have to tell Lane and Nat tonight!" she cried in an agonized tone. "Aagghh! What do you think they're gonna say?"

Hilton shook her head as she lay sprawled on her bed watching TV. "I have no idea but I'm sure they'll be supportive. They better fuckin' be," she added with a grin at Jill. "Or I'll kick their asses."

Jill laughed and sat down on Hilton's bed to watch TV with her. "Are you going to the Turtle tonight?"

"I don't know….I haven't talked to Lane and Nat to see if they're going; what about you?"

"I want to; I need to get out and do something. I shouldn't stay long though….I wish I could drink! I aced my damn test and I wanna celebrate!"

"Yeah, that's definitely a drawback of being pregnant!" Hilton agreed. "We can go for a little while; I'll go if you go."

"Okay," Jill agreed. "I wonder if Adam'll call me tonight."

"I bet he will. If he doesn't then he's a prick, more than he was already." She grinned playfully and Jill grinned back. They heard the front door open and Laney and Natalie came in together, talking.

"Well, I guess it's show time," Jill said with a nervous glance at Hilton. "Here goes nothing…." She stepped out into the living room. Laney and Natalie were unloading their groceries in the kitchen. Hilton came out into the living room with her.

"Jilly has an announcement," Hilton said. Jill was relieved she didn't have to bring it up herself now and sent a silent thank you to Hilton.

Laney and Natalie exchanged a quick glance, then swiftly turned their gazes to Jill.

"Um…I'm pregnant." Jill looked from one to the other, then down at her feet, then at Hilton.

Laney and Natalie just stared at her, but they didn't look that surprised. Then they guiltily glanced at each other again.

"Okay, so we knew," Laney admitted. "Or we guessed."

Jill's mouth dropped open. "How?"

"Well," Laney continued, "with the whole pregnancy test thing, we thought it was really Hilton but then we saw her drinking, so we figured out it was you….I watched you that weekend at Eastern and I figured you were buying fake drinks….I don't know, sorry!" She giggled. "But we're really happy for you!" She ran over and gave Jill a hug and Natalie followed.

Jill smiled gratefully at them. "Why didn't you guys say something? I'm so glad you knew! That made it so much easier than explaining to you!"

"We didn't know if you'd want us to say anything. We knew you'd tell us when you were ready," Natalie explained.

"Whew," Jill breathed, and flashed a relieved glance at Hilton. "Seriously, you guys have no idea how much easier that made things."

"So, how'd it happen?" Laney asked eagerly as she settled into the chair, glad to finally be able to hear the details. "Do you know if it's a boy or girl? Does Adam know? Are you guys staying together? What are you doing next year? Tell us everything!"

The girls all giggled, and Jill told them what little there was to tell, since she had only had one doctor's appointment and didn't know if it was a boy or girl, or the future of her relationship with Adam. She told them about his initial reaction, but said he had apologized and begged for another chance so she thought she had to give it to him.

"Awww, that's so cute!" Natalie said. "I'm sure he was just shocked at first. But he obviously really likes you and is serious about this!"

"Yeah, well…." Jill said guiltily. "Um, I'm not sure how serious I am about him…."

"What?! Why?" Laney and Natalie exclaimed together.

"I…uh…don't know." She had been planning to tell them about Todd, but something stopped her. "I'm just gonna see what happens. Because everything works out for the best." She flashed a smile at Hilton, who grinned back.

"Yay, Jill!" Laney jumped up and hugged her. "This is all so exciting!"

Jill smiled over Laney's shoulder. She didn't feel as excited as Laney, but she didn't feel too badly right now.

Adam did call that night, and the girls met up with Adam, Justin, and Ryan at Mike's, the karaoke bar. They went at nine and got a good table. They hadn't gone to Mike's in awhile, and Jill was excited. She loved the karaoke bar and she wondered why they didn't come more often. Usually it was because they didn't go out till later, she realized. And if they didn't get there before the singing started at 9:30 the line for Mike's could be an hour or more, so they usually just stayed in the Turtle.

It was already packed in the karaoke bar when Mike and Jake, who ran the show, came in and got things started. They stood on top of their separate tables at the front of the room and announced the start of the singing. "Does everybody know the rules?" Mike shouted, cupping his hands around his mouth. "My side versus Jake's side! Money goes here on our tables and which-ever side has the most money gets the next song! But don't start coming up here till after the first song. If at any time you're caught *not* drinking or singing along and not showing some respect for our singers, you'll get to stand on your table and sing all by your-self! Whatever these sympathetic people in here choose for you. Okay? So get out now if this doesn't sound good to you. Oh, by the way, anybody who leaves is a fuckin' pussy!" Mike scanned the room, squinting his eyes and pretending to look for anyone who was leaving. "Nobody's leaving? Good! Okay, if you know the first song, this is how we do it, Jake and I lead the first one and every-body sings with us!"

Jill sat at her table on Mike's side of the room with her friends and her Turtle cup full of cranberry juice so she wouldn't get called out for not drinking, and as everyone in the room sang along to the traditional first song of the night, "I Love This Bar" by Toby Keith, she felt genuinely happy and lost in the moment.

"SO-*CIAL*!" Mike yelled at the end of the song and Jill raised her glass and happily toasted everyone else's.

"All right, we're taking money now! Which side's gonna get the first song?"

Several people shoved to the front of the room to put money on Mike's and Jake's tables.

"We've got ten over here for this girl who wants to sing 'Enter Sandman,'" Mike said. The he turned and wrinkled his nose at the girl as Jill and Hilton looked at each other and covered their mouths to hide their laughter. '*Enter Sandman*'?" Mike repeated. "*You* wanna sing Metallica?"

"No, I'm gonna sing, she's gonna headbang," the guy behind her said.

"Twenty over here!" Jake called. "'Margaritaville'! Yeah, let's hear some Jimmy Buffett!"

"Twenty-five," Mike yelled as the guy who wanted "Enter Sandman" put more money in his hand.

"Thirty!" Jake yelled back.

The "Enter Sandman" guy waved his hand toward Jake. "You can have it!" He and the girl returned to their table laughing.

"All right, way to go, my side!" Jake shouted. "Take it away!"

The winners, two guys, stepped up on the small stage between Jake's and Mike's tables and took the microphones out of their stands.

Jill giggled. She couldn't wait to hear them. This was so fun. They turned out to be half-way decent singers. As Jill sang along to the chorus she felt someone bump her and turned around to see what was going on. Hilton was ducking her head and trying to hide behind Jill and Justin while she listened to a message on her cell phone.

"Hey!" Mike yelled, and Jill realized he was looking at their table. "There's a girl right over here in front on her fuckin' cell phone, not showing any respect for our singers!"

The other side of the room cheered while everyone at Jill's table started cracking up and looking at Hilton, who peered out sheepishly from behind Justin.

"What's the fuckin' rule about cell phones in here?" Mike yelled. "This girl just pissed off everyone on my side of the room! Not only did we not get the first song, but now this shit! Get up on your table, little Miss Too-Good-for-the-Rest-of-Us-Has-to-Talk-on-Her-Damn-Cell-Phone. Everybody quiet! She's going to sing for us! Do you know how it works?" he asked Hilton.

Jill, Laney, and Natalie giggled hysterically as Hilton nodded and good-naturedly climbed up on the table so everyone could see her. Someone grabbed the bucket from Jake's piano with the words NO RESPECT painted on it and passed it over to Hilton, who dug a dollar out of her back pocket and dropped it in the bucket.

"Okay, this is how it works!" Jake yelled to everyone. "This girl is on Mike's side of the room, so she put a dollar in my bucket 'cause she was talking on her fucking cell phone and showing no respect for our singers! Now, whoever on my side of the room puts the most money in this bucket gets to pick the song she has to sing! Let's see some big bucks, my side! We need to win tonight! I'm sick of Mike's side kickin' my side's ass!"

"Come on, my side!" Mike yelled. "If you think she does a good job singing, put money in my bucket! Put more than they pay to hear her sing it!"

Every week it was a competition between Mike's side and Jake's side. There were two buckets on each side, the no respect bucket for people caught not singing along or not drinking, and the song bucket for when people gave money to sing karaoke. At 1:30 the total money in both buckets was counted for each side and every table on the winning side had the opportunity to sing one free song if the people sitting there wanted to.

Someone ended up paying twenty-five dollars for Hilton to sing "Total Eclipse of the Heart" by Nikki French. Jill and Laney and Natalie looked at each other across the table and burst out laughing. Hilton giggled and stood up straight on the table, pretending to be really serious about it as the song started. As she sang, she had her hand on her heart and an over-exaggerated look of pure anguish in her eyes, and everyone at their table was cracking up. She was singing at the top of her lungs and she even spun around on the table several times to sing to different sides of the bar, making gestures to go along with the lyrics. When Mike and Jake finally cut the music off Hilton doubled over in laughter, then stood back up and winked at the crowd, clapping her hands above her head as everyone cheered for her. She climbed down, laughing out of pure enjoyment and batted her eyelashes at Jill. "How'd I do?"

Jill laughed at her.

"That was fuckin' kick-ass!" Mike yelled, clapping for Hilton. "Come on, people, let's beat twenty-five bucks!"

Someone came to the front and put a fifty in Mike's no respect bucket.

"Woohoo, Hilton!" Laney cheered, giggling and clapping. "Someone loves you!"

Hilton leaned over to Jill and whispered, "Luke's called me six times since we've been in here! I just realized; that's why I was trying to listen. I couldn't hear the messages though." She raised her eyebrows at Jill and shrugged, puzzled but not overly concerned. "Oh well." She turned back to the front, where "Margaritaville" had been resumed, and Jill lost herself in the fun of the karaoke bar again.

They left Mike's around 10:30 and everyone else was going to dance in the Turtle, but Jill thought she should probably leave because she was tired. She hated how often she was tired now. She didn't want to go home yet and she felt irritated. Adam offered to go with her and she agreed because she didn't feel like being alone.

When they got back to her apartment they watched a movie and Jill fell asleep on the futon. Adam was sitting on the couch. Things had been pretty quiet on the ride home and even though she was allowing him to spend time with her, Jill hadn't tried to talk to him much since Tuesday. When the movie was over he came and sat on the edge of the futon and woke her up. She still felt really tired so she decided to go to bed.

"Can I stay with you?" Adam asked. "Please, Jill. I know you're still mad and you should be, but I really just want to be with you."

"Okay," Jill told him, smiling a little. She let him sleep in her bed but didn't kiss him or cuddle with him at all.

The next afternoon she made the call she was dreading but knew she had to make.

"Todd. Hey. I just wanted to tell you what happened with Adam. He was waiting at my apartment when I got home from class on Tuesday and he apologized and begged me to give him another chance. And I've let him hang out with me but I haven't done anything with him and I haven't even been that nice to him and I'm not feeling it with him, but Todd, I owe it to him and you and me too, to give it another chance." She was crying now and although Todd was silent she felt she could almost hear when his face stiffened and he sank onto his bed in a resigned way.

"Todd, I want to be with you so much, and you don't even know how much I wish I could do what you said, and be with you and let you raise my baby with me. But that's not fair to you, Todd, because what if a year down the road you change your mind and you're stuck? I can't ruin your life like that, Todd. Please understand." She was crying so hard she was having trouble getting the words out. "I love you so much."

"I understand what you're saying, Jill," Todd said earnestly. "But I would never, ever regret being with you, and I would never feel stuck. I'm sorry you think that and I wish you knew it wasn't true, but I understand if you feel you have to give Adam another chance."

"Todd," Jill sobbed, absentmindedly wiping tears away with the back of her hand. "Todd, thank you so much for everything, and you know I love you, but I think it's best and will be easier for both of us if we don't talk for awhile. I feel like I really should give this a legitimate try with Adam to be fair to him, and I know I can't do that if I'm always talking to you and wishing I was with you instead. This is the last thing I want to do but I don't know what else. It's only three more weeks till summer, right? And we can definitely talk and hang out then, but I think it'd be best if till then we didn't. Okay?"

"If that's what you want, Jill," Todd replied quietly. His voice sounded dead. "But I'm always here for you. So if you do need to talk, please, please call me. Please, Jill. You know you can."

"Thanks, Todd; thank you so much," Jill gasped gratefully through her tears. "I love you, I really do."

"I know," Todd said sadly. "I know. I love you, too. Bye, Jilly." He hung up.

Jill's hand dropped listlessly from her ear and she stared at her open phone in her lap, her mouth hanging open in disbelief. This couldn't be real. She and Todd weren't talking now. And he'd been so understanding and great about everything and she knew she was breaking his heart. It made her feel guilty as hell and it also made her love him even more. She fell onto her back and rocked with her knees pulled up to her chest, bawling, still grasping the phone she had never hung up, trying to cling to the last bit of Todd through that tiny mouthpiece, that tiny earpiece…but knowing there was nothing on the other end to hang on to because she had let him go.

Late April and Early May 2004

Things slowly got better for Jill over the last three weeks of school. She spent more and more time with Adam and remembered how much he could make her laugh and how hot he was and how much fun they had together. The more time she spent with him the less she thought about Todd. Out of sight, out of mind. Their night together was like a dazzling memory frozen in time…a dream perched on the edge of reality…but there was a door between her and the dream and it was slowly shutting, and the sparkling lights that made up the memory were no longer visible. They were still there, and if she would've opened the door and let the lights shine through she could've remembered every detail, but she just never let herself think about it. She finally stopped being cold toward Adam and let things fall back into their old routine for the most part.

That weekend, the day after Jill told Todd they shouldn't talk anymore, Hilton told Luke the whole story and he felt like a complete ass for making such a big deal out of it. Hilton didn't let him get away with it, especially the part where he had accused her of sleeping with another guy. She made him feel even worse, but they finally got back together and by finals week they were completely back to normal and always together (most of the time locked in Hilton's room).

Adam had gotten an internship working for the vice-president of Nichols & Burton, an advertising firm in town. Turned out his grades were pretty good after all, because at least fifty business majors had applied for the three available positions. He wanted Jill to stay in her apartment over the summer so they could be together.

Jill seriously considered the idea, and figured a lot would depend on her parents' reaction to her news. She was dreading the end of finals week when she had to go home and face them. She thought she was beginning to show a little bit, but if she wore a t-shirt it wasn't at all noticeable. She studied hard and thought she did well on all her finals. Not like it mattered, because what good was a psych or pre-law degree with no grad school? she thought bitterly.

On Thursday night of finals week Jill, Hilton, Laney, and Natalie all watched the series finale of *Friends* together and bawled for an hour after it was over. Then they decided to skip the Turtle so they could watch the Friends on *The Tonight Show*. They cried again as the very end of *The Tonight Show* showed the Central Perk set being torn down, and then they put in season one on DVD and watched until they all fell asleep.

After her last test was over on Friday, Jill went to the doctor again. Everything was still looking good. This time she let Adam go with her, but she made him stay in the waiting room too, just as she had made Hilton, telling him she just wasn't comfortable with someone else being in there with her. She did let him come in during the ultrasound though, and when he grabbed her hand and rubbed her back affectionately she felt a few tears in the corners of her eyes.

Jill had everything packed to go home, and she told Adam she'd stay there at least a week, but would keep in touch with him about whether she'd be coming back or not. She also really needed to figure out what she was going to do about next fall. She was due right in the middle of the semester, so she knew she should probably take it off, but she didn't know where she'd be living and she hadn't cancelled her registration yet, or tried to cancel her lease. She figured a lot would be determined in the next week at home.

As she drove home she was so scared she kept getting a nauseous feeling in her stomach and she was actually afraid she'd have to pull over and throw up on the side of the road. She tried taking several deep breaths but she couldn't concentrate and she shook her head furiously, trying to rid herself of her terrified thoughts, but it wasn't working. She suddenly realized she was sitting so tensely that she ached all over from being frozen in the same position for an hour. She had to consciously relax her body and force herself to loosen up a little bit. She drove the speed limit the whole way home…the first time ever for that. She willed time to go as slowly as possible and then she started thinking maybe she didn't have to tell them today.

Jill, stop it! she chided herself. You can't put it off! Stop being a baby about it and just get it over with. If they totally disown you at least you can go back and stay with Adam. That made her feel a little better, but not much.

When she pulled into the driveway and carried a couple of her bags into the house and passed her mom in the kitchen on the way up to her room, she smiled as though nothing was wrong and said, "Hold on, I'll be down in a minute!" She rolled her eyes as she continued up the stairs. You have to do it, Jill! she told herself. And as she laid her bags down in her room and the queasy feeling came back, she knew she did have to. She couldn't go on with all this anxiety building up and making her sick for much longer. She just had to get it over with. She didn't think anyone else was home, which actually made this the perfect time because she could tell her mom first and then hopefully her mom would tell the others, or at least be there when Jill did it. It was a little less scary that way. Jill looked at herself in the mirror, took a deep breath, and turned and walked out of her room.

"Hi, Mom," she said a little sheepishly as she walked into the kitchen and sank into a chair at the table. Her mom was at the stove making dinner. It smelled like spaghetti. Jill's mouth watered. Her mom turned and when she saw her daughter's sad smile her own happy one turned into a sympathetic frown.

"What's wrong, honey? I thought you said on the phone things were going well with Adam and all your finals went well."

"Yeah, they did," Jill said, averting her eyes and looking out the window.

"So it's Adam, then?"

"Well, kinda. I mean, things are going fine with him, but...." She forced herself to turn and face her mom. She swallowed and then said, "I'm pregnant." As soon as she said it she broke into hysterical sobs and buried her face in her arms on the table.

After a minute she felt her mom stroking her hair soothingly. "Jill, are you sure?"

Jill lifted her head and nodded, barely able to see her mom through her tear-soaked eyes.

Her mom pulled her into a hug and held her close. Jill was sobbing again.

"Mom, what am I gonna do? I don't know what to do about school, about my lease; my whole life is so messed up now! I don't know what to do! Dad's gonna be so mad at me!"

Her mom stepped back and looked at Jill.

"He will be at first, but he'll get over it. I'm not that happy with you myself but what can I really do? What's done is done. We'll figure this out, honey." She stroked Jill's hair. "Does Adam know?"

Jill nodded, looking away. She felt like she'd betrayed her whole family. They had raised her so well and look what she'd given them in return.

"He's actually okay with it. He's been really great about the whole thing. He wants me to come back and live down there this summer so he can be close to me."

"Well I know Dad won't want you doing that. If you're expecting us to help support you, he'll expect you to live here."

Jill hadn't thought of that, but she knew her mom was right. She nodded. "Well, I obviously don't have the money to do it myself. That's fine. I hadn't even decided if I wanted to go back down there anyway. He can come here to visit me over the summer."

"Have you thought about next year at all? Have you and Adam talked about it?"

"Not that much. I told him I had to see what happened at home. I would probably just live here and go to DBU and take care of the baby and then see what happens with Adam when we graduate. The only thing is I don't know if I can get out of my lease."

"Could you find somebody else to take it over for you?"

"Maybe." Jill shrugged indifferently. She felt all her hopes vanishing. Like a little girl believing in the all-encompassing power of her mother to make everything okay, she'd somehow wished her mom could offer her some magical solution in which she would still be able to live at Dale next year and go to school there.

"Well, you better start looking for people. Call the apartment office and tell them you're looking for someone. Maybe they could place someone there for you."

"Yeah, well I can't just do that to Hilton and Nat and Laney though. I can't just stick them with someone they don't even know."

"Well you definitely can't afford to pay rent all year with the baby expenses!"

Jill broke into tears again. "I know. I know. I messed everything up so bad; I don't know what to do. My whole life is ruined!"

"No, it's not, honey." Her mom's voice took on a soothing tone again. "The girls will understand. And your life isn't ruined at all. You can go to school here like you said and probably still graduate a semester behind. And Adam can come visit as often as he likes."

"I guess so." Jill mumbled, avoiding her mom's eyes and not even bothering to mention that she'd never get a job without a grad degree. So much for going to visit schools this summer.

"Have you been to the doctor yet?"

"Yeah, I went twice. Everything's fine."

"You went twice already? How long have you known you were pregnant?"

"A long time. I didn't want to tell you sooner because I was afraid you'd make me come home or something. I wanted to finish out the semester."

"So you knew when you brought Adam here for Easter? Dad is not gonna like that at all. He'll be mad you kept it from us all this time."

"Oh, well, I don't care!" Jill snapped. "I did what I thought was best. I'm sorry."

"I know, I know, honey." Jill's mom hugged her again. "Why don't you go upstairs and rest for a while? We'll talk about this some more later."

"When's everyone else gonna be home?"

"Well, Winnie is out to the movies with Croy," her mom answered with a slight smile, and Jill couldn't resist smiling back, a little bit. "And Aaron has a baseball cookout, and Dad has poker tonight, second Saturday of the month. So they won't be back for awhile yet. Try not to worry about it right now."

Yeah, right! Jill thought dejectedly as she dragged her feet up the stairs. At least her mom hadn't yelled at her and was being supportive and offering to help financially, but all Jill could think about was how quickly her future had vanished right before her eyes.

Jill passed out and sometime later her phone woke her up. It was Adam. She shoved the phone to the floor and rolled over. She didn't even have the energy to talk to him. She'd deal with it later.

When she fell back asleep she dreamed she was rocking a baby and singing softly to it. She stood up and put the baby in its crib and covered it up, then turned around and realized she was in her own room at her parents' house. She wondered what to do next. It was only eight at night, and she couldn't even do anything in her room because the baby was sleeping. She wandered into the hallway and peeked into Winnie's slightly open door. Winnie was sitting on her bed with her back to Jill talking excitedly into her phone and watching TV. She has the perfect teenager's life, Jill thought. She has a normal life. I used to have that. She went downstairs and found her parents watching TV in the living room. Aaron was in the basement on the computer. Jill went back upstairs and curled up miserably on her bed. As she lay there her phone rang. She jumped up eagerly. It was Hilton.

"Hey, Hilton!" Jill greeted her excitedly. "What's up?"

"Oh, not much, we're just getting ready to go to Mike's and the Turtle."

Jill's heart sank and she kicked a pillow that had fallen onto the floor.

"I just had to tell you what the bitch did today! She stole my bottle of rum! Nat and Lane and I went to Subway and when we came back she was gone and so was my rum. I'm so fucking pissed! I hate her! Jill, we miss you so much! How's the baby?"

"Oh, she's good," Jill said, trying to sound upbeat. "Oh, hey, Hilton, she's crying. I have to go. I'll talk to you later, okay?"

"All right, babe, love ya."

Jill hung up the phone and went over to the baby's crib to look at her sleeping. She felt tears streaming down her face and she had to look away because she felt guilty for resenting her own daughter. It's not your fault, I know! she cried silently. I'm just such a horrible mother and I can't even stand to talk to Hilton because I'm so jealous of her life! She sank to the floor and sobbed.

Suddenly she jerked awake. She sighed with relief that it'd been a dream, but the relief didn't last long. This was what her life was going to be like in a few months…and she didn't even have any more time to live it up now that she was at home. She felt trapped, like her parents weren't going to let her leave, ever. Not until she got married at least. And how was she ever going to meet someone to marry living at her parents' house and raising a baby? Maybe Adam would stick with her but she wasn't counting on it. She didn't doubt he'd always be in the baby's life, but she couldn't see him sticking with a girl who wasn't even living in the same town and couldn't go out and party. People didn't change overnight, and she had a hard time seeing him giving up the party life, and why should he have to? Jill would feel guilty asking that of him, just as she would've felt guilty letting Todd be her boyfriend right now. She wondered vaguely why she felt guilty about Adam now when she hadn't before, but that thought came and went and she let it. No time to think like that now.

Just then her mom knocked on the door to see if she wanted dinner. Jill went downstairs and ate, trying to be more cheerful and telling her mom about the ultrasounds and how amazing they were. She really did feel better afterward, and her mom suggested she go out and do something with her friends, since her dad wouldn't be home until late.

"We can tell him tomorrow, and I don't want to tell Winnie and Aaron until Dad knows. So go out and see a movie tonight or something. Try to enjoy yourself."

Jill wanted desperately to call Todd, but she couldn't do it. She called Hillary and Lorylyn, some of her old girlfriends from high school instead, and they went to a movie and then hung out at Hillary's for awhile. Jill was glad for the distraction and was able to have a good time catching up with the girls. They reminisced about high school, and she didn't tell them about the pregnancy. The only bad part was talking about high school inevitably meant talking about Todd and how obsessed Jill had been. She laughed it off and told Hillary and Lorylyn they were still good friends but nothing had ever happened between them. It was hard because these were two of her oldest friends; she'd known them even longer than Hilton and they knew her whole history with Todd. She longed to tell them about her night with Todd, but then they'd wonder why she hadn't dumped Adam, and she didn't want to go there yet.

When she got home everyone was in bed and she felt ready to call Adam. It didn't seem like as big of a deal now that she hadn't dealt with it for a few hours.

"Hey," she said lightly when he answered. "So I told my mom."

"How'd she take it?"

"Actually, not too badly. She was supportive and she wasn't mad or anything. At least she didn't let it show. I haven't told my dad yet 'cause he was out with his friends all night. I have to tell him tomorrow, but my mom said she's sure he won't let me live down there this summer. If he's going to help me with money there's no way he'll let me be living somewhere else, and I know she's right."

"That sucks, Jill! So we're just supposed to be apart all summer, then?"

"Well, you can come here whenever you want. But I can't turn down that money from my parents, Adam. If I move back down there this summer my dad will probably disown me and how will we afford it?"

"Well, of course I'll come see you, Jill, whenever I can, but I have a job so it's not like I can come all the time. And it's gonna be really uncomfortable for me to be in your house with your dad being all disapproving and shit."

"Well, then don't come visit me!" Jill snapped. "Look, I'm sorry, but I have no money and I'm close to my family. I'm doing what they want."

"Okay, okay, Jill. Of course I'll come visit you. I don't care if it's weird. But it's my baby, too, and I want to be with you all summer. Your dad should understand that. What are you gonna do in the fall?"

"Well…I think I'm gonna have to stay here and just finish school here, at Dale Brinkley. That's what my mom said."

"What the fuck, Jill?! You're just gonna go along with that? Did you even fight it at all? You must not care that much about being with me, then. I should have as much of a say as your parents do."

"Look, Adam," Jill fumed. "I know it's your baby, and you want to be around it, but do you have the money to pay for everything? Do you actually see us moving into an apartment together and raising the baby while still going to school? You already signed a lease for next year anyway! Plus, I've only been with you for a few months! My family has been here for me all my life and I'm not going to turn down their help now and just walk out on them! I've already caused enough trouble for them! Do you think I want to live here and go to school here?! I'm the one whose life is ruined! You can do whatever you want. You get to keep going to Dale and partying and having fun and I'm stuck here! I'll never be able to go out drinking and barely any of my friends live here during the school year so I wouldn't even have anyone to go out with if I could! I don't even have anyone to hang out with at all!"

"Jill, don't be mad. I was being an asshole. I'm sorry; look, I'll come and visit you as often as I can, and we'll work this out. Okay?"

"All right, that's fine," Jill said tiredly. She thought about telling him not to come at all but she didn't want to do something she'd regret later. She was just too exhausted to think about it clearly. And she understood where he was coming from. "I'll let you know after I talk to my dad. You can probably come next weekend if you want."

"Okay, let's plan on that. I'll call you tomorrow, okay? Night, baby."

"Night, Adam."

The next morning after church Jill and her parents ate lunch in the kitchen while Aaron and Winnie ate in front of different TVs. Jill knew her mom had set it up this way so they could tell her dad.

"Jill has something to tell you, Russ," her mom said as she sat their plates down in front of them. She gave Jill a prompting look.

Jill's dad looked out at her from behind the Sunday paper with curiosity in his blue eyes. "What is it, Jill?"

Jill fidgeted in her chair and looked down at Sunny, the dog. She twisted her fingers around the edge of the seat and finally looked up and looked her father square in the eyes. "I'm pregnant."

Her father's mouth widened into an O and he dropped the paper on top of his food. Then he seemed to gather himself together and quickly picked up the paper, folded it, and placed it aside. His gaze flickered over to Jill's mom, who was watching from the stove.

"Maria? Did you know about this?"

"Only since last night," Jill's mom answered calmly. "I thought it was best if she told you herself."

"Adam is the father, I assume?" her father asked, looking back at Jill. His voice had taken on a stern tone, as though he was a high school principal talking to a troublemaking student.

"Yes," Jill said quietly, looking back down at the table.

"Well, when is the baby due?"

"Next fall, right in the middle of the semester," Jill stated mechanically and glumly.

"Well, you'll be living at home of course," her father said matter-of-factly, picking up the newspaper and opening it again, but holding it below his face so he could still stare right at Jill. "You can take the semester off and then finish school here. Are you and Adam still together?"

"Yes, Dad."

"Okay, well, that's fine. He can come visit you here whenever he likes. I can't believe you were so irresponsible, Jill. Do you know how much this is going to cost us?"

"I have some idea," Jill muttered. "Thanks so much, though, Dad, for helping me out with the money."

"Well, do we really have any other choice?" He raised the newspaper up so that Jill could no longer see his face. "We'll go out to dinner tonight and tell Winnie and Aaron and talk about it as a family."

Jill nodded pointlessly. Once again, it had gone better than she thought it would, but she still felt enormously guilty for disappointing her family. She pushed her food away. "I don't think I'm hungry." She stood up from the table and went out of the kitchen.

Instead of going right to the stairs, she paused outside the door to hear what her parents would say.

"Well, I've dreaded that announcement for six years now," her dad said. "At least it didn't happen sooner. Now she's almost done with college. I probably didn't react that well though."

"It'll be fine," her mother said soothingly. "It's just a shock. I never expected that from Jill; I only worried about it because I guess it's natural for a mother to worry about that with her daughters…."

Jill turned and rushed down the hallway and up the stairs. She hurried into her room and shut the door and collapsed on her bed, sobbing. I'm such a disappointment, was all she could think. I'm such a horrible person.

That night when her family went out to dinner Jill was still feeling horrible and was extremely nervous about Aaron's and Winnie's reactions, especially Winnie's because she had always been close to her little sister and was afraid Winnie's opinion of her would be ruined.

It went a lot better than she thought it would. Her mom actually made the announcement, and Aaron snickered, then quickly covered his mouth and made a straight face when her dad glared at him. Jill didn't mind; she'd rather have Aaron laugh than be upset.

Winnie's eyes widened, and she seemed more intrigued than anything.

Her parents asked Winnie and Aaron not to tell any of their friends at school since it was so close to summer vacation, and that way some people might not have to find out at all. Jill knew this gesture was meant more to protect her than any of the rest of her family, since their friends and pretty much the whole town would find out soon enough. She appreciated it, but she knew

Aaron's friends would know the next day. She didn't care anymore though…better to get it out than keep being nervous about people's reactions.

When they got home Winnie came into Jill's room and asked her lots of questions and Jill was immensely relieved that they were able to talk and joke around just like old times. Thank You, God, she prayed silently, for not letting Winnie hate me or be ashamed of me!

After her talk with Winnie Jill went to bed feeling much better and she didn't have any depressing dreams that night.

Summer 2004

Jill's mood swings continued throughout the summer, but as time went by she felt content more often than she felt depressed. The one thing she hated the most was not being able to put on a bikini and lay around the pool, her favorite summer activity. Adam did end up coming to visit almost every weekend, and a couple of weekends Jill went down to stay with him.

Hilton was living at school for the summer, too, working as an assistant to a guy who ran his own photo shop and did portraits, passport photos, wedding photos, and whatever other odd requests he got. It wasn't the type of photography Hilton wanted to spend the rest of her life doing, but it was interesting enough for a summer job. Her weirdest customer so far had been a thirty-something woman who came in wanting to hire a photographer for her dogs' wedding. She wanted the package to include what it would for a normal wedding party: shots of the bride alone, the groom alone, the bridesmaids, groomsmen, parents, etc.—because apparently there *was* going to be a wedding party of eight other dogs—and she also wanted there to be photos of the ceremony. Hilton didn't have the nerve to ask who would be presiding over this ceremony. Not only that, but the woman requested that someone come to her house the week before the wedding to look at her yard and decide where the altar should be set up so as to have the best lighting for photos of a sunset wedding. Hilton was alone in the store when this happened, so she took down all the information as seriously as possible and promised to have her boss call on Monday. But when Hilton called back on Monday at her boss's request to ask the woman to come in again, she was informed that another photographer had already been hired. Jill and Hilton rolled on the floor in the living room of their apartment as Hilton told the story, gasping for breath and barely managing to spit out the words over her laughter. So those weekends at school were the most fun. Plus, Jill was relieved just to get away from home for a couple of days.

She was working at the same therapist's office she had worked at every summer and Christmas break since she graduated high school. She was a receptionist/secretary/assistant and she really liked her job. She didn't have to see too many people she knew there and the ones she did see were only vague acquaintances of her family and they weren't prone to starting long conversations with her or even asking her about the pregnancy, and she knew they wouldn't talk about seeing her because most of them didn't want people to know they were in therapy in the first place. It was as awkward for them as it was for her and they wanted to get in and out with only the necessary amount of small talk and eye contact.

Since she was busy with her job and Adam and making preparations for the baby, she didn't have a lot of time to think about Todd. It felt weird knowing he was in the same town but not having any contact with him, but she forced herself not to dwell on it.

She still didn't want to know whether she was having a boy or girl, and Winnie was enthusiastically making lists of names that kept getting longer and longer. Jill and Winnie and their mom went shopping to pick out some toys and clothes but they couldn't buy a lot since Jill didn't know the sex.

Jill wanted to keep seeing her doctor from school, but her mom insisted she go to their family doctor. Jill felt nervous about this because she didn't want to explain to him the circumstances of how she'd gotten pregnant. She had known him since she was a little girl and knew it would be embarrassing, but most of all she didn't want her mom in there hearing her tell about it. She finally agreed to go because she really had no choice, but she made her mom stay in the waiting room.

One day near the end of June she had just gotten to work and hadn't had a chance to look at the day's schedule yet when the door opened. She glanced up from her desk with a smile and a polite greeting ready but her mouth opened in shock instead when she saw Todd's mom.

"Uh…Mrs. Blake. Hi." She quickly plastered on a smile. "What are you doing here? I mean, I'm sorry, please come in and sit down. Are you the nine o'clock? Dr. Jennings should be right out…." Jill couldn't believe she hadn't thought of the very likely possibility of running into Todd's mom here. Mr. and Mrs. Blake had started couples' counseling back when Jill and Todd were in high school, and after their divorce Mrs. Blake had continued to come for individual sessions. The last couple of years she had cut her sessions down to one every month or so, but was still a regular client.

Mrs. Blake smiled at Jill and approached the desk. "Hi, Jill, honey, how are you? We've missed having you around this summer."

"I know," Jill said with a sigh. "It's just, I've been really busy….I'm sure you've heard about the baby and all…." She leaned back to point at her stomach, which was still only obvious when she wore tight clothing. She flashed her eyes guiltily at Mrs. Blake.

"I know you've been busy. Is everything going all right with your pregnancy?"

"Oh, yeah, it's going great! And I'm sorry I haven't been around; it's just that it's complicated now…." Jill looked down at the desk.

Mrs. Blake reached out and touched Jill's hand. Jill looked up to meet her gaze.

"I know, Jill," Mrs. Blake said and by the look in her eyes Jill knew she did. "But I think Todd would really like to hear from you."

Jill gave her a sad smile. "How is he, anyway?"

"Oh, he's good. Been hanging out with the boys a lot, you know. But I think he'd really like it if you gave him a call."

Jill looked down at her hands. "I know."

She thought about calling Todd all day. She wanted to more than anything, but things were going so well now and it would just screw everything up again. Plus Todd was used to not having her around by now, so why screw things up for him, too? Finally, after sitting on her bed debating for two hours, she threw her phone at her closet door and left her room to go outside, where the rest of her family was cooking burgers and lounging around the pool.

Bennett had a party every Fourth of July because he had a huge backyard and the fireworks were visible from his house. Jill had planned on spending the night with Adam down at school, but his parents wanted him to come home because they had a huge extended family and it was a tradition for them to watch the fireworks together every year.

"I'll come with you," Jill had suggested. She hadn't met Adam's parents yet and figured she probably should do so soon. She realized she really knew nothing about his life outside of Dale, nothing about his high school friends or interests, nothing about his family. She knew she was his first serious girlfriend in college, but he must've had one in high school? It freaked her out a little that she hadn't even wondered about his childhood and his hometown before. But she wanted to know now and this would be the perfect opportunity to learn all about him.

"Well..." Adam had said. "I haven't exactly told my parents you're pregnant yet."

"*What*?!" Jill had fumed. "You told me you told them right at the beginning of the summer, like I did!"

"I know...."

"So are you *planning* on telling them?"

"Well, yeah, but I'm just afraid of what their reaction will be."

"Well, you might want to tell them soon; they might want to know before the baby's born!" Jill exploded. "Are you planning on my family paying for *everything*?" Then a horrible, terrifying thought struck her. "You aren't planning on telling them, are you? Because you're afraid they'd make you live at home, or move here with me, and you have no intention of doing that! You don't plan to stay with me that much longer, so why should your parents know, right?" She was shaking.

"Jill, of course not! Are you fuckin' serious? Come on. Of course I plan to tell them. I'll tell them over the Fourth, if you want. But I think it'd be best for me to go by myself and tell them, rather than show up with a pregnant girlfriend. It'd be like, 'Hey, Mom and Dad! Surprise!' Don't think they'd go for that one."

"Fine. But you better tell them, Adam!"

"I know, don't worry, Jill; I will."

That was a week before the Fourth, and things were tense between Jill and Adam after that. No matter what he told her and no matter how much she tried to reassure herself, she couldn't shake the feeling that it was weird he hadn't told them yet and something was very wrong with that situation.

Hilton came home on July 3 to spend a few days with her parents, so Jill decided to go to Bennett's party with her. She hadn't planned on going because she hadn't seen most of the people who would be there since the news of her pregnancy spread around, and she wasn't looking forward to dealing with them. Hillary and Lorylyn had both called but Jill hadn't called back. In the end, though, Hilton convinced her it would be better to go and talk to them and give them some real information instead of letting them continue to gossip.

Jill had been too worried about Adam to consider the fact that Todd would most likely be at the party, but as soon as she and Hilton walked into the yard, there he was, playing basketball with Dirk and Bennett and another guy from high school on the half court in the backyard.

Jill and Hilton yelled hi to Bennett and then walked over to a group of their girlfriends without saying anything directly to Todd. They chatted with their girlfriends for awhile and Jill was having a good time. Everyone was very curious and interested and she didn't feel like anyone was talking about her behind her back or being disapproving. She didn't know now why she had automatically expected that reaction. Some of these girls had been her best friends in high school and tonight it didn't really feel like that much had changed. It was a comforting feeling.

Finally Jill left to use the bathroom and on her way through the garage she ran into Todd coming out. Why didn't I pay more attention so I wouldn't run into him like this? she wailed to herself. She wasn't sure if he would even talk to her but for some reason she stopped in front of him instead of walking past.

"Hi, Todd."

"Hi, Jill."

"How have you been? I ran into your mom; she probably told you."

"No. She didn't."

"Oh…." Jill pulled at her fingers absentmindedly. She looked around the garage, everywhere but at Todd. She could tell he was just staring at her. Finally she looked back at him and said, "I thought about calling you. A couple of weeks ago."

"I would've liked to hear from you," Todd said. Suddenly his shoulders slumped and his cool, indifferent look dissolved. "Damn it, Jill, I would've loved to hear from you. I've missed you so much. It's killing me not to be able to talk to you. Can't we try just being friends?" He reached out and touched her arm lightly with his hand.

Jill looked into his eyes and felt like she was seeing everything she was missing in her life. This was Todd, her best friend. How had she gone without him this long? Her whole body relaxed and she smiled. "Of course we can." She stepped into his arms and he hugged her tightly and kissed the top of her head.

"I still love you, Jill," he whispered. "I think about that night…all the time."

Jill jerked back. "Damn it, Todd! Why did you have to say that? I thought you wanted to be friends!"

"I do! I'm sorry. I thought it would be okay to say that. I'm fine with just being friends, though. I need you in my life."

Jill shook her head quickly, trying not to cry. "No, Todd, I can't do this. I can't do it to me or to you. Being friends is going to be too hard for us now! We'd just hurt each other. It'll hurt less to just make a clean break….It was going well before tonight, for both of us. That's why I didn't call you when I got home from school, like I said I would….Your mom said you were doing great….I'm sorry, Todd." She ran past him into the house.

She locked herself in the bathroom and sat on the toilet lid and cried, then quickly wiped her eyes and got up to fix her makeup in the mirror. She didn't want anyone to notice she'd been crying.

She considered telling Hilton she was ready to leave, but thought that would just spark questions and speculation, so she decided to stay. When she came back out of the house everyone was spreading out on blankets to watch the fireworks. Jill found Hilton and sat down beside her. Todd was sitting across the yard by Dirk and Hillary. He didn't look at her.

"Jill, what's wrong?!" Hilton asked as soon as they got in the car to leave. She was slightly drunk and Jill was driving.

"Todd told me he still loves me."

"Ohhhh….So what did you say to him?"

"I just told him we couldn't be just friends and it would hurt us too much to try. I said I thought it was better if we made a clean break."

Hilton gave Jill a sympathetic frown. "That sucks, but you have to do whatever seems best."

"Do you think that is best?"

"I don't know, Jilly." Hilton shook her head and patted Jill's arm. "But you'll figure it out. Everything happens for a reason."

"Yeah, I know. You're right. It'll all work out." It was easy to say, but it was harder to keep believing it.

That night she had a dream about Todd. She couldn't remember it when she woke up, but she knew things had been good between them because she had the feeling of being disappointed it was a dream.

The next day Jill cancelled her registration for the fall semester at Dale, but what she didn't tell her parents was she had only told the registrar's office she was taking a semester off; she hadn't requested a transfer to the Brinkley campus. She wasn't sure how she'd be able to go back to Dale in the spring, but she couldn't quite make herself shut that door just yet. You never knew what could happen….

Adam called her Monday night when he got back to school and told her he'd told his parents. "They weren't thrilled, but they were happy we were staying together," he told her. "They want to meet you."

"Good," Jill said with a sigh of relief. "Thank you, Adam. Oh, my gosh, I feel so much better now!"

They planned for Jill to go down the next weekend and meet his family, but unbeknownst to Jill, her mom, Winnie, and Hilton had planned a surprise baby shower for that weekend, so for the second weekend in a row, Jill didn't see Adam at all.

The baby shower was lots of fun and Jill got lots of good presents. Hilton's mom got her a book about caring for an infant, and Hilton got her a tiny Dale sweatshirt that either a boy or a girl could wear. Laney and Natalie came, too, and Laney got her an infant-sized Dale stocking cap and pair of socks, while Natalie got her a Dale t-shirt and bib.

"You guys, these are so cute!" Jill giggled. "Thanks so much!"

After the shower, Laney, Natalie, and Hilton stayed for the rest of the weekend at Jill's house and they went out to dinner and a movie that night, then stayed up all night eating and talking and watching movies. It was just like a lazy night at school. After they all left on Sunday Jill felt nostalgic but good and ready to face another week.

The following weekend she finally got to meet Adam's parents. She went down to school on Friday night and on Saturday she and Adam drove to his house an hour and a half south of Dale and spent the day with his parents out on their boat. They had a huge house right on a lake outside of a small town, and Jill got the impression the lake was the core of the community. They passed lots of other people on jet skis and boats, and Adam and his parents seemed to know them all. He was an only child, which Jill had assumed because she'd never heard him talk about any siblings, but she hadn't known for sure. She had hoped to meet some of his old high school friends, since apparently none of them went to Dale, but when she asked if any of them would be around, Adam said his best friend had died in a drunk-driving accident the summer after their senior year, so Jill dropped the subject.

Jill was worried because his family was Catholic and she thought they'd disapprove of her and the whole situation, but they were really fun and laid back. They took a case of Budweiser out on the boat and it was gone by the time they came in that evening. She thought it was hilarious that their cat was named Magnificat. They seemed to have made peace with the fact that their son was having a child and they were friendly to Jill and she felt accepted. She really liked them and was glad she'd gone.

On Saturday night she and Adam went back to Dale and played euchre all night with Hilton and Luke, and Jill had a blast. Maybe she wouldn't have to lose this totally….She could come down here after school started on the weekends, too, and Adam would still be coming to visit her and Hilton would come home for the weekends once in a while….It was going to be all right. Jill drove home Sunday feeling the happiest she had in a long time. She patted her stomach on the way and talked to the baby, whom she had started imagining was a girl. She thought about names and the only ones that came to her were names of characters on TV shows she watched.

"What?!" Winnie cried in frustration when she heard Jill telling her mom some of the names she liked. "Those are all TV characters! That's just stupid! You're so uncreative! I have lots and lots of better names than that!"

Jill agreed it was probably stupid to name her baby after a TV character and she didn't really even know it would be a girl. She promised Winnie to keep considering her lists of names.

The hardest time of the whole summer for Jill was at the end of August when all her friends went back to school. She hadn't found anyone to take over her lease because Hilton, Natalie, and Laney refused to let some stranger move into the apartment. They had firmly informed her they would each pay a third of her rent rather than have someone else move in, and that way she could come back and visit whenever she wanted and still have her bedroom. They wanted her to move back in for the spring semester, with the baby, and they pointed out that surely with all of them and Adam and all her other friends, there would always be someone to take care of the baby when Jill was at class. So Jill's name remained on the lease.

Jill hoped with all her heart this could actually work out, but it sounded too good to be true. She knew it wouldn't fly with her parents and she was just setting herself up for disappointment. Still, she couldn't stop hoping and she was glad she hadn't requested a transfer to the Brinkley campus yet. She told her parents she hadn't found anyone to take over her bedroom, but when she had explained her circumstances to the apartment managers, they had let her drop the lease.

She spent the weekend before school started at her apartment with her roommates and Adam, Justin, and Ryan had a big party on Saturday night. The weekend was fun, but it was depressing as hell driving back home to her new life on Sunday while her friends prepared for the first day of classes. A year ago she never would have imagined she could possibly end up in this situation.

September 2004

Hilton hated it at school without Jill. She liked Natalie and Laney but it just wasn't the same without her best friend. She spent more and more time with Luke and skipped the girls' nights. She knew it annoyed Natalie and Laney and she felt bad, but whenever the three of them hung out the room felt empty. Laney went to Eastern a lot anyway and so Natalie was hanging out with Justin and Ryan on the weekends. Maybe she'll just start dating Justin, Hilton thought. Then I won't have to feel bad for ditching her. But really, she wasn't *that* close to Natalie anyway. Any story she had, she would've told Jill or Laney before Natalie. Even though Laney was kind of gossipy, at least she was a good listener. Natalie wasn't really a *bad* listener; she just never expressed the same amount of interest Jill or Laney would. Hilton knew Jill felt the same way about Natalie. Laney was the only one who was extremely close to her.

Jill had been planning on trying to come down a lot of weekends, but she was getting big now and her parents didn't like the idea of her driving down alone all the time. So Adam went up there most weekends and Hilton went once when he didn't, but she wished Jill could come down to the apartment. She was still hoping Jill would be able to move back in next semester because right now her senior year was sucking big time. Even when she was with Luke the town still felt empty. She needed a close girlfriend, damn it! She had no one to tell her little everyday stories to. She talked to Jill on the phone but it just wasn't the same….Luke was getting annoyed with her because she was shitty with him a lot. And the worst part was it had only been three weeks. And her change of majors sophomore year from architecture to photography had pushed her graduation date back a semester. She had over a year left. She decided to do whatever she could to get Jill back down here next semester. And, she thought, no matter how bad this is for me, it's a hundred times worse for Jill.

The third weekend in September Laney went to Eastern again and Natalie decided to go with her because she was sick of sitting around being bored. It was like being home alone since Hilton was never there and she didn't want to become an annoying tagalong for Justin and Ryan. Plus Ryan's girlfriend was coming anyway, so it would be a good weekend to get away. She was afraid of being a third wheel at Eastern, but Laney assured her Del's roommate was hot and would go out with them.

As it turned out, he was extremely hot and Natalie was really glad she'd come. His name was Sean and he went out to dinner with them, but then at dinner Del asked him if Kari had called and Sean said no but he hoped she would call later and he and Del shared a knowing smile. Natalie's heart sank and she looked at Laney and narrowed her eyes.

Laney scrunched up her face in a look that said, Oops, my bad, and Natalie just rolled her eyes. Great, she thought. So I won't be the third wheel, I'll be the fifth wheel. She hoped she could at least find a guy to dance with at the bars. She hoped they went to a bar that had dancing.

Later as they were sitting at a table in one of the bars on Tenth Street, Todd came over to say hi to Del and Laney.

"Oh, hey, Nat. I didn't even see you over there."

Natalie smiled in a bored fashion and lifted her beer bottle to him in greeting.

Del started talking to him about Eastern's football team and Todd sat down at their table.

After a while Sean and Kari got up to dance and Laney and Del followed.

"You don't have to stay here," Natalie told Todd. "You can go find your friends; don't feel bad."

"Oh, no, I don't even know where they are." Todd leaned back against the wall. "So, how have you been?"

"Oh, kinda bored," Natalie said vaguely. "Not the most exciting year so far."

"Yeah? Me either, I guess. Same ol', same ol'." He smiled and took a long drink of beer.

"No shit. I mean, Laney comes here every weekend, Jill's not around, and Hilton's always with Luke so it's usually just me being a tagalong to our guy friends. I'm sure they're getting sick of it 'cause they never get a boys' night; that's why I came here. But I'm just a tagalong here, too." She laughed a little and gestured toward the dance floor with her beer bottle.

"Yeah, I know how you feel. It's always just me, Conrad, and Lizzy it seems like. That's my roommate and his girlfriend. I mean, tonight I'm here with some other guys but they all just wanna get some ass and I just haven't felt like it lately. I don't know what my deal is…." Todd smiled.

"Hey, that's not a bad thing, though."

"Yeah, I just don't feel like getting on a different girl every weekend anymore. Not like I actually got on a different girl every weekend before," he added quickly. "But before I always felt like it and now I'm just not interested."

"Yeah, I know what you mean. At first I was thinking I could find a guy to hook up with here and then at least I wouldn't feel left out, but I just don't even want to. I'd rather just chill here."

"Yep, I hear ya." Todd raised his bottle and Natalie clinked hers against it. They both laughed.

Natalie was thinking how easy Todd was to talk to. She'd never really had a long conversation with him before but they really seemed to get each other, at least with the third wheel thing. An hour later when Del and Laney returned to the table Natalie and Todd were still sitting there talking.

"Come on, you lazy asses!" Laney cried. "Come dance with us. Stop sitting there! Sean and his little slut left so we need people to dance with!"

Natalie and Todd looked at each other and smiled, and Todd stood up and offered his hand to her. She took it and they followed Laney and Del back to the dance floor.

He is so hot, Natalie thought as they danced together. But how can I even be thinking about him like that? He's Jill's! Wait, no he's not! She's having a baby with Adam. I guess I'm just used to thinking Jill and Todd would end up together….Just because he's her friend, that doesn't mean I couldn't date him! Plus he hasn't even asked about her tonight….Well, that's probably because he knows what's going on with her. I'm sure they talk all the time still. And plus, if he thought it would hurt her he would never even do anything with me. So I'll just let him make the first move.

She smiled to herself, happy with her decision and excited that she'd finally met a guy she could see herself dating. The more she thought about it the better it sounded. She could always come down to Eastern with Laney and if Jill moved back in they could even double date with her and Adam….It was almost too perfect to be true.

Todd finally kissed her and they spent a few minutes making out on the dance floor until Laney grabbed her arm and told her they were leaving. Todd didn't even try to get her to go home with him, which made her like him even more.

"Maybe I'll see you tomorrow," was all he said, and then he rushed off to find his friends, Natalie assumed.

"What the hell?!" Laney cried as she pulled Natalie into the bathroom. But she wasn't yelling; Natalie could tell by the little smile she was trying to hide.

"I know, I know. Jill, Jill, Jill. But it's not like they ever even dated!" Natalie defended herself as she played with her hair in the mirror. "And she's having a baby with another guy! She never even outright admitted to us that she liked Todd. And plus," she looked pointedly at Laney, "he wouldn't do anything that would hurt her."

"I don't know!" Laney cried. "I mean, he did kiss her that one time!"

"What?"

"Yeah, you know, the time last spring that she came down here with me. It was after she knew she was pregnant. Oh, come on, I know I told you! Yeah, he kissed her and then the next night they were really weird around each other! They hardly talked or touched or anything!"

"Okay, you definitely never told me that! But they're okay now, right?"

"I don't even know if they talk anymore. After that I never heard her talk about Todd."

"Oh, shit," Natalie rolled her eyes. "But still, it's not like I did anything wrong and all we did was make out. I'm sure nothing will come of it."

Laney looked at her knowingly. "You want something to come of it! And I'm not saying it's wrong; Todd doesn't belong to her and you guys can both do whatever you want. But do you think he's just using you to get back at Jill? I mean, they have a huge history. He could still be pissed about whatever happened. Like if he kissed her and she blew him off. And we don't even know what's happened since that one weekend I know about."

"No, he wasn't using me; I know that," Natalie said confidently. "We talked for like an hour, and we really just got each other. It was the most natural first conversation I've ever had with a guy. And he didn't even try to get me to go home with him or anything like that. So I know he wasn't using me." Natalie stared at herself in the mirror and slumped over onto Laney. "Damn it, Lane, I really like him!"

"Well go for it, then!" Laney said with a mischievous smile. "Jill has no claim on him and he must be over her if he ever did like her." Laney raised her eyebrows and shrugged. "And she's got a boyfriend and she's having a baby so don't even worry about it. If anything maybe she'll be glad he found someone else, if he did like her and she didn't like him."

"That's true," Natalie said, even though they both knew Jill had definitely liked Todd for several years. Damn it though, Natalie said to herself, she never even admitted it to us, so how was I supposed to know, right? And if she gets upset about it then screw her; I can do what I want and so can Todd. She's with someone else so Todd and I shouldn't hold back just from the fear of hurting her!

She hoped she'd see him tomorrow.

Todd didn't even look for his friends but decided to walk the two miles to his apartment. He was incredibly confused and needed to think some things over. He really liked Natalie and hadn't met a girl he could talk that easily with since Melanie, not counting Jill of course. And he knew he should move on from Jill;

it's not like he had a chance with her so it was just stupid and use-less to wait around. He had been thinking since the semester started that he needed to meet someone to actually date, not just hook up with. And now he had met someone with definite poten-tial, but she was Jill's friend. Todd knew dating Natalie wouldn't make him think of Jill because Natalie didn't look or talk at all like Jill or anything like that, and it's not like he was used to hanging out with the two of them together, but he was just afraid it wouldn't work out in the end because Jill would be too upset or he would be forced to be around her sometimes.

But you can't worry about her being upset, he told himself. She chose Adam over you so you're free to do whatever you want.

She was probably totally over him anyway, because Natalie wouldn't have kissed him if she thought it would hurt Jill. Even if it did hurt her, did he really care? Were they even friends any-more? No, she had specifically told him she didn't want to be.

Fuck you, Jill, he thought. You're not making me miss out on *another* relationship.

The next afternoon he called Natalie at Del's and asked her to dinner. He had thought about just asking her to meet up later at the bars, but he decided he might as well go all out and see if this could lead anywhere.

He cooked fettuccini alfredo. Natalie looked really hot and once again, the conversation was great. They were totally at ease around each other and Todd really liked her.

After dinner they sat around watching TV and ended up mak-ing out on the couch. Conrad and Lizzy called from the bars and wanted Todd to come to the midnight movie, so he and Natalie joined them. As they were leaving the movie Laney called, asking for a ride home from the bars, so Todd and Natalie went to pick them up. Outside Del's apartment, Natalie lingered in Todd's car for a moment after Laney and Del went inside.

"Nat, I've had a really good time with you this weekend. Would you, like, wanna keep seeing each other?"

"I'd love to." Natalie grinned at him and kissed him quickly on the lips. "I had a great time, too. I'm so glad we got a chance to get to know each other."

"Well, I'll give you a call sometime this week, then. Maybe we could get together next weekend. Meet in Indy or something."

"That'd be fun! Give me a call."

They kissed again and then Natalie climbed out of the car. She watched with a smile as Todd waved and recklessly reversed out of the parking spot. There was something about him that was so arrogant, but in a cute way. She giggled to herself as she turned and headed for the apartment. Finally! she thought. I've found the perfect guy!

"So what are you gonna tell Jill?" Laney asked on the way back Sunday afternoon.

"I don't know," Natalie said carelessly, flipping her hair over her shoulder and looking out the window. "I'm not. At least not yet. I mean, we'll see if it becomes anything and if it does then I'll tell her. Or he can tell her. Maybe he'll tell her today. We don't know how much they talk. They might still be really close."

"Yeah. So are you gonna tell Hilton?"

"I don't know; do you think I should?"

"No, she'll just go and call Jill right away. You know she will."

"Yeah, you're right. Okay, I won't tell her either."

"Guess what, guys!" Hilton exclaimed, bouncing and clapping her hands as soon as Natalie and Laney walked in the door. She was standing at the stove making dinner.

"What?" Laney asked.

"Jill's coming next weekend! Her parents are gonna let her come one more time before she has the baby! They just don't want her to drive down here alone so Adam's going up on Thursday night and driving her down, then taking her back on Sunday."

"Wow, that's a lot of driving for him," Laney said in a voice that implied she thought it was a stupid idea.

Hilton frowned. "Aren't you excited for her to come?! I can't wait! She hasn't been able to come at all yet the whole semester!"

"Yeah, that's awesome!" Natalie said, trying to sound upbeat.

"Yeah, I'm excited," Laney said. "I just hope she'll be okay, this close to being due."

"Well she still has like two months," Hilton said. "'cause she got pregnant at the end of February. So she's due at the end of November, I guess. I haven't asked her the exact due date."

"Yeah, that's true," Laney agreed. "I'm sure it'll be fine then."

As she and Natalie headed toward their bedrooms they sneaked an annoyed look at each other that said, Well, so much for keeping that a secret….Natalie had told Laney about Todd suggesting they meet in Indy, and Del was coming to Dale next weekend, so there was always the chance Todd would try to catch a ride with Del if he and Nat decided not to go to Indy.

Hilton looked after Natalie and Laney suspiciously and saw the glance pass between them. She was pissed. What the hell was their deal?! She knew they were annoyed with her for not hanging out with them much but that didn't mean they had to be annoyed Jill was coming. Did they just not like Jill all of a sudden or what? That was ridiculous. They better not get shitty about paying part of her rent, Hilton thought. Oh, well, I'll just pay it all myself if they do. I'll just have to tell my parents I need more money, or try to get more hours at the photo shop. Since school started, she'd only been working one night a week for three hours or so, just to have a little extra money for the bars and because it would look good on her resumé. She glared at Laney's and Natalie's closed bedroom doors and decided she'd have to figure out what the hell was going on before Jill came down here because she didn't want them being shitty with Jill.

Todd called Natalie on Wednesday. "Still wanna go to Indy?"

"Sure!" Natalie had decided not to mention that Jill was coming. If Todd had liked Jill, Nat didn't want to get him thinking about her and ruin all this. She had to at least find out if the whole thing with Todd was going to be anything before she let the Jill situation become a problem.

"Well, that's good, because I already made dinner reservations and booked a hotel room downtown."

Natalie's eyebrows rose. "Wow, I'm impressed!"

"The hotel room has two beds..." Todd said sheepishly. "Don't think I'm trying to do a bunch of nice stuff just to get you into bed."

Natalie laughed. "Well, we'll just see how the night goes..." she said suggestively.

"I'm not gonna be here this weekend," Natalie announced later that night when she, Laney, and Hilton were in the living room watching TV and doing homework.

Hilton looked up sharply. "Why not?"

Laney hid a laugh; Natalie had already told her she was for sure going to Indy with Todd.

"I'm going to Indy...." Natalie kept her eyes down and continued writing in her notebook.

"What for?" Hilton asked with a sideways glance at Laney, who stared at the TV.

"Well…." Natalie finished writing and looked up, meeting Hilton's gaze steadily. "I'm going there to see Todd."

"*What*?!" Hilton jumped up out of her chair. "Jill's Todd? Is something going on between you guys?"

"Okay, he's not *Jill's* Todd; she's with Adam, remember?" Natalie snapped.

Laney laughed and covered her mouth with her hand. She was still staring at the TV.

"And," Natalie continued, "we hung out last weekend at Eastern and had a really good time and we're seeing each other now."

Hilton felt like someone had punched her in the stomach. How could Todd do this?! Of all the shitty, fucked-up ways to get back at Jill! She had never thought he would be capable of something so low.

"Natalie, what the *fuck* are you thinking?! I can't believe you'd betray Jill like that!"

"Betray Jill? Like I just said, the last I knew, Jill was dating Adam. Oh, and she was also having a baby with him. So tell me how exactly I'm betraying Jill?"

"You fuckin' know she's been in love with Todd for years! And okay, I'm not saying he shouldn't be able to date someone else, but this will kill Jill! She'll be devastated, Natalie. I can't believe you would do that to her." Hilton was almost shaking.

"Well she never once told me she was interested in Todd, so how was I supposed to know?" Natalie asked innocently. "And plus, why would Todd do this if it would hurt her?"

Hilton realized she couldn't answer that question; she'd forgotten Natalie didn't know what had happened with Todd and Jill. She probably thought they were still best friends. Still though, how could she sit there and say she'd never known Jill was in love with Todd? What a bitch.

"She may have never said it, but you knew! Don't lie and say you didn't." She turned to Laney. "You think it's funny? You think that one of your best friends getting her heart broken is going to be funny? Wow, what great friends you guys are. Fuck you both." She stormed into her room and slammed the door.

"I just think it's funny you're so upset about it!" Laney yelled after her. "And Natalie's right; Jill has no claim on Todd. You're the one being a bitch about it, Hilton! Natalie finally met a guy she really likes; she should be able to date him! Jill probably won't even care!"

She looked at Natalie and burst out laughing. "She's so protective of Jill. Her best friend. You'd think she never even liked us, they way she's blown us off this year."

Natalie shook her head. "It's not funny. I feel bad about it. But still, it's not my responsibility in life to watch out for Jill. I have a right to make myself happy. And why the hell did Hilton get so upset about it?! What a bitch."

Hilton was so mad she didn't know what to do. She could barely see straight. How could Natalie even consider dating Todd? There were tons of guys she could date. And how could Todd do this to Jill? She knew she had to tell Jill and she didn't know how. But she couldn't let her come here this weekend and find out that way. She would be heartbroken. She was going to be anyway.

Hilton debated for a long time about how she should tell her. She didn't want to tell her over the phone but she also didn't want to wait until Jill got down here because that might make it too hard for her to be here. Finally she called Adam and begged him to let her go get Jill tomorrow instead.

"I'm having some problems with Luke and I really need to talk to her, just me and her," she pleaded.

"Can't you just call her, or talk to her when she gets here?"

"Please, Adam, please. I need girl time with her; you wouldn't understand. Just let me do it. That way you can go out tomorrow."

"All right, that's cool. Thanks, I guess."

"Oh, my gosh, thank you! You rock, Adam. Later."

Hilton didn't talk to Natalie or Laney at all before she left the next afternoon. It was a long drive home. She'd just told Jill she was coming instead of Adam so she'd have a chance to talk to her privately and catch up.

They went out to dinner in Brinkley and as soon as they'd ordered Hilton reached across the table for Jill's hand and looked her sadly in the eyes. Jill had bangs now and her hair was longer. She looked adorable. Hilton couldn't stand to hurt her....She hated Todd and Natalie.

"What is it, Hilton?" Jill asked, thinking something was wrong with Hilton.

"Jilly, I don't know how to say this. I wish I didn't have to tell you, but...I think Todd and Natalie are dating."

Jill dropped Hilton's hand. "What?" she choked out in a half-whisper. Tears came to her widened eyes almost immediately and she quickly looked around the restaurant, then wiped her eyes with the back of her hand. She stared at Hilton, pleading with her eyes for it not to be true.

"I just found out yesterday....Natalie went with Laney to Eastern last weekend and they didn't say anything to me about it until last night when Natalie said she'd be gone this weekend because she was going to Indy to meet Todd. She said they hung out last weekend and were going to keep seeing each other."

Hilton was almost crying, too. "Hon, I'm so sorry. I bitched her out. And Laney too because she was sitting there laughing." Hilton looked away in disgust. "What fucking bitches."

Jill stared down at the table. She was in shock. Finally she looked up and brushed her bangs out of her eyes. "I don't know what…I don't know…I just don't know." Tears started to run from her eyes again and she quickly and violently wiped them away. "You didn't tell them, did you? About me and Todd?"

"No, I didn't tell them anything. They think there's nothing wrong with it; they said you have no claim on him and Natalie can do whatever she wants. But I yelled at her and told her she knows you've loved him for years. And she denied ever knowing it. What a bitch! Uhhh!" Hilton shook herself violently. "I can't stand either one of them!"

"Do you think Todd is just trying to get back at me? Or…does he really like her?" Jill looked at Hilton beseechingly. If Todd really liked Natalie Jill would be devastated. Even though it was the worst way she could think of for him to get back at her, she hoped that was all it was. She knew it was a selfish thought, but she couldn't stand the thought of Todd with one of her best friends. She had never felt so betrayed.

"I have no idea, Jill." Hilton shrugged. "I guess we'll have to wait and see…."

Jill looked down and nodded.

"So that's why I came. I didn't know if you'd even want to come down now."

Jill hesitated. She had no idea. This was way too much to handle at once. She was still in shock. "Well, they won't be there, right?"

"No, they won't."

Finally Jill looked up, still sniffling away tears. "I'll go, then. Fuck them," she said defiantly. "I won't let them ruin this weekend. I've looked forward to it all week."

"Good," Hilton said with a smile. "And you know what, Jill? You've struggled over what to do about Todd, but if he really likes someone else, at least you'll have your answer. You'll know you made the right decision." She squeezed Jill's hand.

Jill nodded and squeezed Hilton's hand back, but she stared out the window instead of meeting Hilton's eyes.

They decided not to go back until the next day and Hilton stayed over at Jill's house.

Jill dreamt she was dancing with Todd at the party in her apartment, and Natalie came up and started dancing behind him. Jill grabbed Todd's face in her hands and stood on her toes to kiss him firmly. He was hers tonight, damn it. She had completely forgotten that Adam had left with that other girl.

Todd kissed her back hungrily and their kisses got sloppy because they were so drunk. He was rubbing her ass and Jill knew they were putting on quite a show but she was too drunk to care.

"Get a room!" she heard somebody yell. It sounded like Justin. Some people started laughing. Jill laughed against Todd's mouth.

"We're so drunk!" she giggled. "Why are we making out?!"

"'Cause it's fun." Todd tried to kiss her again but Jill backed away.

"Come get another drink with me," she said, grabbing his hand and leading him into the kitchen.

"Get it, Jill!" Hilton shouted.

Jill looked across the room at her and both girls doubled over in laughter. A minute later Hilton was at Jill's side.

"You better hook up with him tonight!" she whispered loudly in Jill's ear. "I'll be so disappointed in you if you don't!"

Jill pretended to glare at her but she couldn't pull if off and started giggling again. "*Shhhh, Hilton,*" she said in an exaggerated whisper.

Then all of a sudden Hilton was calling her name and Jill knew she was in bed, and she had the panicky feeling that she was naked again. She hurried to cover up before Hilton came in her room but then she realized she was wearing sweats and a long-sleeved t-shirt and was in her bed at home. Hilton was talking to her from the floor.

"Jill! Wake up! It's eleven…do you wanna get going pretty soon?"

Jill blinked and quickly sat up, holding the covers around herself. "Yeah, sure, that's fine. Man, that was a weird dream!"

"What was it?"

"It was about a party at our apartment last year and I was making out with Todd…."

"Oh, I remember that!"

"You do? It really happened then?" Jill asked with a frown. "I've dreamed about it a couple times but I don't remember it happening…."

"Yeah, it did. I had forgotten about it till now but I definitely remember. I so wanted you to hook up with him that night! You big wuss!" She smiled.

"Did he hook up with anyone that night?"

"I have no idea; Luke made me go to bed right after you were making out with Todd. He thought I was so wasted and I totally wasn't." She looked at Jill and giggled. "Okay, well I was, but I was just having a good time. I didn't need to go to bed. But anyway, I don't know if Todd hooked up with anyone, and he must've been gone by the time I got up the next day….Wait, you don't think he hooked up with Natalie that night, do you?" Hilton's eyes had widened and her voice was suspicious.

Jill shuddered and shrugged quickly. "Who knows. Okay, well I'm gonna get in the shower." She jumped out of bed and walked quickly into her bathroom, shutting the door behind her.

❦   ❦   ❦

The car ride to Dale was more upbeat than the dinner conversation had been. Hilton updated Jill on everything going on at school and told stories about Luke, classes, and professors. She was taking a black and white class, her favorite of all her photography classes so far. They got to the apartment around three and Laney wasn't home. Both girls were glad to put off dealing with her for awhile and sat around in the living room watching TV.

Laney got home around five.

"Hey, Jill!" She ran over to give Jill a hug. Jill didn't bother to stand up but let Laney bend down to reach her. "So how's everything going?"

The three of them sat in the living room and talked for awhile. Hilton was really short with Laney but Jill decided to just be friendly with her because it was easier than being a bitch and making things awkward for the whole weekend. Plus, at least Laney wasn't the one dating Todd.

"Is Del coming this weekend?" Jill asked.

"No, this is the first weekend this semester we haven't seen each other. But it's okay. It'll be nice to have a weekend with just the girls! I told him not to come because you were coming."

"Awe, that was nice," Jill said. She saw Hilton glare at Laney and could almost hear Hilton thinking, What a two-faced bitch! Jill thought Laney sincerely wanted to spend the weekend with them though, and she couldn't understand how Laney could want to do that and be truly excited to see her, yet still think it was okay for Natalie to be dating Todd. But I guess her feelings of friendship toward me haven't changed; she just thinks Todd and Natalie are free to do whatever they want, Jill decided. And she had to admit to herself that it did make sense. They *could* do whatever they wanted. She had no hold on Todd and no right to be mad at him for dating someone. She still felt betrayed by Natalie though. She tried to think what she would do if she was in Natalie's situation and really liked Todd. She didn't know.

Jill and Laney and Hilton went out for dinner then went over to Adam, Justin, and Ryan's apartment. They played six-handed euchre since Jill couldn't play a drinking game, and when they got bored with that they moved on to drinking games anyway and Hilton and Laney took turns taking Jill's drinks for her.

Jill wanted to spend the night with Adam, so Laney and Hilton crashed in the living room. It had been so long since she'd spent the night here. It made her sad.

"So, are you ready for the baby to come?" Adam asked when they were in bed.

"I think so….I mean, I've been reading some books and stuff and I have my mom to help me so I think I'll be okay. I'm just kind of getting nervous about the actual giving birth part…."

"I hope I can be there for it. Hopefully I'll have enough time to get there after you go into labor."

"Yeah, well the first labor is usually long I've heard. So I'm sure it'll work out."

"What about names?"

"Oh, my gosh, you've seen the lists Winnie's made. And she keeps adding to them! I don't really have one that's really struck me as right…not for a boy or a girl."

"What do you want it to be?"

"I don't know, you?"

"It doesn't matter to me. I'll be happy no matter what. As long as it's healthy. And you, too."

"Don't worry, I'll be fine." Jill smiled and snuggled up to Adam.

❧   ❧   ❧

Natalie and Todd went out to dinner in downtown Indy and both of them had a really good time. It was a nice night so afterward they walked around the city for almost two hours, holding hands and talking.

"I'm having such a great time, Todd," Natalie said with a smile. "This is so fun; thanks for a wonderful night." She kissed him.

"I know; I'm having a great time, too," Todd replied. He looked her in the eyes and offered her a genuine smile as he swung her hand back and forth.

When they finally checked into their hotel they decided to use the hot tub. It was almost eleven and no one else was around. They fooled around a little in the hot tub and then decided to go back up to the room.

"I'm getting in the shower," Natalie said, taking her ponytail down and shaking her hair out.

"Can I join?" Todd asked with a wink.

"No, not tonight. I kinda wanna take things slow…if you don't mind."

"No, not at all. Don't feel pressured. That's fine." Todd kissed her quickly and smiled.

Natalie felt relieved. She was having a blast with him and things felt so natural, but she didn't want to get carried away and regret it later. Before she slept with him she wanted to be sure this was going somewhere because she didn't want it to end in two weeks and then always feel guilty around Jill for having slept with Todd. The thought was also still in the back of her mind that he might only be interested in her because he couldn't have Jill, the girl he really wanted. She didn't want to be his second choice.

✿   ✿   ✿

The rest of Natalie and Todd's weekend went well. They slept in separate beds both nights and Todd didn't make any more comments about getting in the shower with her. They did fool around a little but he didn't try much. He didn't seem to mind holding back and she was glad he wasn't pressuring her. Maybe he was actually a nice guy. Could she be so lucky?

Natalie wasn't sure what time Jill would be leaving to go home on Sunday, so after Todd left around noon to head back to school, Natalie stayed in Indy and did some more shopping. She and Todd had gone to the Circle Centre Mall on Saturday but she didn't want to make him wait while she tried on a bunch of clothes, so she went back and spent four hours going to all the places she had seen things she liked. She ended up spending two hundred dollars but didn't feel bad about it because it had been such a great weekend, so why not give herself a little treat to end it?

She hoped she wouldn't run into Jill because she was afraid it would ruin her mood. Luckily, only Laney was home when she got back around six.

"Hey, how was it?!" Laney greeted her enthusiastically.

Natalie sighed with pleasure. "Oh, my gosh, it was so great, Lane!"

Laney grinned.

"So did Jill leave?" Natalie asked.

"Yeah, she left like an hour ago. Adam's driving her back."

"Where's Hilton?"

"Luke's."

"So how was it this weekend?"

"Fine. Really good actually. It was good to see Jill. The you and Todd thing didn't come up at all. I'm sure Hilton told her, but she didn't seem upset or anything, so she must've been okay with it." Laney shrugged and got her food out of the microwave.

"Good," Natalie said with a sigh of relief. "I guess Hilton just overreacted then."

"I guess."

Jill was exhausted by the time she got home. She had pretended to sleep in the car so she wouldn't have to keep up a conversation with Adam, but she was really trying to make herself mentally okay with Natalie and Todd. She had tried to act upbeat all weekend, and acting it helped her feel it, but every time she thought of Todd and Natalie together in Indy, cuddling at a movie, or Todd buying her dinner, or the two of them making out or having sex, she felt sick to her stomach. You have to get over it, Jill! she told herself. It's just something you're gonna have to live with.

By the time they were half an hour from her house, she'd convinced herself she was okay with it because she realized she'd had fun this weekend, even knowing the two of them were together, and she told herself it'd just keep getting easier as time went by. And she knew she should be happy for Todd since she'd broken his heart….She should be glad he'd found someone else to make him happy. She told herself it was selfish to want him to still want her and love her and she promised herself she'd try as hard as she could to stop thinking like that.

The last half hour of the ride she talked to Adam cheerfully and when she got home she felt almost happy. It had been a good weekend and she was proud of her resolution to get over being upset about Todd and Natalie. Adam came in and ate dinner with her family, and Jill walked him out to his car when he left.

They kissed goodbye.

"See you next weekend, baby," Adam said, patting her head.

Jill smiled at him as he lowered himself into the car. "See you then."

October 2004

On Thursday, October 16, Jill went into labor. It was long like she'd thought it would be…eighteen hours. Adam and Hilton were there four hours into it and she felt bad they had to stay overnight.

"I told you it'd be long," she told Adam. Then she jokingly added, "You should've gone out to the Turtle and come tomorrow morning and you probably wouldn't have missed anything…."

The baby was finally born at 6:17 Friday morning. It was a beautiful baby girl with dirty blond hair like Adam's. Jill cried as the doctor passed her baby to her for the first time. She was so glad her hair was the color of Adam's. She hoped it would stay that color forever.

"Does she have a name?" the doctor asked.

Jill looked at Adam. "Adria. Adria Nicole." Adam smiled, running his fingers through Jill's hair.

Winnie and Hilton were both disappointed with Jill's name choice. They had both wanted Aspen Nicole. Winnie had actually wanted Aspen Capri.

"You guys, I can't name her Aspen! She would get made fun of so bad when she's young! Do you know what kids would come up with for that name?"

"Whatever, that's what I'm naming my first girl," Winnie said defiantly.

"Well, then, our girls will have the same name," Hilton said and they smiled at each other and giggled.

"You could have at least named her a city name!" Winnie cried exasperatedly. "I really like the city names."

Jill laughed. "I know." Two weeks ago Winnie had abandoned all the name lists she'd made so far and started focusing only on city names. She thought they were really cool and unique and Jill liked some of them, but couldn't ever find one that seemed just right.

"At least I picked your first choice of all your other names you came up with," Jill pointed out.

"Yeah, it's okay; I guess I can live with it," Winnie said with a dramatic sigh. "At least you didn't name her after a stupid TV character!"

"Yeah, I guess I can live with it too..." Hilton agreed, rolling her eyes and pretending to be annoyed.

All three girls burst out laughing.

"No, really, Jilly, I love it," Hilton said. "She's so beautiful. She has your eyes."

Jill smiled. "And Adam's hair. I love Adam's hair."

Hilton smiled and thought that she would've said Adria's hair was a little darker than Adam's...more the color of Todd's.

Hilton hadn't wanted to wake Natalie and Laney with the news, so she called the apartment around noon to tell them. Natalie answered and said Laney was at class but she would make sure to tell her as soon as possible. She sounded really excited and said she would talk to Laney about coming up next weekend to visit, once Jill was settled at home.

After Natalie hung up she decided to call Todd and tell him. They had seen each other every weekend, and even though Todd had a project to do this weekend, he had promised to come and stay for three days next weekend to make up for it. Jill's name had come up once but Todd had brushed it off easily, saying only that he and Jill didn't talk much anymore because she was several hours away and busy with Adam and the baby, but he hoped she was doing well. Natalie still didn't know if there had ever been anything going on between Jill and Todd, but she thought Todd might think it was weird if she didn't call and tell him, plus she was really excited to tell someone and Laney wasn't home.

"What?!" Todd exclaimed in shock. "She had the baby already? Is everything okay? Is she okay?"

"Of course, why wouldn't she be?"

"Well she's like a month early! Right?"

"Oh, yeah, I guess so." Natalie hadn't even thought about it. But now she remembered Hilton saying Jill should be due in late November. "Huh, weird. I hadn't even realized. Hilton didn't say anything about any problems though when she called just now, so I guess everything's fine."

"Huh, okay, well that's good then," Todd said, but he didn't sound convinced. "Hey, well, I've gotta go meet Conrad for lunch, so I'll give ya a call later tonight. Sorry I can't come see you this weekend, but I just really have to get this research project done. But thanks for letting me know about Jill."

"Okay, bye."

Natalie flipped her phone shut with a small frown on her face and stared at the kitchen table for a moment. Weird reaction, kinda, she thought. How would he remember exactly when she's due if they don't talk anymore? Oh well…it's probably no big deal. She shook her head to clear her thoughts and went into her bedroom.

❦   ❦   ❦

Todd sat on the edge of his bed with his head in his hands. Shit, he thought. He hadn't been expecting the call about Jill and it had thrown him off. He had immediately worried about her and the baby and he was afraid it had showed too much. He didn't want Natalie to get the wrong idea. He liked her a lot and really thought this thing between them was going somewhere. But now all he wanted to do was call Jill to make sure she was okay. He had already forgotten about his research project, which had been all he could focus on for the last week. He didn't know what to do. Finally he called Conrad.

"Hey, dude, sorry, but I can't make lunch. Jill had her baby…."

"Oh, shit, are you goin' home then?"

"No, I'm not plannin' on it. But I just need to think about some shit I guess. It kinda threw me off. Sorry, man."

"Dude, don't worry. It's cool. I'll see ya at home later, okay?"

"All right, later, man."

Then on an impulse Todd called Jill's house. He knew she wouldn't be home and asking her parents about her would be better than calling her cell. He knew he shouldn't do anything that might upset her right now.

Jill's mom answered the phone.

"Hi…Mrs. Sherer…it's Todd. I, uh, heard that Jill had the baby and I just didn't know if I should try to call her or anything but I just wanted to make sure she's okay and everything, since she was early and all…." He trailed off, wanting to shoot himself. He sounded like such an asshole, and he had no idea how much Mrs. Sherer knew about what had happened between him and Jill.

"She's fine, Todd," Mrs. Sherer replied in a slightly confused voice. "And she's not early at all; she was actually due two days ago."

"What?" Todd exclaimed, figuring quickly in his mind. In March she'd said she was about a month pregnant, April, May, June, July, August, September, October, no, he hadn't miscounted. She should only be eight months along.

"But…" he faltered. "I thought…she told me…." His heart was racing. "Oh, holy fucking shit. Oh, shit. Oh, shit. I'm sorry, Mrs. Sherer. Never mind. I was thinking about something else. I was just wrong. Sorry." He hung up. He was breathing so hard he thought he was going to hyperventilate. She's not early. That means January. Oh, God. Wow. He grabbed his keys and ran to his car.

Jill's parents had taken the day off work and stayed with Jill till around eleven. After that they went home to rest since they'd been up all night, and after school they brought Winnie back to the hospital. Winnie had insisted on staying with Jill all day, but Mrs. Sherer had made her go into school at eleven.

As soon as they got back to the hospital Winnie rushed into Jill's room, beaming. "Guess what?! Adria *is* a city name! It's in Italy! I looked it up at school!" She was extremely proud of herself.

Jill grinned. "Well, see, quit giving me all that crap about not picking one of your city names!" she teased. "I knew it was a city the whole time…."

"You did not!" Winnie giggled and twirled around the room. "I'm glad you picked Adria now! It sounds so…tropical or something. Exotic! That's it! I love it!"

After Winnie went to get a snack and Mrs. Sherer got a moment alone with Jill, she told her about Todd's call. She had debated whether she should or not, but finally decided Jill would want to know.

"Todd called today," she said softly.

"What? He called the house?"

"Yeah. He sounded all flustered and said he didn't know whether to call you or not. He was really worried because he thought you were a month early."

Jill quickly glanced down, then looked back at her mother with a confused expression. "What did you say?"

"I told him you were actually due on Wednesday and then he started acting really weird, almost freaking out. Then he said he must have just figured wrong about when you were due and he hung up. It was really very strange."

"He was acting weird?" Jill sat up straight. "What did he say when he was acting weird?"

"Just a lot of cuss words and then 'I'm sorry, Mrs. Sherer. I was just wrong.' And then he just hung up."

Jill sat back against the pillow and looked down at her hands, which were gripped together so tightly they hurt. "Huh. Weird. Oh, well, who knows I guess." She shrugged and gave a small laugh. "Well, I'm pretty tired, Mom; I think I'm gonna get some sleep now."

"Okay, honey; I'll check back later."

Jill turned her head away as her mom walked out of the room and pulled the covers as tight around her as she could.

At 4:30 Hilton was sitting in the waiting room reading a magazine when Todd burst in.

Hilton looked up and visibly jumped. "Todd, what the hell are you doing here?!"

"I need to see Jill. Where is she?" He was out of breath and looked completely distraught. He wouldn't even look right at Hilton.

"She's sleeping. Todd, seriously, what the hell is wrong with you?"

"Nothing. I just wanted to make sure she was okay. Natalie said she thought Jill was early. So I was worried about her."

"Yeah, she is early, I think," Hilton said. "But she's fine. No problems at all."

"You think she's early?" Todd stopped glancing around nervously and stared at her.

"Well, I never even asked her for sure what her due date was." She stared at Todd. A crazy idea was taking shape. "I was thinking November sometime, but I don't remember for sure when she first had sex…with Adam. So I could be wrong."

"Oh." Todd looked around again but Hilton didn't miss his slight flinch at her words. "Where's her mom?"

"I don't know. Maybe eating or something. Why don't you sit down?"

"No, I really need to see Jill. Please just tell me what room she's in."

Hilton told him and as he practically sprinted off down the hall she watched him with narrowed eyes as she thought back to last spring and figured quickly in her head. Then she remembered the conversation she'd had with Jill last month about their party back in January and she was almost sure now that she was right. But it was almost just too far out there….

Todd peeked in Jill's room before he opened the door. He wanted to make sure no one else was in there. It looked empty so he looked quickly around to make sure Jill's mom was nowhere in sight, then he knocked twice on the door as he pushed it open.

Jill wasn't asleep and she sat straight up in bed as soon as he opened the door.

"What are you doing here?" she asked in an almost scared voice as she looked at him through her devastating brown eyes. His gaze was drawn automatically to them, even though they were partially hidden by her bangs.

Then he didn't know what to do. All he'd known was he had to get here and tell her, but now he started to wonder if he'd made a huge mistake. He froze in the middle of the room and just stared at her.

The silence seemed to stretch on forever. Then all of a sudden she whispered, "It was you, wasn't it?" Then she burst into tears and slid down, covering her face with the blanket.

Todd rushed to the bed and knelt beside her. "Yes, Jill, yes, it was me. Please don't cry. Please." He reached out to touch her hair, some of which was showing from under the blanket.

"Why didn't you tell me?" she sobbed. "Why didn't you tell me? I was your best friend. How could you let me go on not knowing? Do you know what *hell* that was for me?" She lifted her face from under the blanket and the look on it broke his heart.

"Jill, I don't know, I don't know. I mean, I thought you'd remember and we'd talk about it later; I just couldn't deal with it that morning. Then when you didn't say anything, I realized you didn't remember and so it was just easier not to tell you. I thought I was doing the right thing. I thought we'd never be able to be friends if I told you. I thought you'd hate me and think I took advantage of you."

Jill sat up again and angrily wiped her tears away. "You didn't think we could be *friends*?" she hissed. "You didn't think we could be *friends*? Well you could have at least told me when you found out I was pregnant! But no, you just told me how you were in love with me and let me fall in love with you too and you still didn't tell me! Do you know I was in love with you all of high school? It took me so long to get over you and I was *so* happy when I did! And then you told me you were in love with me and I fell for you all over again. And you were afraid we couldn't be friends anymore."

"How was I supposed to tell you when I found out you were pregnant? I didn't want to interfere. You remember the night you told me you were pregnant and how weird my reaction was? Well that's because I thought it was mine, Jill! I thought you were telling me you were having my baby and you'd known we slept together all along! Then you asked if I wanted to know who the father was and it totally shocked me! And then I asked you if Adam was the first guy you had sex with and you said yes! So I thought maybe you didn't even know you had sex the other time! What was I supposed to say, 'No, actually you're wrong, it wasn't your first time, because you slept with me at a party two months ago?' You know what, Jill?" Todd's voice had taken on a desperate tone. "I wanted to kill myself for not telling you right away. Because I thought if I had maybe I could've had you. You could've been my girlfriend. This whole time I've partially blamed myself for you getting pregnant. If I hadn't been such a pussy for so long maybe you would've ended up with me and not been pregnant. That's what I kept thinking."

Jill snorted in disgust. "You partially blamed yourself for me getting pregnant? How ironic. Well now you can fully blame yourself for ruining my life! I won't say you took advantage of me that night, because I've had dreams about it and I remember…some things from earlier in the night. But after a certain point I've never been able to remember the rest of it, till waking up naked in bed by myself the next morning! Until about a month ago I wasn't sure if what I was dreaming about had actually even happened at all! But then I told Hilton about the dreams and she told me she remembered that night…but she didn't know if you hooked up with anyone or not. When she told me we had actually been making out that night, well that was the first time I wondered if it was you. Before that I never thought it was a possibility. I thought the dreams were just…wishful thinking. But I guess dreams do come true," she snapped bitterly, angry again. "You walked out on me the next morning and you didn't even tell me! How do you think I felt when I found out I was pregnant?! And I didn't even know who I slept with that night. I didn't even know who I lost my virginity to. I thought it was someone I didn't even know…and I couldn't bear that humiliation, Todd. So I slept with Adam."

She started crying again but quickly brushed away the tears. She turned away and her face was expressionless. "I never expected anything to come of it and then he would've been off the hook easy when I told him I was pregnant; I would've just said I didn't expect anything from him or maybe I wouldn't have even told him it was his, but at least I would've been able to tell my parents and friends I knew whose baby I was having. But then Adam liked me and I thought, why not? Why not start dating him and be happy? I thought everyone would just think I was a month early…except my mom. I told her when I was really due….She and my whole family think I've been dating Adam since right after Christmas break. So look what you've done, you fucking asshole! You ruined my life and made me ruin Adam's!"

Todd was angry now too. "I did not *ever* make you sleep with Adam! Once you told people you were pregnant, I would've come forward and told you that we slept together, Jill! It was your choice to sleep with him, and a pretty bitchy thing to do if you ask me! How could you pick some guy out to sleep with and just say, 'Okay, he's hot, so I'll let him think he's the father of my baby. I choose him.' That's bullshit, Jill! That's not you! The Jill I knew would never do anything like that! What the fuck were you thinking?"

Jill didn't look mad anymore. She looked ashamed. "You're right. I know. The whole thing just made me crazy. I couldn't believe it when I found out I was pregnant, Todd. Me, Jill, the good girl. The virgin. Or so everybody thought. And then to tell people I didn't even know who the father was because I was so wasted I couldn't remember who I lost my virginity to? It's not like I knew it was you and knew you would come forward! I thought it was somebody random, maybe even someone I didn't know, and would never see again! You don't know how awful that was, Todd! I have never felt worse about myself, so I had to cover it up somehow! So I slept with Adam, and like I said, I expected it to just be a one night stand and then I was just going to tell him he didn't have to be any part of it. But then I just got so caught up in him and I had this perfect picture of having a nice little family and I just couldn't stop myself! I really don't even know how to explain it. I know it was the worst thing I could've done, to do that to him, but it was like I was a different person. I started to feel guilty about Adam a little, and that's when the idea of having an abortion came to me, but I just couldn't do it. And I guess I rationalized it a little to myself by thinking about how many girls Adam's slept with and how he almost deserved something like this to happen to him. And then as time went on I almost started to forget that it was all a lie. I thought about Adam like he was really the father! I know that sounds crazy, but it's true! Like when I told Adam I was pregnant and he freaked out, I was actually pissed he didn't want his own baby! I really felt like it was his!"

"Wow, Jill." Todd was silent for a minute. He couldn't believe it. He really did see her as a different person in a way now. He couldn't believe what she'd done. But he could see from the way she was talking now and the way she'd acted around him last spring how desperate she'd been. But pulling someone else into it and completely ruining that person's life just to help herself look better?

Jill was staring at him, waiting for some kind of reaction.

"You know, you think it's shitty that I didn't tell you we slept together," he finally said. "But now, since I didn't, all this has happened and I've gotten to see the person you really are. And what I'm trying to figure out right now is how you can be someone totally different than who I thought you were. And I'm especially trying to figure out how the fuck it's possible that I still love you, because I do." Todd broke down and covered his face with his hands so she wouldn't see the tears. He didn't see her face go cold.

"I can't believe you're blaming this on me, Todd. It's not like I really had a choice, okay? You have no idea what it was like for me! And now, on top of all that, to find out my supposed best friend didn't have the balls to admit what happened! He just walked out the next morning and left me by myself. But then later, when I'm with someone else, oh, he has no problem telling me he loves me then. You know what, Todd? It seems like all you do is fuck up my life. Why did you even come here? I wish you'd never told me! Get the fuck out of my room. Get out of my life."

"Jill, no!" Tears were running down Todd's face now and he suddenly felt like she was slipping away from him. He felt panicky. He couldn't lose her. "I know it was a huge mistake, okay? I won't blame you! I don't know what it would've been like to be in your position. Please, just talk to me some more, Jill. Please. I want to be with you. I want to be the father of our baby. You know what I thought today when I found out it was mine? My first thought was, Oh, God, thank You, this is the best day of my life. Jill, I was so happy when I found out. I'm still so happy. Please let me be a part of this. Please."

Jill gave him a look that could have frozen hell over. "You had your chance to be with me and be this baby's father nine months ago. You ruined that chance and you ruined everything for me. So I'll say it again, and I mean it, Todd," she said in the coldest voice he'd ever heard. "*Get...out.*" She slid down and pulled the blanket over her head again.

Todd sat there in shock for what seemed like forever. Jill didn't move. Finally he stood up and walked mechanically out of the room. He walked down the hall to the waiting room, seeing nothing, and sat down in the first chair he came to.

"Did you see her?" said a voice in front of him. He looked up to see Hilton standing there staring down at him.

"I saw Jill," he muttered, annoyed. Wasn't that obvious? Where did Hilton think he'd been this whole time?

"I mean your daughter. Did you see your daughter?"

Todd's head jerked around and he stared at Hilton. "It's a girl?" he asked in a soft, amazed voice.

"You know what, Todd?" Hilton said airily. "I'm glad it's yours. I like you and Jill together. I always thought you guys would end up together. But I don't know if that's going to happen now. You fucked things up big time and I don't know where Adam is but you better get the hell out of here before you make an even bigger mess of things." Hilton turned and walked down the hall toward Jill's room, leaving Todd staring after her.

A girl, he thought. Jill and I have a baby girl.

When Hilton walked into Jill's room Jill was sobbing with her head in her hands. She looked up at Hilton and just shook her head. Hilton rushed over to the bed to hug her.

"Don't worry, Jilly, it's all gonna be okay."

"Hilton, you have no idea…."

"No, I know. It's okay."

Jill looked up at Hilton with wide eyes. "How do you know?"

"I figured it out. Just now. I saw Todd out there...." She motioned toward the waiting room. "So why...did you pretend it was Adam's this whole time?"

"Because I didn't know whose it was!" Jill shook her head again, wiping angrily at her eyes. "I didn't even know I slept with Todd! It was that party at our apartment last year right after we got back from Christmas break, you know, the one I was asking you about a few weeks ago."

Hilton nodded. "Yeah, that's what I thought. I figured it out after Todd came in. I remembered that convo we had...."

"I didn't remember anything from that night when I woke up the next morning, but I was in my bed naked by myself, and I was sore, you know, so I knew...that I slept with someone but I didn't even remember who. And then as soon as I found out I was pregnant I started having dreams about that night. And I remember making out with Todd but I could never remember anything past that. But it really wasn't until I talked to you about my dream that morning that I really started to wonder if it might be him. Things just really started to make sense...like him all of a sudden wanting me and trying to make out with me and stuff. But I still wasn't sure, not until just now when he came in here...." She broke down again.

"So did you...purposely sleep with Adam then?"

Jill was silent and didn't look up. Hilton drew in her breath. This was almost too crazy to believe.

Finally Jill looked up and her eyes pleaded with Hilton to understand. "I couldn't deal with telling people I didn't know who I slept with! And I never expected to start dating Adam! I thought it would be a one night stand and then I would just have told him I didn't expect anything from him and it would've been over and done with. It wouldn't have messed things up for him at all...but then he liked me and I just don't know what the hell I was thinking. I should never have started dating him....I am such a bitch. Oh shit...I'm just realizing what I've done to him....Hilton, I've ruined his life. And Todd fucking told me what a bitch I am, too. And now I'm gonna have to tell Adam....Oh, my gosh, what is he going to say? Wow, I'm so horrible, Hilton. I can't believe I did that. Please don't hate me. I hate Todd for not telling me the next day! I hate him!" Her voice was muffled through her tears.

Hilton hugged Jill and widened her eyes at the wall. It was hard to believe Jill was capable of anything like this. And she had pulled it all off so well. Hilton couldn't believe she'd had no idea. Thinking back now, there were some signs....

"So when did you know you were pregnant? Did you really not know until spring break? Because you were drinking before that...."

Jill pulled back and shook her head. "No, I wasn't. I found out around the end of February....The first time we went out after I found out, I was DD so it didn't even matter. And then after that, I was just pretending to drink. I never went in on beer remember? I always 'mixed' my own drinks? There was never any alcohol in them. And the night we made margaritas and packed for break...I kept going into my bathroom and dumping a little of it down the sink. And I was having morning sickness, Hilton....Oh, my gosh, it was so hard to hide. Like, the morning after I first slept with Adam, Laney took me home and thought I was sick 'cause I was hung over but it was morning sickness...and when you bought me the pregnancy test, I'd already taken one. And that's why I wouldn't let you go into the doctor's office with me...I didn't want you to hear her say when I was due or hear us talking about how far along I was. There are lots of other things I did to cover up, too...like I told you guys Adam and I used a condom that first time but we didn't and I purposely made sure we didn't so it'd be more realistic that I would've gotten pregnant from that night. Like the weekend before that I'd heard him telling Justin that he'd just gotten test results back and he was clean so I knew it'd be safe....Please don't hate me for lying to you. It wasn't because I didn't trust you....I wish I would've just told you all along; it would've been so much easier on me having someone who knew and you could've helped me know what to do, and maybe I wouldn't be in this mess now. But I couldn't tell anyone. I felt like such a slut!"

Hilton hugged Jill again. "Don't worry, babe. Of course I don't hate you! I can't imagine what I would've done in your situation, but probably the same thing! And if Todd said you were a bitch, then fuck him, because if he would've had any balls in the first place and not walked out the next morning, none of this would've happened." She rubbed Jill's back soothingly.

"Thanks so much, Hilton. I'm so glad someone under-stands....Ugh, how am I ever gonna tell Adam?"

"You know what, Jilly?" Hilton said decidedly. "It doesn't mat-ter how you tell him....Adam will be pissed and hurt at first but in the end he'll be relieved. It's going to be okay. Aren't you at least a little glad it's Todd's?" She pulled back and looked Jill in the eyes. "He's the one you really love...and you always have. See...every-thing happens for a reason...maybe you and Todd *are* meant to be together. I always thought so. And there's a reason you drug Adam into it too, even if that reason's not really clear. But it doesn't have to be; you just have to know there is one. At the very least maybe he'll learn something from this and not sleep with as many girls as he did before you guys hooked up. And maybe that'll save him from getting an STD or something."

Jill snickered bitterly. "Yeah, I doubt Adam's going to see the future good this could do him."

She turned glum again. "But how could Todd do this to me, Hilton? How could he not have told me? You know, the night I told him I was pregnant, he sat right there and listened to me say Adam was the first guy I ever had sex with and he didn't even tell me then! But then later he told me he was in love with me and let me fall back in love with him too! What a fucking *asshole*! I don't even know if I could love him or trust him anymore….And even if I could, I told him to get out of my life. I said I never wanted to see him again. So…"

"Yeah, he did fuck up. But maybe one day you'll want to give him another chance. You never know."

"I doubt it. But I need to get this over with. So could you find Adam and tell him I need to talk to him?"

"Jill, what's wrong?!" Adam asked, rushing to the bed and grabbing her hand as soon as he walked in. "Why are you crying?"

Jill quickly pulled her hand back and looked away. "Adam, I have to tell you something. And I just want you to know that I'm so sorry and I know I'm a horrible person and I know you're going to hate me and I shouldn't have even put you in the situation where I would ever have to tell you this, but I have to tell you now so this doesn't go on any longer."

"Jill, what in the hell are you talking about?" He tried to take her hand again and this time she jerked it out of his grip and looked at him coldly.

"Adam, Adria's not your baby."

"What?" He frowned at her. "Why the hell would you say that?"

"Adria is not your baby," Jill repeated slowly. "I was pregnant for four or five weeks before I ever slept with you."

"What?! How the fuck is that possible? How did they not tell you that before, when you went to the doctor or anything?"

Jill was silent. Adam froze and backed away from her.

"You knew. You knew this whole time she wasn't mine."

Jill nodded, the cold look still in place.

"So who the fuck's is it then?" Adam shouted. "Does he even know about it? Did he ditch you and so once you started dating me you just decided to let me believe it was mine?" Then an even worse thought crossed his mind. "Did you start dating me *because* he ditched you? You did! You fucking bitch. You used me because whoever the fucking father was dumped you and so you needed to find someone else."

Adam shook his head in disbelief and looked wildly around the room. "Jill, I…I loved you! I was going to stay with you and you were just going to let me, all that time laughing to yourself that you'd fooled me….Wow, you are the biggest fucking bitch I've ever met. Go to hell, Jill."

He turned and stormed out of the room, letting the door slam behind him.

Jill stared after him. For once her eyes were dry. She couldn't even describe how guilty she felt about what she'd done to Adam, but she realized she wasn't sad they would no longer be together.

She was relieved.

Luke, Hilton, Jill, and Todd were all dancing on the coffee table, with Hilton and Jill in the middle. The girls were giggling uncontrollably, but Jill couldn't even remember why. All of a sudden Hilton's high heel slid across the table and she grabbed onto Jill for balance, dropping her Turtle cup as she did so. Her mouth widened and she covered it with her hand. "Uh oh!" she exclaimed, watching her cup as it seemed to tumble to the floor in slow motion, finally hitting and splashing red all over the white carpet. Jill widened her eyes and looked at Hilton. Then they both cracked up again.

Luke stepped down from the table and grabbed Hilton, picking her up and placing her on the floor. "You need to go to bed, honey! I'll be right back." He hurried into the kitchen to get some paper towels and carpet cleaner.

Jill looked around and noticed that almost everyone had left. Justin, Ryan, Kylie, and Kylie's friend were playing a card game at the kitchen table and some guy Jill didn't know was passed out on the couch. Natalie and Laney must have gone to bed. Luke came back and started cleaning up Hilton's spilled drink.

"I'm so sorry. So sorry, honey," Hilton kept saying.

Jill giggled again. Hilton looked up at her and grinned.

"He looks funny cleaning it up," Jill said in a loud whisper.

"I know," Hilton whispered back.

Luke laughed and grabbed Hilton's hand as he stood up. He started dragging her toward their room. "It's bedtime for you, baby. Say goodnight to Jill."

"Night, Jill!" Hilton cried, blowing Jill a kiss. Then she pointed at Todd and widened her eyes, nodding her head rapidly and grinning. She gave Jill a thumbs-up.

Jill giggled and waved her away, turning around to make sure Todd hadn't seen. She looked back at Hilton and put her finger over her mouth to get Hilton to be quiet.

"You better do it, Jill!" Hilton exclaimed giddily as Luke pulled her into the bedroom. "Tell me about it tomorrow!" She winked at Jill and then Luke shut the door behind them.

Jill turned around to see if Todd was still behind her. He was at the keg getting another beer. Jill went up and started dancing behind him.

"Hey, Jilly," he said, turning around and smiling. "Wanna make out some more?"

"*Noooo, shhh,*" Jill said in a silly voice. "See, there's other people." She pointed at the kitchen table.

"Oh, okay, let's go in your room then," Todd said carelessly. He grabbed Jill's hand and started walking casually across the living room.

"Hey, we're takin' off," Justin said as he stood up from the kitchen table. "Have a good night, guys."

"Oh, stay! We wanna play a drinking game!" Jill cried, loving the feel of Todd's hand firmly gripping hers.

"Sorry, the cab's outside, gotta go," Justin said with a grin, shrugging. "I know you want me, Jill; you're welcome to come back to my place."

"Oh, shut up; just go!" Jill said with a laugh. "Bye, boys!" She went over and kissed Justin and Ryan on their cheeks and hugged Kylie and her friend. "Have fun!"

"Bye, Jill. Later, man," Justin said, shaking Todd's hand, then the four of them headed out.

Jill locked the door behind them and turned back to Todd. "We're all alone," she pouted. "That guy is passed out." She pointed to the stranger on the couch.

"That's cool with me," Todd said, grabbing Jill around the waist and dancing slowly, talking nonchalantly to the ceiling above her head. "So now that there's no other people we can make out some more, right?"

Jill giggled. "I don't know…" she said, as though she was considering it.

"Please, Jilly? I wanna make out with you," Todd said playfully, pulling her closer and still dancing.

Jill giggled again. "Okay, I guess…."

"Hell, yeah," Todd said, and Jill laughed even harder, tipping her head back. Todd grabbed her neck and pulled her head up, smashing his mouth against hers. He was being sloppy on purpose again and Jill loved it. She laughed into his mouth.

"You dork!"

"Whatever, you love it," Todd said.

"I know," Jill said easily, and then he kissed her again. It was hard and hungry. She kissed him back this time and they stopped dancing, standing still and pouring all their energy into the kiss. Todd's arms were still wrapped tightly around Jill's waist, and then he began to run his hands up and down her back. She sank into him, trying to get closer even though her body was already pressed against his.

"Weren't we going in your room?" Todd murmured, his mouth still on hers.

"Yeah, let's go," Jill replied breathlessly.

As Todd took her hand and led her into the bedroom Jill tried to make herself believe this was actually happening, but it seemed too good to be true. She followed him in a blissful daze.

Todd closed the door behind them and pinned Jill up against it, assaulting her mouth with his again. A thrill ran through her whole body. She had never wanted anyone this badly before.

Todd took a step back and put his hand on the door above Jill's head, breathing hard. "Jill, I want you so freakin' bad right now. Damn. I really do." He leaned in and kissed her again, only for a split second this time, then pushed away a little bit, his hand still on the door, and stood looking down at her.

Jill looked into his eyes for a second, thinking this was the best moment of her whole life. "I want you too, Todd," she said simply.

Todd rolled his eyes in relief. "Thank God."

Jill giggled as he kissed her again, and then she grabbed his hand and led him to her bed. He laid down beside her and they kissed some more. Todd rubbed her leg with his foot and she threw her leg over his and rolled on top of him. As she leaned down to kiss him he reached down to her waist and pulled her shirt up over her head. She felt that thrill go through her body again as he unhooked her bra.

"Wow, Jill. Wow. You're so gorgeous."

She smiled at him from underneath her hair, which was all in her face now. Todd pushed it out of the way as she brought her mouth down to meet his again.

"Jill," he moaned, rolling her off of him and onto her back. He sat up and pulled his shirt over his head, then quickly hopped off the bed and took his pants off. Jill watched him as she lay on her back, and she couldn't stop smiling.

Todd grinned as he climbed back onto the bed, straddling her on his knees.

"Wow, you look really good," Jill whispered with a suggestive grin. He was wearing boxer-briefs and his whole body looked so muscular and hot. Jill couldn't wait to touch him. "Come here," she said.

Todd leaned down over her and kissed her briefly on the lips, leaving her longing for more. Then his lips moved to her chin, her neck, her chest, and then he was licking her nipple.

"Oh," Jill moaned, arching beneath him. "Ouch!" she giggled suddenly as he began sucking on it. "Don't!"

Todd grinned mischievously. "Sorry." As he kissed her lips again he grabbed her hand and placed it over his boxer-briefs. Jill rubbed him through the fabric and felt his whole body tremble.

"That feels so good…hold on." He pushed himself off of her for a second and quickly tore his underwear off. Jill couldn't help but stare.

Todd grinned at her. "You like it?"

Jill grinned back. "I love it." She wrapped her fingers around him and rapidly moved her hand up and down.

Todd moaned, throwing his head back and losing himself in her touch. Finally he couldn't wait any longer.

"Jill," he whispered thickly as he unbuttoned her jeans and pulled them off.

"Todd," she breathed back, pulling him back down on top of her and kissing him hungrily as his fingers shot into her. She inhaled sharply and arched beneath him. "Oh, yes…come on, Todd…."

"Are you sure?" he asked between kisses.

"Don't stop," she said, lifting her head to keep kissing him. "I'm sure."

She felt a thrust and a sort of sharp pain, but then it didn't really hurt anymore. It felt so good. Like he fit perfectly inside her. She rocked beneath him, trying to get her body in sync with his.

"Are you okay?" Todd whispered, pushing her hair away from her face.

"Yeah, I'm okay. It feels so good. Keep going, keep going…."

The next morning Todd came back to the hospital, determined to talk things out with Jill and hopeful that he could win her forgiveness. He had agonized all night over how he could still love her after what she'd done to Adam, but then he realized he'd never liked Adam anyway and Jill was right; Todd *had* forced her to do something desperate. If only he'd had enough balls to face her the morning after….But none of that could be changed, and all he knew was that he still loved her and would no matter what, and he had to do something before he lost her, if it wasn't already too late.

As he approached Jill's room, Mrs. Sherer stepped out and shut the door behind her.

Todd froze and felt like running in the other direction.

Mrs. Sherer looked up and gave a sigh of relief and a smile. "Oh, hi, Todd! I'm so glad you decided to come. I'm sure Jill will be really glad to see you; she could use a friend right now." She lowered her voice to a whisper. "Adam broke up with her last night. I can't believe it; I didn't see that one coming." She shook her head sadly. "If he really couldn't handle it then I'm glad he's out of the picture. But what horrible timing. She's been pretty upset."

Todd's mouth dropped open. "What?! He broke up with her? Wow…." He looked quickly at the ground. "That's horrible…."

"Yeah, well, I'm sure you can cheer her up. Go ahead and just go on in." Mrs. Sherer smiled at him and touched his shoulder briefly as she walked away.

Todd took a deep breath and then opened the door and went in. Jill was sitting up in bed looking at a magazine. She dropped it on her lap when she saw Todd and her stomach felt like she'd just ridden the Power Tower at Cedar Point that shot you down 240 feet at sixty miles per hour. She wasn't ready to see him after dreaming the rest of it and she hated that she half wanted him. She quickly pulled herself together and hardened her eyes.

"Look, I told you—"

"So you told Adam, huh?"

"I told him she wasn't his," Jill replied in a clipped tone. "That's all. That was enough. He was out of here pretty quickly. I thought it was the right thing to do."

"So you just told your mom he broke up with you?"

"Yep."

"So you're just not planning on telling people the truth, or what?"

"No, Todd, I'm not. Why should I tell anyone she's yours when I never plan on seeing you again? Plus, it would ruin your relationship with Natalie." She paused, then added, "Hilton's the only one who knows and she's the only one who will."

"I don't care about Natalie," Todd snapped. "Do you really think that's even a factor here? Jill, I want to be part of your life, and our baby's life. You have no right to tell me I can't be. She's as much my daughter as she is yours!"

Jill was silent. She stared out the window.

"So you're really just going to go on letting everyone think it was Adam's and he broke up with you. That's really fucking smart. You think he's not going to tell people you said it wasn't his?"

"Of course he'll tell people. They'll know she isn't his, but they won't know who the real father is. And I don't really care what people at school think 'cause it's none of their business. And I probably won't see them much anymore, anyway, 'cause there's no way I can go back there next semester now after all this with Adam. But he won't say anything to my family, obviously. So they'll always think she was Adam's."

"And you're actually cool with that? With living a lie?"

Jill turned away from the window, picked up her magazine, and started flipping through it. "I have nothing else to say to you, Todd. You can let yourself out."

Todd threw his hands in the air. "This is fucking ridiculous, Jill. There's nothing else I can say to change your mind?"

Jill continued flipping through her magazine and didn't look up.

This was not what Todd had expected and he was at a loss for words. He was so furious he wasn't even sure he'd be able to put together a coherent sentence. Maybe it would just be easier to leave. He'd walked out on her before; why not do it again? It was what she expected anyway. If nothing else, at least I can live up to her expectations, he thought with disgust.

"Wow, well at least you're making it pretty fucking easy to walk out on you. A lot easier than it was the first time. Because this time I don't feel bad at all." Todd turned and stormed out, just as Adam had the night before.

Jill didn't cry this time either; she was all cried out. But there was no sense of relief, just one of emptiness. But a minute later when the door opened and the nurse brought Adria in, the empty feeling started to vanish and Jill sat up and held out her arms with a loving smile.

When Todd left Jill's room a nurse was coming down the hall wheeling a baby in a little bassinette. Todd stopped dead in his tracks and stared. It was a little girl with his exact hair color.

"Excuse me," he said quickly to the nurse. "Is that...Jill Sherer's baby?"

"Yes, it is," the nurse said, smiling. "Adria. Are you a friend of Jill's? She's about to nurse Adria. I can ask her if it's okay for you to come in."

Todd couldn't take his eyes off of his daughter. "Adria," he murmured. "What's her middle name?"

"It's Nicole," the nurse said with a small frown. "Would you like me to ask Jill if you can come in or not?"

Todd was still gazing at Adria when an approaching voice called his name.

"Todd?"

He jerked his head up. Natalie and Laney were coming down the hall toward him. He hastily turned away from the nurse without answering her and rushed to meet Natalie.

"Hey," he greeted her, running his hand through his hair and looking over her shoulder because he couldn't really look at her at the moment.

"What are you doing here?" Natalie asked with a frown.

"I just decided to drive up last night at the last minute to see Jill and make sure everything was going okay." He tried to smile light-heartedly at her.

"Oh. Yeah, us too. We were gonna wait till next weekend, but then we heard about Adam breaking up with her....Well, was that Adria?" Natalie pointed at Jill's door, where the nurse had gone inside. Her tone was excited now.

"Um, yeah, that was her," Todd said.

"So is Jill really upset? About Adam?"

"Um…yeah, I think she seemed pretty upset."

"Okay, well we're gonna go in and visit with her. Wait for me, okay?" Natalie kissed Todd quickly on the cheek and then she and Laney hurried down the hall.

Todd thought briefly of getting the hell out of there but before he really knew what he was doing he was sitting down in the waiting room across from Jill's parents and Hilton.

Mrs. Sherer looked up from her book. "How was she?"

"Oh, I think she's doing better now," Todd lied, looking away. "Plus Laney and Natalie are going in there now."

Mrs. Sherer looked pleased and continued reading. When Todd glanced at Hilton she gave him a lingering stare that he couldn't quite read, then she looked back down at the magazine on her lap.

Half an hour later when Todd left with Natalie, Hilton said, "Bye, Todd," in a neutral tone as he walked past her, but for a split second her gaze was almost as icy as the one Jill had given him yesterday. The next moment she was smiling at Laney and Natalie and telling them goodbye, but Todd knew he hadn't imagined it.

March 2005

Natalie was at the grocery store picking up some snacks for the drive to Texas when she ran into Adam. Ever since Jill and Adam had broken up, the girls had fallen out of touch with Adam, Justin, and Ryan. They saw them occasionally at the Turtle and talked to Justin but were never invited to parties at the boys' apartment anymore. It wasn't a big deal since all three girls had boyfriends anyway. Laney and Natalie always went to Eastern together on the weekends or went out together when Del and Todd came up, and Hilton and Luke were usually doing their own thing. Last year Luke had basically lived at the girls' apartment, but now Hilton basically lived at his. She hung out with Laney and Natalie occasionally but things weren't the same between the three of them.

Jill hadn't come back second semester. Natalie assumed it was because of Adam. She was a little tight for money and was annoyed about still having to pay part of Jill's rent, but she didn't say anything because she still felt a tiny bit guilty for dating Todd and she felt horrible for Jill that Adam had broken up with her. Natalie knew if she was in Jill's situation she probably wouldn't want to come back to Dale either. Adam should be the one paying the damn rent, she thought. But, Jill was paying a fourth of it now so at least it was a little better than it had been last semester.

"Hey," Adam said, and Natalie looked up to see him walking down the aisle toward her.

She gave him a clipped smile and immediately turned back to the bottled water in front of her. She thought he was a complete asshole and wasn't in the mood to talk to him.

"What the hell was that?" Adam asked, laughing and punching her lightly on the shoulder. "Can't you say hi?"

"I generally try not to waste my breath on people who aren't worth it," Natalie said as she selected a case of water and put it in her cart. She turned and pushed the cart down the aisle.

"Not worth it? What the hell did I ever do to you?" Adam asked. He didn't sound mad, just confused.

Natalie stopped her cart and turned to face him. "Are you, like, serious here or what?"

Adam threw his hands in the air. "I have no clue what I did to you."

"You didn't do anything to *me* but you totally fucked over my friend!" Natalie snapped irritably, then glanced around to see if anyone could hear.

"*I* fucked *her* over?!" Adam cried. "Are you fucking serious?!"

"Yeah, I'm fucking serious! The day she had your baby you walked out on her, after leading her on all that time! I can't really think of anything shittier to do to someone!"

Adam looked like he couldn't believe what he was hearing. "Well how about, on the day you have a baby, telling your boyfriend it's not really his and you knew you were pregnant before you started dating him, but let him believe it was his because the guy you fucked before him ditched you?"

Natalie's mouth dropped open and she just stared at Adam.

Adam smirked. "Yeah, I thought that was worse. See ya." He walked away and left Natalie gaping after him.

Hilton was watching TV at Luke's when her phone rang. She grabbed it off the coffee table. "What's up, Nat?"

"Hilton, I just ran into Adam and he told me Adria wasn't his baby! Is that true?"

"What?! What the hell are you talking about?" Hilton quickly walked out onto Luke's balcony, closing the door behind her.

"He said Jill told him the day Adria was born that Adria wasn't his baby and Jill had been pregnant before she started dating him and that the other guy she slept with had dumped her! So you didn't know?"

"No! That's crazy! I had no idea," Hilton lied.

"Okay, I find that hard to believe, but whatever. But I have to ask you something, Hilton, and you *have* to tell me if you know the answer." Natalie sounded close to tears now. "Is Adria Todd's baby? Is that why he went to see Jill in the hospital? I mean, I know it sounds horrible I would even think that and I'm probably totally off, but I just can't help thinking that because I can't think of any other guy Jill could even have slept with, and—"

"Who knows, Nat, why don't you ask him?" Hilton snapped her phone shut and returned to the living room with a small smile on her face.

Natalie could hardly breathe. So it was Todd. Her instinct had been right. She hated the way Hilton had told her to ask him, like she'd been waiting for Natalie to figure it out all along. She was bawling. Without thinking what she was going to say she dialed Todd.

"You fucking asshole!" she yelled through her tears as soon as he answered his phone. "You just thought I was never going to find out?! What kind of sick deal do you and Jill have going on? You guys are so fucked up! Why are you even wasting your time with me? Why don't you just go be with her! You both deserve each other! I don't understand and I don't want to!" She hung up and collapsed on her bed in tears.

Laney knocked on the door. "Nat?"

Natalie hadn't even heard her come home. She couldn't answer because she was crying too hard.

Finally Laney opened the door and came in. "What the hell is going on? What were you yelling about? Was that Todd?"

"Jill—" Natalie gasped. "Jill...and Adria...I saw Adam today and he said...." She rolled over as a new wave of tears spilled down her cheeks.

"Nat!" Laney shook her. "Sit up and tell me what you're talking about!"

Natalie managed to roll over. "Adria is Todd's," she said, then immediately covered her face. "And Jill knew before she started dating Adam that she was pregnant."

"*WHAT*?!" Laney cried. "Are you fucking serious? Tell me the whole story!"

Natalie told her what had happened with Adam at the store and with Hilton on the phone.

"I just don't understand!" she sobbed. "Why wouldn't they just have been together? Why would she start dating Adam and let him think it was his baby? Why would Todd date someone else? That's so fucked up! And how could they not tell me?! I really can't believe Jill let Adam think it was his! What a bitch! This is just all so crazy....Yeah, so I guess spring break's ruined now. Sorry."

"No, Nat, you're going, damn it! Fuck Todd; we can still go."

"Yeah that'll be so fun for me, being the fifth wheel! And with Lizzy and Conrad there...and what if Todd still goes?"

Laney, Del, Natalie, Todd, Lizzy, and Conrad were supposed to go to South Padre Island.

"Don't worry about it; we'll figure something out."

"No, we won't, Laney!" Natalie snapped. "I'm not fucking going! Even if Todd doesn't go, Lizzy and Conrad will and I can't be around them! I don't want to see any of them again!"

"Fine, you know what? Let's just ditch them all. Let the three of them drive to South Padre by themselves. Let's go somewhere else."

"Where? It's Wednesday! We leave in two days!"

"Don't worry. I'll figure something out."

"*Whatever!*" Natalie buried her face in her pillow as Laney left the room. Who even cared about spring break right now? She wished Laney would shut up.

Natalie had fallen asleep when Laney knocked on her door again a couple hours later. "Come in," she called with a yawn.

Laney opened the door and flipped the light on. "Surprise!" she said with a grin, holding out a piece of paper.

"What is it?" Natalie asked tiredly.

"It's a receipt for a plane ticket to Miami! We're going to a spa for two days! And then we're going to party in Miami for the rest of the week!"

"What?! Lane, how'd you pull that off?"

"Well, I called your mom and told her you and Todd broke up and you couldn't go to South Padre anymore, so she's paying for your plane ticket and the hotel for the whole week! So it should end up being about the same price as South Padre!"

"What about Del?"

"Oh, he doesn't care. He was being shitty about going anyway 'cause he's so broke right now. This gives him an easy way out. I mean, I told him he can still go with them all if he wants, but I doubt he will." She giggled. "Aren't you excited now? Do you feel better?"

"Yeah, a little. It's just crazy though. I still can't believe it. I don't even want to think about it. But thanks, Lane, this really helps."

Later that night Hilton decided to go back to her own apartment and see what was going on. She was curious about what had happened between Natalie and Todd. To her surprise, when she walked in loud music was coming from Laney's room and Laney and Natalie were giggling. Hilton poked her head in the doorway.

"Hey guys, what's going on?"

Laney and Natalie were trying on clothes and drinking. They laughed and waved Hilton into the room.

"We're packing for Miami!" Natalie exclaimed, taking a huge drink of her margarita. Then she giggled again. She wanted Hilton to think she was happy and didn't care about Todd.

"Miami? What about South Padre?" Hilton hadn't even thought of what would happen to Natalie's spring break if she and Todd broke up.

"Fuck South Padre," Natalie said with a wave of her hand. "We're not going." She motioned to Laney and herself. "We're going to Miami."

Drunk ass, Hilton thought. "So you ditched the rest of them?"

"Don't know what they're doing." Natalie waved Hilton's question away. "Don't give a fuck."

"What about Del?" Hilton asked, trying not to laugh at Natalie.

"Oh, he didn't wanna go anyway," Laney told her. "So he doesn't care."

"Oh, I see. Well, have fun." Hilton smiled wryly to herself as she walked into her own room. It served Natalie right for ever getting involved with Todd. And now maybe things between Todd and Jill could finally be resolved. Then an idea struck her. She closed her door and sat on her bed to think. Could she really pull it off, or was it just going to cause more trouble?

Finally she picked up her phone and called Luke.

The next day Jill was sitting at work in Dr. Jennings' office reading a magazine when her cell phone rang. She smiled when she saw it was Hilton. She hoped there wasn't a change of plans; Hilton was bringing Luke home for part of spring break and they were all supposed to hang out together.

"Hey, Hilton!"

"Hey, Jilly! Guess what?" Hilton sounded jubilant.

"What?"

"We're going on spring break tomorrow!"

"What?"

Hilton giggled. "You're coming on a trip with me! To South Padre!"

"What? I can't, Hilton! I have to work, and Adria…"

"No, no, it's okay. I already called your parents and they said it was okay. They said you needed a vacation and they'll watch Adria and they didn't think Dr. Jennings would mind. I mean, come on, if you were at school she wouldn't have you working there anyway so how can she mind if you're gone for a week?"

Jill finally laughed. "So we're going to South Padre?! Are you serious? That's awesome!"

"Yeah! Well hurry and get the hell out of there and pack! I'm driving up tonight to pick up some stuff and take you down to school! So I'll be there like around eight."

"Okay! See you then!" Jill grinned as she hung up. She could hardly believe it. She was going to get to go on spring break! It seemed too good to be true.

❦   ❦   ❦

"So why did you decide on this so last minute?" Jill asked on the way down to school that night.

"Well, it's kind of a long story. Natalie and Todd broke up last night."

"What?! Why?"

"She found out, Jill. She ran into Adam and I guess they were talking and he told her Adria wasn't his baby…."

"Oh, shit." Jill felt sick to her stomach.

"Yeah, and then she called me and asked if it was Todd so I told her to call him and ask. So I guess she did…so anyway they broke up."

"Wow. Shit. Oh, my gosh, I don't want to see her now!"

"Oh, don't worry, we're staying at Luke's tonight."

"Oh, okay….So what does that have to do with you deciding to go on spring break?"

"Well…." Hilton hesitated. "Natalie and Laney were going to South Padre, but now they're going to Miami. And Del was going with them, but I guess he's just staying home now 'cause he didn't wanna spend the money."

"So why'd they change their plans? Are we taking their hotel room in South Padre or what?"

"Well, yeah….Okay, Jill, you're gonna kill me but…." Hilton was trying to hide a smile.

"Oh, my gosh, Hilton, is Todd going?! Oh, my gosh! I can't believe you did this to me! Take me back right now! I'm so not going! Did my mom know Todd was going?"

"Yeah, she knew, but she thinks you and Todd are still friends. I told your parents it was Todd, Lizzy, Conrad, Luke, and me, and we wanted to take you on a trip. And it's true. I just told them not to tell you who all was going because everyone wanted to surprise you."

Jill was panicking. "So Todd knows I'm going?"

"Yeah, I called him first. He wants you to come."

"Hilton, I cannot believe you did this! Are you trying to play matchmaker or something? Todd and I can handle it ourselves! And there's nothing even to handle! I told him to get out of my life and he said I was making it easy for him to walk out on me again! Todd and I are done with each other! I'm not going."

"Yeah, I knew you'd be pissed." Hilton looked over and hit Jill's arm lightly. When Jill turned to look at her Hilton was smiling.

"Come on, Jill," she urged. "I know you guys could handle it yourselves, but you wouldn't do anything about it. You'd just keep being apart and being unhappy. I know he really let you down, but he's one of your oldest friends. Are you really going to shut him out of your life for good? And it's not fair to Adria to let her grow up without a father. You and Todd don't have to be together, but it'd be good for both of you and Adria too if you were at least on good terms with each other."

Jill looked down at her lap and finally nodded. "I know. You're right. You're totally right. I can't do that to Adria. I already ruined eight months of Adam's life that he'll never get back and I'm not going to ruin Adria's. If Todd wants to be part of her life then I guess he can. But I can't believe he even wanted me to come on this trip…that's just crazy. It's gonna be so weird seeing him."

"It won't be for long. You guys have known each other forever. And come on, Jill, you can't tell me you weren't the tiniest bit happy when you found out she was Todd's baby." Hilton gave Jill a knowing look.

Jill looked at Hilton out of the corner of her eyes and cracked a small smile. "This was a really fucking risky idea," she said.

Hilton beamed. "I know. You're always saying that to me. But my risky ideas always work."

"So it was nice of them to give us our own car; I love how that worked out," Todd joked uncomfortably. It was Friday afternoon and the six of them had just set out for South Padre. Hilton, Luke, Conrad, and Lizzy were all in Conrad's car and Jill and Todd were in Todd's truck.

"Well, your truck doesn't fit three people too comfortably, so how did you think it was going to work out?" Jill muttered. She was staring out the window. She was extremely nervous and not at all sure how to act.

Todd was silent for awhile. He wasn't sure what to say but he figured he had plenty of time. It was a long drive.

It was silent for the next half hour. The only time Jill moved was when she changed the radio station. Then she immediately went back to staring out the window with her hands in her lap.

Finally Todd couldn't stand the silence any longer and he had to say something. He had wasted enough time not letting Jill know how he really felt.

"Jill, I still love you," he said. His voice was hoarse.

Jill turned and looked at him for several seconds. "I just don't know," she finally said. "You kept such a huge thing a secret from me for so long. I don't know if I trust you anymore."

"Oh, come on, Jill, aren't you going to give me a break? Look at you! You're not such a trustworthy person yourself! You got drunk, lost your virginity, got pregnant, didn't know who the father was, so you picked some guy you thought was hot to sleep with and place the blame on. And if you didn't find out it was me you never would've told him he wasn't the father! You're a fucking bitch, Jill! And you won't even give *me* a break, just because I kept one thing from you?"

To his surprise, Jill laughed. He turned and looked at her.

"Wow," she said. "I know; I am a horrible, horrible person. I don't know why I laughed. So if you think I'm so bad then why do you want me? At the hospital after you told me what a bitch I was, you walked out on me and said I was making it easy. So what's changed? Why do you love me now?"

"Because you're you," Todd said, shrugging his shoulders helplessly. "I've loved you for over a year now. I never stopped; you just really hurt me and pissed me off in the hospital and I didn't know how to handle it, so I just blew up. I don't know. I can't really explain it I guess. But you did all that shit because of what I did to you. You were right about what you said to me in the hospital. I corrupted you. I made you do a lot of bitchy things and ruin someone else's life. If I would've been honest none of that would've ever happened. So I guess we deserve each other."

"It's not all your fault," Jill said, shaking her head. "I should've just been honest about not knowing who the father was. And then you would've come forward and everything would've turned out so much better."

"Maybe not," Todd said with a shrug. "Maybe we wouldn't have fallen in love. Maybe we would've been upset we were having a baby and it would've torn us apart. I think it was not being able to have each other that made us want each other."

Jill cocked her head. It made sense. She liked that theory. "That's true. I hadn't thought of it that way. So Hilton has been right all along. Everything does happen for a reason."

Jill looked over at him and smiled a mischievous smile. "And now with all our baggage, no one else is going to want us."

"That's for fuckin' sure."

Jill reached over and squeezed his leg. Then she became serious. "I'll give it a try, Todd. I mean, if you still want to. Why not, right?"

Todd looked at her with wide eyes. He hadn't expected it to be this easy. "Are you serious? I mean, are you sure, Jill?"

"Why, don't you want to?"

Todd took his eyes off the road and looked steadily into Jill's eyes. "Of course I want to, Jilly." He reached over and took her hand off her lap, interlacing his fingers with hers. A tear trickled down his cheek, making Jill's eyes water too. "I want this more than anything."

Jill let the tears run down her face. "Me too, Todd." She leaned over to kiss him on the cheek.

Then she grinned. "I can't wait for you to meet Adria!" She squeezed his hand.

"I know. I can't wait either. What's she like, Jill? I've been dying to know all this time." He sounded really choked up and Jill removed her hand from his to wipe more of her own tears away.

"She's amazing, Todd." Jill's smile was radiant now, even though tears were still trickling down her face. "She looks a lot like you already and it's been so hard looking at her, but also so wonderful. She's so beautiful and I love her so much. It's so weird how I thought I had ruined my life when I got pregnant. She's the best thing to ever happen to me. Besides you of course." She attempted a laugh through her tears and squeezed his leg again, leaving her hand there this time.

Todd covered her hand with his and smiled back at her. He was still crying, too.

"So what are we gonna do?" Jill asked suddenly. "I mean, I took this semester off to save some money, but I'm going back to school next semester and I'll graduate next May. I was just planning on going to DBU and living at home….Do you know where you'll have a job yet?"

"I actually have an interview the week after spring break. It'd be an awesome job. I really hope I get it."

"What is it?"

"It would be working for a gym, and members could like, hire me as their personal trainer. I mean, eventually I probably want to work somewhere bigger, or be on my own instead of through a gym, but it's a really great starting point, you know?"

"That's awesome, Todd! So where is it?"

"It's actually like ten minutes from Dale. In town."

Jill's eyes widened. "No way!" Then the realization hit her. "You wanted that because of Natalie, didn't you?" Natalie didn't have a job yet, so she was planning on staying at Dale next year to live with Laney, who'd gotten a job at an accounting firm in town. Natalie wanted to work on her portfolio some more and start sending her work to designers.

Todd looked at her sheepishly. "Yeah. But you know I'm so over her already, Jill. I mean, that never meant anything to me compared to this."

"I know."

"Really? It just surprises me that you're so willing to give us another try. I mean, I expected it to be really hard to talk you into it or something."

"Well, I understand how Natalie didn't mean that much to you, 'cause Adam never meant that much to me. And the reason I first wanted to try to work things out with you was because Hilton pointed out it would be better for Adria if you and I were on good terms. But then when I saw you today, I just realized I will always love you. And then what you said to me, about what an awful person I am but how you still love me…I don't know. It just made me realize how lucky I am to have you and how I never want to lose you again, and I realized it was time to just get over the past and move on, you know? Losing our relationship was the worst thing ever. You know, when I first found out I was pregnant, one of the things I was most upset about, even more than telling my parents, or how it messed up my school, or my lease, was how our relationship would change, and how I wouldn't be able to come visit you at Eastern anymore...how we just wouldn't be *us* anymore." She was getting choked up again just thinking about it. She tried to hold the tears back but couldn't.

Todd turned her hand over in his and interlaced their fingers. Their eyes met and locked, Jill's shimmering with tears, Todd's dark and passionate, and in the split second before Todd had to turn back to the road Jill had never felt as close to another person as she felt to Todd right now. She knew the two of them shared things no one else could ever understand and they could never explain. She couldn't imagine ever wanting to be with anyone else.

She smiled happily as she turned to look out at the road ahead, her fingers still interlaced with Todd's. "So, maybe we could live together then? And I could go back to Dale? Or I could live with Hilton and you could live with Luke? 'Cause neither of them graduates till December. And then I could just apply for grad school at Dale. They actually have a really good program. I just wanted to go somewhere else, you know, but now that doesn't even really matter. As long as I'm with you." She gave him a teasing smile, knowing she sounded corny.

"Yeah, thanks, no pressure to get that job," Todd said, then suddenly his expression turned serious. "What about your parents?"

"I told them. I had to. I couldn't live with my family not knowing who Adria's real father was anymore. I told them it was you and that we had slept together but that I started dating Adam before I found out I was pregnant, so Adam and I just decided to stay together and I pretended the baby was his that whole time. That actually didn't upset my parents too much, once they got past the fact I lied to them for so long, because you know they love you, you're like a longtime friend and Adam was kinda random...I think they were actually relieved. Plus it sorta explained to them why Adam would've broken up with me the day Adria was born."

"Are you serious? That's unbelievable. That's awesome! I'm so glad they know. Even if it's not *quite* the whole story." Todd grinned. "I'm so glad to have you back, Jilly. I missed you so much."

"Me too," Jill said, unable to stop grinning. "I love you so much, Todd. I'm so glad things worked out this way."

Shortly after dark Jill called Hilton.

"We're gonna have to stop at the next rest stop or exit or something," she said. "This isn't working out for Todd and me."

Hilton sighed. "Really? Okay, well…we need to stop for gas and dinner soon anyway. I guess we can switch cars after dinner….I'm sorry, Jilly."

"It's okay; just stop as soon as possible."

They pulled off at the next exit and followed Conrad's car into the parking lot of a local diner. Hilton jumped out of Conrad's car and ran over to Jill's window.

"Are you sure you want to eat here? This reminds me of the place where Laney got sick last year….We can just switch cars and go to the next exit."

"I don't think we can wait," Jill said, motioning to herself and Todd. "We're really hungry…."

"Yeah, we're starving," Todd said with a grin. "We couldn't wait any longer. That's why we asked you to stop." Then he rubbed Jill's leg and winked at Hilton.

"Oh!" Hilton exclaimed, shaking her head and pretending to glare at them. "You guys are awful!" She giggled happily and grinned at Jill in surprise and delight, then punched her lightly on the shoulder. "Well I guess we'll go in and get a table then! Take your time!" She giggled again and ran off to join Luke, Conrad, and Lizzy.

Jill turned back to Todd and smiled. "You're starving, huh?" She straddled him in the driver's seat. "Me too," she whispered, then took his face in her hands and kissed him.

Todd responded immediately and their bodies melted into each other. Jill pulled his shirt over his head and kept kissing him.

"Wait," Todd said, drawing back. "Damn, my condoms are buried in my suitcase somewhere. Maybe we should just wait till later 'cause we probably shouldn't do that again…."

"Oh, what the hell, what's another baby?" Jill said carelessly, then giggled and ran her hands through Todd's hair as she kissed him again. "Just kidding," she said when she came up for air. "But I am on the pill now." She giggled again.

"Oh, yes, oh, yes," Todd moaned. "That just made my day."

"*That* made your day?" Jill giggled. "What about me saying I'd be your girlfriend?"

"Oh, please," Todd said arrogantly, grabbing her ass and squeezing it. "You know I'm just in it for the sex, Jilly."

Jill squealed and laughed. "Oh, you are, huh? Well, I guess that's okay, 'cause the sex is pretty damn good." She lowered her mouth to Todd's again and thought of nothing but how good he tasted.

A little while later as they walked across the parking lot toward the restaurant, Jill held Todd's hand and swung it casually between them.

"So was that good for you?" she teased.

"Well…you know how I said before that you were the best sex I'd ever had? Well, yeah, that's still true." Todd grinned at her.

"Yeah, that was totally hot," Jill agreed with a laugh. "I've always heard make-up sex is hot. Maybe we should fight more often. You know, you did call me a fucking bitch today…."

"You are a fucking bitch," Todd said. "So do you want me now?"

"Oh, yeah, more than ever," Jill teased, backing him against the wall of the restaurant and kissing him teasingly on the lips. "But you'll just have to wait," she said as she backed away and grabbed his hand again. "I need some food!"

As they walked into the restaurant holding hands, Jill realized she hadn't felt this carefree and happy since the night of that party over a year ago. She smiled and leaned her head against Todd's shoulder.

As she and Todd joined the others, Jill shared a private smile with Hilton and whispered, "Thank you." She squeezed Hilton's leg under the table.

Just then the waitress approached to take Jill's and Todd's drink orders.

"I'll have a frozen strawberry daiquiri," Jill said with a relaxed smile. It felt so good to be back to normal again. Actually, no, Jill thought happily. This was way better than normal. Now she had Adria, and Todd. She reached for Todd's hand under the table and he leaned over and kissed her.

Hilton touched Jill's arm and Jill leaned over.

"See, everything happens for a reason…" Hilton said quietly, her eyes sparkling, and she and Jill giggled and grinned at each other.

978-0-595-36273-8
0-595-36273-7

Printed in the United States
39831LVS00001B/52-90